Divinely Entwined

The Fallen Guardians Series:
Book 1

Written By:
E.F. Rose

Divinely Entwined
The Fallen Guardians Series, Book 1

Written by E.F. Rose
www.facebook.com/DarkestRose13

ISBN: 978-0-9898906-3-2

Edited by: Kim Young

Cover Design by: Diana M. Photography
www.facebook.com/DianaMuniz.Photography

Warning

This book is intended for mature audiences only (18+). This book contains some explicit language, sexual content, and violence.

Dedication

This book is dedicated to my family, both by blood and by choice, who never stopped believing in me.

Prologue

1944

The pain was almost instant as he regained consciousness. Curling on his side, Christian groaned, every inch of him screaming in protest. As his body became alive with feeling he was suddenly aware of several factors. One, the air was extremely cold; two, the ground beneath him was nothing but rock and dirt; and three, he barely had any clothes on.

Wonderful!

A chilling breeze whipped through the air, sending shivers down his spine. Clamping his jaw shut to keep his teeth from chattering, he concentrated on the sounds around him. In the eerie silence, he could just make out groans breaking through the quiet. Recognizing the sounds, Christian sighed. His brothers were also with him and, by the sounds of it, beginning to come around.

What the heck happened?

He tried to think back, pushing his mind to remember something, anything. He remembered banding together with his brothers, there had been some kind of argument, a blinding white light, then darkness. Every muscle in his body ached as he reached his arm out, running his fingers over the dirt and rocks beneath him.

Earth!

This couldn't be right, though, could it?

Christian slowly opened his eyes. "Shit..." he hissed. Even his eyelids ached. It was dusk, which made it hard for him to focus on anything other than what was right in front of him. Everything was grey and green blurs shifting in the wind. Blinking repeatedly, he sighed as his vision began to clear. He could now see his brothers, who were also sprawled out on the hard ground. Some of them were beginning to move about, attempting to get up, while others still lay motionless.

Groaning, he worked his arms under his body and began to sit up. He felt like he weighed a ton. His arms were shaking from the strain when he finally pushed himself to his knees. Looking down, he was not surprised to find dirt, dried blood, and bruises covering his entire upper body. He ran his hands over his stomach, wincing at the pain from even the slightest touch. This was not good! Looking around, he could now see that his brothers were slowly getting up, looking as confused as he felt.

"What was that?" his brother, Darren, asked as he looked at him, his sapphire eyes glowing in the dimly lit forest. Narrowing his gaze, Darren looked first to the ground, then off into the trees. "And where in the world are we?"

Shaking his head, Christian looked up towards the sky, which was quickly getting darker from the thick clouds rolling in. He had a feeling he knew exactly what had just happened to them, and he felt his throat begin to close up. Hearing a sharp hiss and ragged cough, Christian looked over towards Cyrus, meeting his cool, black eyes.

"This looks like Earth," Cyrus hissed, wincing. "Why would He put us here?"

"I don't know, but He must be really mad," Darren whispered, wincing as he raised his arm to run a hand through his blond hair. Christian could practically hear his teeth grinding as he looked around him.

A sudden grunt had them all looking towards Nicholas. His eyes were fiery red as they stared back. "What in the...?" he groaned, shaking his head as if trying to clear it. "I think every part of me is bruised." Christian watched as he moved into a sitting position, holding his head in his hands. Suddenly, Nicholas looked up, his eyes wide. "Where's Manuel?"

Looking around, Christian realized Manuel was nowhere to be seen. Feeling a sense of panic, he began to fear the worst.

Christian was just about to get to his feet when they heard a rustling coming from the nearby bushes. Crouching down, he felt himself tense as he stared towards the noise. His brothers also began to ready themselves for a sudden attack. "Who's there?" Christian hissed.

A groan was the first thing they heard, then a sudden flash of movement, followed by a set of glowing amethyst eyes squinting out from between the leaves. "How is it I have the luck of ending up in the freaking bushes?" Manuel groaned as he began to pull himself into the open. His whole upper body and face were covered scratches.

With a sigh, Christian shook his head. "Crap, Manuel... Get over here." He looked over at the rest of them.

"What happened?" Manuel asked, crawling his way towards them. Getting as close as his bruised body would allow, he sat down with a huff. "Does anyone know?"

"I think I have an idea," Christian whispered as he looked at the tall trees around them. A soft drizzle had begun to fall, slowly dampening the hardened ground.

"Well, tell *us*," Cyrus spit out. "I mean, any insight would sure help right about now. So, please, feel free."

Blinking a couple times, Christian just stared at him. "I think we're being punished for acting out."

"That's ridiculous!" Cyrus stated, shaking his head, "We're His Watchers, the Guardians of His precious humans. He forgives their misconduct and misplaced faith with such ease. Why would he treat us any differently? There's just no way this would happen to us over a few comments."

"A *few* comments?!" Nicholas exclaimed. "You wouldn't be talking about the constant arguing and criticizing we all did, would you?"

"Speak for yourself!" Manuel shouted. "I told you to shut up. I told you guys to stop questioning His level of forgiveness for the humans. I told you all to just stay on point and stop going on and on about it. But no..." Looking over at Cyrus, he rolled his eyes. "You just *had* to be heard!"

"Hey, we *all* had a problem with what was going on, so don't give me that crap," Cyrus hissed out.

"Yeah. I didn't hear you disagreeing with us when the subject of the humans' behavior came up, did I?" Darren said to Manuel. His usually calm mannerisms seemed to vanish in the blink of an eye. "You can just take this shit about it being because of all of us, yet having nothing to do with you, and you can kiss my–"

"Okay. Come on, guys," Christian piped up. "Let's just take a deep breath here. We've obviously been sent down here for upsetting Him, but He wasn't upset enough with us to have us fall completely from Him." Clearing his throat, he looked around, meeting each of his brothers' eyes in turn. All of them nodded as the realization of just how bad this could have been sank in. "He must still care enough for us to give us a chance to fix the wrong we've done. We just need to figure out what He wants us to do."

"Okay. So what do we do now?" Nicholas asked, picking up a nearby stone, passing it from one hand to the other.

"I'm not sure," Christian said, looking around, silently hoping for some inspiration or sign of what they needed to do. He knew it had to do with the humans because they were the main theme behind all of their issues. Other than that, he had no idea where to start. Looking back at his brothers, he realized they were all waiting for him. He had always known what to do and where to start, but this time... "I just don't know," he whispered.

Silence fell upon the group as they all worried over what could possibly become of them. Glancing down at the ground, so cold and damp beneath his knees, Christian closed his eyes and prayed. He prayed for wisdom. He prayed for forgiveness. He prayed for strength.

Chapter 1

Present Day
Fhallon Heights, California

Father James stirred in his sleep, mumbling softly to himself. Sweat started forming on his forehead, his body beginning to shake. This went on for hours before he woke up. Sitting up, he looked wildly around the room. His hand shook as he reached up and ran his fingers through his silver hair.

It was the same dream every night.

In the dream, he always found himself walking through the church garden late at night, sighing over the many rose plants lining the gravel walkway. Reaching out, he picked one of the bright red roses and twirled it in his fingers, then dropped it as he felt one of the thorns prick his skin. He stood there, watching as a deep red drop of blood began to make its way down his finger. The droplet hypnotized him, its brilliant red slowly becoming the only color he could see. He stared at it, watching it slide down his wrist, until he was suddenly startled by a deep chuckle coming from behind him.

As he slowly turned towards the sound, he could just make out a shadowy figure standing by the garden's aged angel statue. The angel's head was slightly turned down as if she was in despair, her eyes hollow and sad. The shadowy figure was always just that in the beginning...a gray figure against the darkness. Father James squinted at the figure in an attempt to make out any kind of detail.

"Who's there?" he whispered. The air suddenly became thick around him, causing him to vigorously rub his hand over his chest. The shadowy figure chuckled again with a low rumble, causing Father James to shiver.

"Who I am is of no consequence, Father," the deep voice rumbled as he tilted his head. "All you need to know is that I am here to help you."

"Help me? With what?"

"With your shaken faith, of course."

Father James licked his lips, slowly shaking his head. "I don't know what you mean by that."

"Oh, Father, there is no reason to lie to me. Like I said, I am here to help. I am not one of your little choirboys you need to lie to so as not to wreck my poor little world." With another chuckle, the figure took a slight step forward. The moonlight showed just a hint of pale skin as he stepped away from the statue. "Now, what do you want, Father? What can I do to help you regain your faith?"

"I don't–"

"Father!" the figure chided. "Just tell me what you want. I promise, whatever it is, it will stay just between us."

Father James licked his lips again, glancing around before letting out a shaky sigh. "I didn't want to believe that this had happened, that I had lost my faith. But I did and I want it back. I feel so hollow inside, like I've lost a part of my very soul."

"You want to believe again." The dark figure smiled, stepping further into the moonlight, his white teeth flashing slightly.

"Yes," Father James whispered as he stepped towards him, his hands shaking at his sides.

"I can help you, Father. All I need is for you to do one little favor for me. Just one little favor, then your faith will return."

"A favor?" Father James gulped as he reached into his pocket, running his fingers over his rosaries. The act did little to calm his rapidly beating heart. "What kind of favor?"

"Nothing big. I just need you to find something for me, something your church has been holding onto for a long time now."

"What do you need me to find?"

"An old book, Father. A *very* old book! *Libro dei Damnati*. I know you have seen it. It is the thick leather book with the gold symbol on the cover."

Father James gasped, taking a step back. "Th-that book is unholy! I can't... No, I won't get that for you!"

The stranger moved closer to him, sneering as he tilted his head to the side. "You *will* get that book for me, Father James. You will do it not only to save your faith, but to save your very soul. You see, Father, I have the ability to give you everything you have ever wanted. All I want is for you to find that one little book. I do not even want you to give it to me. I just want you to find it."

Father James nervously licked his lips. "If you don't want it for yourself, what do you want me to do with it if I find it?" He watched as the stranger smoothed his porcelain fingers down his black coat.

"All I want you to do," the stranger whispered, giving Father James a knowing smile, "is read from it."

Father James could feel his chest tightening as he gazed at the stranger. "What are you?" he whispered, a cold breeze cutting through his robe.

"As I said before, that does not matter. What matters is what you are willing to do to get your faith back."

"You just want me to read from it? Nothing more?"

"Just read, Father. Out loud would be best."

"And you can return my faith to me? Help me find the light again?"

"Anything you want, Father. Do this tiny little favor for me, and I'll give you everything you want and more."

At this point, the dream usually came to an abrupt end, Father James being jarred awake. However, this night, the dream was lingering, swirling through his head as he looked around his dark room. Glancing at the clock, he noticed it was 3am.

Shaking his head, he attempted to rid his mind of the dream, but it just would not go. He could hear the stranger's promises repeating over and over.

Slowly climbing out of bed, Father James slid on his robe, deciding that a walk through the corridors would do him some good. With a slight squeak from the hinges, he opened his door and stepped into the hall. Looking around, he stood there, waiting to hear if his movements had woken anyone else. After a couple moments of silence, he let out a soft sigh.

Gazing at the walls as he walked, Father James looked at the wonderful pictures and statues adorning the hallway. All of them were as gorgeous as they were old. Gliding down the stairs, he rounded the corner and stepped out into the cool night air. Finding himself in the garden, he quickly made his way past the roses and heavenly statues, stopping at the angel statue from his dream. He gazed up at her, yearning for the feeling of comfort and awe that her presence usually brought him.

However, right now, he only felt hollowness, a bleakness that had followed him around for the last nine years. He wanted everything to go back to the way it was, the way things had been before the events happened that shook his faith. Looking upon the angel's face, he felt a tear slide down his cheek. Wiping it away, he began walking again, moving cautiously through the garden, winding up at the entrance to the church's cellar.

Quietly, he stood there, staring at the old wooden doors which lead down into the corridors below. The corridors which were filled with the oldest of things...books, maps, paintings. Closing his eyes, he could picture the closed room that should never be opened, a room filled with items that should never be touched. Father James shivered as he opened his eyes, realizing he was reaching for the door knob.

"What am I doing?" he whispered, feeling a cold breeze pushing against him, almost warning him to back away. Shaking his head, he chose to ignore this silent warning, needing to know if his dreams were more than they seemed. He turned the knob, hearing the door groan as it gave way to the damp stairs leading to the cellar.

Reaching into the dark, he let his fingers slide around on the cool cement walls until he found the light switch. With a quick flip, he watched as the lights lining the ceiling flickered a couple times, then softly lit the way.

As he began to make his way through the door and down the stairs, Father James felt his hands begin to tremble. The stranger's voice in his head was louder than before, his promise still echoing through his mind.

He passed one door after another, all of them open for him to see the splendors within. The halls felt like they went on forever, turning one corner after another, until he was deep into the corridors beneath the church. If he had never been down here before, he would have surely found himself lost by now. Swiping at the cobwebs hanging from the ceiling, he rounded the last corner and stopped in front of the final door, the only one that was closed.

This door was much darker than the rest. There were dark stains weaving gracefully through the wood, as if it were marble, many spots looking black. Father James felt a coldness in the pit of his stomach as he stared at it.

"I shouldn't go in there," he whispered. "I must be out of my mind."

He stood there for a minute more and then, shaking his head, began to turn to go back the way he had come. Just as he turned away from the door, he felt the air around him shift. Stopping, he heard the stranger's voice in his head again, but instead of it being echoes from his dream, he heard it like he was standing right next to him.

One favor... That is all you need to do and I will return your faith to you!

Shaking, Father James looked around. "You're real?"

Oh, I am very real, Father, as is my promise to you! All you have to do is get the book.

"What if I can't find it?"

You will find it, Father. Just go through the door and it will be right where you last saw it.

"How do you know I've seen it already?"

I know much more than you can fathom, Father. Just get the book, take it up to your room, and read it. That is all I am asking of you.

Turning back towards the door, Father James felt drops of sweat beginning to fall down the sides of his face, soaking into his collar. Hugging his robe around him, he took a step towards the door, slowly reaching out to the door knob with his right hand. "What will happen once I read it?" he whispered, feeling the cool metal beneath his fingertips.

A soft sigh echoed through his head as he began to open the door. *Once you read the book, Father, you will have your faith returned to you. That really is all you need to know. Do I ask so much of you? Is this tiny request too far out of your reach?*

"No, I can do this," he said with conviction, opening the door wide. Walking into the dismal room, his nose was immediately assaulted by the stench of mold and filth that seemed to be creeping out from every dark corner. Gulping slightly, he paused, allowing his eyes to grow accustomed to the dim light filtering in behind him.

Slowly sliding his gaze across the room, he saw a slight glint of light reflecting from the far right corner. Inching towards it, he reached down and, with a shudder, ran his fingers over the old dark leather. The gold emblem on the cover shimmered in the soft light, as if the light itself was in the room solely for that purpose.

Now, take the book up to your room, Father. You have done well and, soon, you shall have exactly what was promised to you.

Father James picked up the book, feeling the weight of it in his arms as he pulled it against his chest. Every fiber of his being was telling him he should leave it, turn away from this dark room, and never return. But part of him, the part that wanted nothing more than to have his mind put at ease and his faith returned, made him turn, book in hand, and make his way from the cellar. Heading towards his room, he felt eager to begin his reading, to complete his side of the deal, and become whole once more.

†

"So... Is it going to work?"

Andras slowly opened his eyes to find Hantu, his demon of choice when it came to frightening another into submission, standing before him. "Of course it is going to work, Hantu."

"I just wanted to make sure you still wanted me to stay out of this," he said, tilting his head to the side. His thick black hair cascaded over his right shoulder, smooth against his porcelain skin. His coal black eyes glowed as he looked up and meet Andras' stare. "Just say the word and I will go to this priest, make sure he does what you want him to."

"No. That is quite all right, Hantu," Andras said with a crooked smile. "I believe I have Father James more than happy to do what I want him to."

"What do we do now?"

Andras leaned back in his chair and looked around his office. It wasn't much, but when in Hell, you can't expect too much extravagance. The walls were a dark wood, cabinets and shelves built into them. Not that he had much to put in them, but they were good for the few files and old scripts he had acquired throughout the years. All the furniture was a dark red oak with finely carved edges, which was a nice contrast to the thick, black carpet beneath their feet. All in all, it was a rather fitting office for him, one he was hoping to be free of in the near future!

Andras tapped his fingers on the dark oak table as he looked back at the demon standing in front of him. He was always fascinated with how Hantu could look so normal one minute, then turn into every human's worst nightmare the next. That was the main reason Andras kept him around. Among his devoted soldiers, Hantu was definitely one of the most...handy.

"Sir?" Hantu asked as he eyed Andras, slightly unnerved by his silence.

Clearing his throat, Andras leaned forward, resting his elbows on the table. "We just need to be patient. The priest has the book with him and, as we speak, is taking it back to his room. Now, go and tell the others to start preparing. I have a feeling it will not be long before we can put the next part of our plan into effect."

"Yes, sir," Hantu murmured with a slight bow of his head. He turned on his heels and left the office, quietly closing the door behind him.

Andras let out a sigh, reaching up to massage his temple. It had been a long time since he had broken through a human's subconscious to invade their thoughts. He had forgotten how taxing it was and about the migraines that always followed. Luckily for him, Father James' mind had not been a very difficult one to breach. It was so filled with doubt and anger, Andras hardly had to fight at all to get in. Sure, getting him to actually go down into the church's cellar and get the book had taken a little finesse but, in the end, everything had worked out exactly how Andras had planned it.

Feeling the migraine begin to pound through his head, Andras reached into his desk drawer and pulled out a bottle of whiskey. Taking a long swig, he just hoped he wouldn't have to do that again with Father James. All he needed the old priest to do was read through the book. Of course, what Father James didn't know was that with each page, he would be undoing an age-old curse which kept Andras, as well as more than a dozen other demons, from ever gaining access to Earth.

Andras had a few soldiers under his command who were able to make the leap, to go topside, but not many. When a demon was of "pure blood", born instead of made, they weren't held by the same restrictions as the rest of them. Not that being "impure" in blood caused a demon to be less powerful, of which Andras was proof of, but it did have its downfalls. To be able to tip the balance in his favor, he was going to need as many as he could get. Once the priest started reading, the veil holding them back would begin to weaken, allowing him to slip a couple more of his demons through.

Now if I could just keep the priest from asking too many questions or second-guessing my reasoning behind doing this!

Then there was also the fact that people would begin to go missing. Andras chuckled to himself. After all, what was a little curse lifting without some human sacrifice? Of course, if the priest found out about this little "side effect" of his reading, he would have to be taken care of. Then Andras would have to look for yet another human to open the gates. Grinding his teeth, Andras thought over how long it had taken to find the priest to begin with. This had to work!

Taking another drink of his whiskey, Andras closed his eyes, calmly concentrating on the feel of the smooth, woody liquid as it rolled over his tongue and down his throat, burning like hot coals on its way down. *If only everything could be as simple as whiskey*, he mused, leaning back in his chair. Feeling the warmth in his stomach beginning to spread, he reached up and ran his hands through his short black hair. If this all went south, the whole mess was going to give him an ulcer.

Hearing the door open, he groaned. Andras kept his eyes closed in the hopes that whoever it was would take the hint and go away.

"Andras?"

He cracked one eye open and glanced at his second-in-command, Agalon, who appeared to be on edge. Lifting his head, he looked at him and suppressed a snarl. "Agalon, I do not remember calling for you. What is it you need to see me about? Something of grave importance, I am sure."

"I did not realize you were going to connect with the priest today."

Seeing this was said more as a statement than an actual question, Andras simply raised his eyebrow in response. As the seconds ticked by, they continued to stare at each other until, finally, Andras tilted his head in question.

"I just thought you would want *me* in here, not Hantu," Agalon hissed.

Sighing, Andras rose from his chair and walked around his desk. Running his fingers over the fine edges, he came to rest against it in front of Agalon. "I did not think it was going to be a big deal," he responded with a shrug.

"Well, it *is* a big deal. I am your second-in-command!"

"Yes, and being my second-in-command means you need to be watching over the soldiers when I am otherwise indisposed. So while I was in here taking care of the priest, what were you doing?"

"I was gathering your soldiers for the meeting we are supposed to have later," he snarled back.

"Well, there you go. You were doing your job."

"Are you going to fill me in on what transpired, or am I supposed to wait until the meeting and find out with everyone else?"

Leaning back a little on the desk, Andras just stared at him. He really was an intimidating brute with his silver hair and blue, piercing eyes. Andras knew the only reason he was acting like this was because he truly hated being second, although he put up with it because he was loyal to Andras. The thought that Hantu found out information before he did was just eating him up, especially since it was information on a mission that, if done right, had the potential to alter the status of the major players involved.

But wasn't that why he had called Hantu into his office in the first place? He needed to keep Agalon on some kind of leash. He didn't want him to start feeling like he had all the answers because then he may think he could go against Andras. That just wouldn't do because then he would have to dispose of Agalon, and he was way too valuable to risk that.

Andras sighed again and crossed one ankle over the other, allowing some of his agitation to show. "I was planning on telling you before the meeting, Agalon. I was just waiting for my migraine to go away. Is that okay with you?"

"Oh... Of course, Andras," he said, clearing his throat. "It has been a while since you have had to do this. I forgot about the headaches that followed." Agalon looked at the ground for a second, obviously trying to decide what to say next.

While Andras waited for his second-in-command to gather his thoughts, he looked over his shoulder towards the papers stacked on his desk. So much had gone into finding the perfect person to do what he needed. There were files upon files of individuals with weak faith, shattered hopes, and lost souls. So many minds completely open to him, yet he needed the perfect one, the one who would not only do what he asked, but one who wanted something. That was what Father James had. He not only had a weak mind and lost faith, but a want, a need, to have something to believe in!

This is definitely something I can give him, Andras thought with a slight chuckle.

Hearing Agalon clear his throat once again, he looked back towards the demon.

"Would you like me to give you some more time, sir?" Agalon said hesitantly. "I could come back later, once you're ready for me."

"Yes," he said slowly. "I need you to go finish gathering everyone up. I need to have everyone present."

"Yes, sir," Agalon said with a slight bow of his head. Andras watched as he turned towards the door, his large frame taking up the entire doorway as he moved away from him.

"And Agalon?" Andras said.

Turning his head slowly, the demon meet his gaze. "Yes, sir?"

"Do not question my reasoning or my actions again." His voice was a cold whisper crackling through the air. Each word was laced with the threat and promise of what would happen if his warning was not heeded.

Agalon blinked, casting his eyes towards the ground. "Of course, sir. I apologize for any disrespect." Andras watched as his throat tensed up. "It will never happen again, Andras."

"Make sure it does not," Andras sneered, keeping his cold gaze upon Agalon as he quietly left the room.

Chapter 2

Eight Days Later

Christian looked across the dimly lit bar. He could hear the ice crackling in a glass as the bartender poured the cheap whiskey over it. Sloshing it over the side, he quickly shoved it towards the awaiting patron so he could get back to fawning over the pretty little blond sitting at the end of the bar.

Not that she was lacking attention.

Flipping her hair behind her shoulder, she leaned in to whisper something to the man sitting next to her. His eyes gleamed as he glanced down her shirt, his brow sweaty with anticipation. Chuckling at whatever witty comment she had made, the man winked and leaned in a little closer.

Christian could see the woman squint for a brief moment, her pupils dilating, most likely in response to the sour odor emitting from the man. When another guy took a seat on the other side of her, the man looked past her and glared, possessively placing his hand on her thigh.

She played the men like her own personal toys, offering everything to them, giving nothing away. Her breathy laugh rolled through the air as she accepted another free drink, as well as many other inviting gestures from the men around her.

Shaking his head, Christian looked towards the other end of the bar. Sitting quietly against the wall was the woman he was here for. She truly was rather beautiful in her own right. He stared at her, taking in her dark chestnut hair, creamy skin, and slender figure. He didn't know much about her, other than what he saw, but he knew she would need him...soon.

If the itching in his shoulders was right, and it always had been, there was something evil around. This sense of his was both a gift and a curse. Usually it would lead him to some evil soul or demon; however, in this instance, it was telling him this woman was one he needed to protect. He wasn't quite sure what was so important about her, but he was never one to ignore his instincts. There had been a couple times in the past when he found himself fighting a demon to save an innocent life, but those instances were rare – at least lately.

It was his calling to either capture evil souls or send demons back to Hell, and although he always enjoyed the fight with the assailant, he got tired. Then there there was the common question he was sure to get. "Are you my guardian angel?" He usually answered with a glare or snarl before quickly taking off. Just because he ended up saving someone's life didn't mean he wanted to be friends.

Guardian angel my ass, Christian thought, rolling his shoulders. He may have been a Guardian for the longest time...still was, to a certain degree...but he was *no one's* guardian angel!

Focusing his attention back on the woman, he breathed deeply, smelling the soft lavender soap still clinging to her skin. He watched her play with her straw, swirling it through her drink, shyly averting any stranger's questioning glance. She put out an air of innocence and to those who didn't look closely, or know what to look for, she would have them fooled. However, Christian could see that behind those shielded, honey-colored eyes was a fire. She was drawing just enough attention to pique everyone's interest, but not enough to draw a crowd. It was obvious to Christian that she was hunting for someone, but who?

†

Ella couldn't believe her luck. She had only been in the bar for a short time and it was already paying off. When her informant, Dave, told her about this place, she had been skeptical. Going from one sleazy bar to another, she had been trying to find the person responsible for all the recent disappearances around town. At first, this had just been a side job, something that had piqued her curiosity, but now it was personal! Ever since a girl she knew had disappeared a few weeks back, and seeing that the local police decided they were just going to wait around for a body to show up, Ella decided to put her P.I. know-how to work.

This morning, after hours of questioning anyone and everyone she could, and spending the last day or so hitting her informants hard, she had finally gotten a break.

Glancing in the mirror behind the bar, she had a clear view of the whole establishment and it didn't take her long to spot him. Scruffy hair, shabby clothes, and an air about him that made Ella feel like she needed to run home and take a shower. He looked just like Dave said he would, although he was a lot bigger than she imagined.

She reached into her purse and ran her finger over the cold steel of her revolver. *Never leave home without it*, she thought. Dave said he didn't think this man was responsible for the missing people, but he could probably lead her to those who were. A lead was a lead.

Shifting in her chair, Ella looked back down at her drink. Luckily, the bartender was so busy with the blonde at the other end of the bar, he didn't seem to notice how long she had been babysitting her drink. Ella wanted to stay as alert as possible, so she decided on a maximum of one or two drinks, even though she could really have used a double.

Glancing around again, Ella caught movement out of the corner of her eye. *Oh my!* she thought, her eyes landing on the mysterious stranger to her right. If she thought the man she was here to find was big, this guy was a giant! His black Korn t-shirt hugged his broad shoulders, and as he slowly rolled them, she could see every muscle in his chest ripple before he settled back into a relaxed slouch. He absently ran his hand through his short brown hair, politely smiling at the server walking past him.

Shivering, Ella couldn't help but stare. Even though she kept looking away, her gaze was constantly being pulled back in his direction. She caught the slightest glimpse of steel blue eyes as he surveyed the bar around him, gazing intently in the direction of the blonde before smiling and looking away. Narrowing her eyes, she fought the sudden urge to laugh. Of course he would look that way. Most of the men in the bar were!

Swallowing hard, Ella realized this feeling of jealousy had to stop. She wasn't here for a night out on the town. She was working. So, taking her gaze off of Mr. Dark and Mysterious, she decided to take one more glance over her shoulder.

Yep, she thought, taking a sip of her drink. *It's time to get this ball rolling.*

†

Licking his lips, Christian glanced around the room. He needed to figure out who she was after because it looked like she was getting restless. He turned his head to the side and concentrated, scenting out those who were nearby, seeing whose interest was hotter for the shy brunette than anyone else. He could feel the familiar tingling in his back as he narrowed his gaze on each man individually. Each man sitting near the mystery woman was glancing her way. Some looked out of pure curiosity, some out of a healthy wonder about what could be...but one had a look of fierce need. His was an animalistic desire, one which would have made even the most brazen woman back away.

We have a winner, he thought, casually looking back towards the bar. This man had such a black soul, Christian could almost taste its oiliness.

Christian's eyes darted back towards the woman at the bar. He could see her continue to look into the bar's mirror, making only the briefest eye contact with the man to his left, then quickly looking away. Instantly, he felt the rush of heat coming off the man in question. With a subtle glance, he could see the wildness building within the man's eyes. Christian seriously doubted humans knew how much the eyes could really tell you. This man wasn't just another lonely soul looking for a good time. There was something very dark residing in him.

Christian closed his eyes and concentrated on the man. He could practically feel his warm breath, hear the acceleration of his heartbeat, smell the stench of alcohol oozing from his pores. Repeatedly, the man's hands tensed into fists and relaxed in his lap as he ran his tongue over his chapped lips. Even though Christian was not able to read minds, he felt he had a pretty good idea what this man was thinking, and it was nothing good.

As his eyes opened, Christian saw the woman glance towards her dark admirer. After the briefest moment, she turned her head away, a small smile playing across her lips. She was playing with fire and didn't even know it. Fluttering her eyes and shyly smiling at the bartender, she passed on another refill and began to slowly gather her stuff to leave, casting an occasional glance in the stranger's direction. She glided easily off her chair. Her shoes barely making a sound, she made her way to the back exit, heading out into the chilly night air and dimly lit alley. With a last heated glance over her shoulder, the brunette stepped through the door. Gritting his teeth, Christian glanced out of the corner of his eyes and saw the stranger staring intently after her. A heartbeat later, he silently got up to follow.

A sudden sense of urgency came over Christian as he got up from his chair. He knew this was not going to play out like the woman intended, yet instead of following the doomed pair out the back, he headed for the front entrance. As he hit the door, he could hear soft grunts and curses coming from the alley.

†

Ella's eyes widened as the man stumbled out the door after her. *Maybe this wasn't such a good idea*, she thought, backing up towards the street. It was time for her to change tactics. "Hey, buddy, you're lookin' a little sloshed. Do you need me to get you some help?" Ella forced a smile as she continued to move away from him. "I could go call you a cab or something."

"You know what, sweet cheeks?" the man drawled. "I think you know exactly what you can do for me." With a burst of speed Ella wouldn't have thought the drunk could muster, he rushed towards her. She started to reach into her purse, but he grabbed her arm, ripping the purse from her hands. She backed away as he threw it into the closest dumpster. "Hope ya didn't need that!" he laughed, moving closer to her. "Now, why don't ya come here and let me get a look at that pretty little smile of yours. You know, the shy one ya been sending my way all night."

"Shit!" Ella said, whirling around in an attempt to make a dash for the street. She felt him quickly close the distance and grab her hair, slamming her into the wall. Adrenaline quickly took over and Ella began to fight back with all she had. He roughly pushed her up against the wall, seductively rubbing himself onto her back. Feeling fear and anger begin to run down her spine, Ella glanced over her shoulder.

"That's it, sweet cheeks!" he sneered. "Get angry. It's always more fun that way."

†

Christian could smell the undeniable scent of fear beginning to waft through the air, realizing the hunter had just become the hunted. Rolling his shoulders as the sensation in his back began to build, he rushed around the corner, in time to see the stranger roughly shoving the woman into the wall.

"Bastard," the woman hissed. "Get your hands off me!" She began to wiggle and squirm, pushing off the wall in an attempt to get some room between her and the cold cement. He could see the muscles in her arms straining at the effort, but the man had too much weight on her. Her assailant just grunted and grabbed the back of her head, pressing her face into the wall.

He leaned in and heavily breathed against her soft skin. "Isn't this what ya wanted?" he whispered in her ear. "Isn't this whatcha were lookin' for?"

Whimpering, the woman closed her eyes and grit her teeth. Christian could see her strength beginning to dwindle. She was not going to be able to fight this man off much longer, and she knew it.

As he started quickly moving towards them, he saw the man wrap his hands around her throat, pulling her head back, harshly pressing his body into hers. Christian released a low growl just before charging into the man at full force. Slamming his body into the man, Christian could hear the cracking of at least one rib, if not two, as he sent him flying off to the side. A loud grunt was heard as his body struck the ground. Rolling to his feet, Christian faced the man, crouching low. He was ready to rush him if he moved to attack. The man groaned and, gripping his side, slowly began to rise to his feet.

"What the fuck?!" he coughed, attempting to catch his breath. "Who the hell are you? Can't ya see we're busy?"

"From the looks of it, I don't think the lady wants anything to do with you, although I can't imagine why!" Christian taunted, taking a step towards the man. He could sense the woman behind him, curling tightly against the wall. Her hand tentatively reached up, going to her throat, as she stared at the two of them. Fear was vibrating from her body, causing him to pause. Inwardly, he was shaking, but Christian forced his concentration to remain solely on the man in front of him. It wouldn't do either of them any good if he allowed himself to get sidetracked, would it?

†

Ella felt her neck, repeatedly running her fingers over the now tender area. *What in the hell?* Ella wondered, her heart racing. Only moments ago, she was being pressed to the wall by a smelly drunk. How she ended up on the ground, bruised and out of breath, she had no idea.

Hearing the grunts and vile cursing coming from the drunk, she looked up, blinking rapidly, and couldn't believe her eyes. Her mystery man was standing there larger than life...and angry as hell. He was just staring down at the man who had attacked her. She could see his back muscles straining against his shirt.

Where did he come from? she thought, wildly looking around her. There was no way he could have gotten out of the bar, around the corner, and down the alley in such a short amount of time...was there?

As she stared back at her protector, she saw his back muscles repeatedly bunch up and relax. *Strange*. Suddenly, she saw his muscles bunch into an odd, almost impossible shape, then flatten out. What in the...?

Not taking his eyes off the man, Christian began to slowly walk to the side, drawing the stranger further and further from the woman. The man, now visibly shaking with anger, growled at Christian, "You're gonna pay for this, ya sorry piece of shit!" Reaching into his back pocket, the foul man produced a rather impressive-looking blade. Waving it in the air aggressively, the man dared Christian to come at him.

Not yet, Christian thought, rolling his shoulders. He could feel his skin start to vibrate as he glared at the man. Lunging at him, Christian slammed the man to the ground and they rolled in a mass of fists and growls. The stranger's knife cut into

Christian's arm as he turned to grab his wrist, snapping it like a twig, producing a howl from the man's lips.

Leaping back, Christian could feel a slight trickle of blood running down his arm. The stinging pain only caused his anger to increase. He took in a deep breath, feeling the tingle in his back turn into a warm throb. Not knowing how much longer he was going to be able to play nice with his smelly sparring partner, he was going to have to act fast.

Breathing deeply, Christian knelt down and ran his hand over his wounded arm. He watched the stranger reach over with his good hand to retrieve the knife from where it had fallen. Running his tongue over his now swollen and bloody lips, he sneered at Christian, "You're going to pay for breakin' my fuckin' wrist, boy!" He turned his head and spit blood onto the cement. "Now it's my turn!"

The man rushed at Christian, awkwardly stumbling over himself in his attempt to knock him off his feet. Anticipating the move, Christian met him and punched the man in his jaw. As he flew sideways from the impact, his hand flew out wildly, slicing Christian's cheek with his knife.

Standing over the man, Christian reached up and touched his face, bringing his hand away with blood-stained fingers.

The rush he now felt would not be calmed with a deep breath or any other kind of mantra he'd been taught to use.

Christian could feel the heat rushing through his body, his back muscles beginning to move. Slowly, he brought his gaze up to meet the man's and saw an instant and familiar fear come across the man's face.

"Your eyes," he whispered, as though to speak any louder would make what he was seeing all the more real. "What in the fuck is happening to your fuckin' eyes?"

Christian knew his once ice blue eyes were now a pure midnight black. They were always the first to change. He peered at the man and, savoring the fear coming off him, Christian groaned inwardly. He could feel the pressure in his back releasing as it split open, ripping his t-shirt down the middle, producing a devilish set of black wings which stretched far above him. The black feathers shined in the dim light of the alley as he extended them to their full length, their tips just brushing the ground.

†

Ella's eyes felt like they were going to pop out of her head. She had only dreamed of such things happening. Sure, there were the characters in the many books she liked to read and the movies she liked to watch, but seeing wings spring from this man's back was absolutely unreal. Maybe it was just the night playing tricks on her, or maybe there was something in her drink causing her to hallucinate. Whatever the case may be, Ella was staring right at the back of a man with the most magnificent, largest pair of black wings she had ever seen.

She watched as they stretched high into the air and, curling slightly at the tips, they cut through the night. She could practically see the man shiver. Whether from pain or ecstasy, Ella wasn't sure. She continued to blink rapidly, still not allowing herself to entirely believe her own eyes. The words *not possible* became a mantra running through her mind.

Yup, she was losing it. She was one eye twitch away from a straitjacket.

Feeling a pressure in her chest, Ella suddenly realized she had been holding her breath. Stars began to twinkle before her eyes as she drew in large gasps of air. In the shocked stillness of the alley, her gasps were deafening. Clasping a hand over her mouth, Ella shrank back against the wall, never taking her eyes off the scene unfolding in front of her.

†

As he stared down at the man on the ground, Christian was only somewhat aware of the gasping woman behind him. In his heightened state, he could see every individual bead of sweat running down his face, and he could hear the irregular beat of his heart. The fear in the man was intoxicating, almost overpowering, causing Christian to sway a little under the feel of it.

His nose was suddenly assaulted with the sharp scent of urine, which Christian could now see was soaking through the stranger's jeans. *Humans*, he thought with disgust, glaring down at the man.

"Wh-what are you?" the man gasped. He began to pull himself backwards with his good hand, his knife now completely forgotten where it lay. Cradling his wrist against his chest, the man grimaced as he stretched behind him, sliding himself further and further away. Avoiding Christian's dark gaze, the man again asked, "What in the fuck are you?"

Christian crouched down, bringing himself to eye level with the man. His black eyes drilled into him as a slow grin spread across his face. "I'm the fucking tooth fairy. Now show me those pearly whites."

The man's face blanched and he began blinking rapidly as a sob escaped his lips. That he was just a couple blinks away from fainting further infuriated Christian.

Oh, I don't think so, he thought, reaching out and wrapping his hand around the man's neck. *You're staying with me for the whole show.*

The man's good hand wrapped around Christian's wrist as he slowly started to stand, bring the man with him. Yanking his face close, Christian stared into his terrified eyes. Looking past the delicious emotion swirling within them, he forced his mind to open and see straight into the man's soul. he saw all the rapes the vile male had committed, all his petty thefts, his many assaults, and his fears.

That's what Christian wanted, what he was always looking for, what he craved. Feeling a sense of need come over him, he focused all of his will on that blackness.

He felt his lips pull back as the man gurgled and kicked in a sorry attempt to free himself. Drawing his wings around them, Christian felt himself aggressively begin to pull at that blackness, willing it to come to him.

The man had stopped struggling and was screaming soundlessly, mouth open and eyes bulging. As the darkness began to make its way to Christian, it became like a gray fog, slowly pouring from the man's eyes, mouth, nose, and skin. It lifted off him in a cloud-like swirl until it engulfed the air around him.

The sheer force of the fog caused Christian to quickly release him, allowing the man to crumble to the ground like a deflated mattress. *A screaming, smelly mattress,* Christian thought, rolling his eyes skyward, feeling the blackness begin to seep into him.

In agony, the man bucked on the ground. His body shook as he finally managed to pull himself to his knees. Reaching up, he grabbed his head with both hands, causing his knuckles to go white, his face twisting in agony. Leaning back, his mouth fell open and he let out a final ear-piercing scream, the last of the blackness bursting from his lips. It swirled wildly in the air, seeming to move blindly around them both, before finally slamming into Christian. The force of the impact caused him to clench his teeth and squeeze his eyes shut. In a rush of feathers, swirling blackness, and shivers, Christian fell to the ground.

"Shit...," he hissed.

Chapter 3

Ella could only stare. The whole thing had happened so fast, but it felt like it had gone in slow motion. As the dark mist that had been surrounding the two men faded away, she was left staring at the back of the now wingless man. He was trembling and had a sheen of sweat covering every inch of his exposed skin. She could hear him hissing slightly as he pulled air in through his teeth. Her attacker, on the other hand, lay unmoving on the ground, staring vacantly at the wall, mouth still slightly open from his final gasp for air.

Curiously, Ella looked back at the shuddering man. Leaning a little to the left, she attempted to see a side profile of him, cautious not to make any noise. No need to draw any attention to herself. Staring at him, she realized she wasn't afraid. Maybe she was in shock? *Yeah, that's it*, she thought.

Now he looked like he was in pain. His hand shook as he brought it up to his face, running his fingers through his damp hair. The cut on his arm was no longer bleeding, but she could see the bruising beginning to blossom around the edges. Ella wondered if he had even felt the cut.

Looking again, she realized that the cut on his face was practically gone!

"Um... Are you okay?" she asked, feeling foolish as soon as the words left her lips. "I mean...um... Are you hurt?"

Yup, that was much better!

†

As the chills began to fade and Christian could feel his mind clearing, he reached up and ran his hands through his hair. It didn't knock him on his ass like it used to, but it still took a lot out of him.

Hearing the woman's voice sent a jolt through his spine. Twisting his head around, he just stared at her. Her brown eyes, though a little wide, were staring straight at him. "What?" he breathed.

"Are you okay? It's just... You're bleeding and... Well, you *were* bleeding. I just wanted to know if you were okay." Licking her lips, she glanced past him at the body. "And thanks for...for showing up when you did." She looked back at him, unblinking. He could see her shaking a little, her right hand moving a strand of misplaced hair from her face.

"I'm good," he stated, continuing to look at her. She wasn't as upset as she had been, and he couldn't sense any fear in her. She was shaken, but not from fear. *Interesting*. Christian's eyes narrowed as he looked deep into hers. Besides the whiteness of her soul and her lack of fear, there was no insight as to what made her so special. Why had he been drawn to her?

Well..., Christian thought as he tilted his head. It didn't really matter why he had been drawn there, did it? He took care of what he needed to, but he guessed it didn't hurt to indulge her a bit while he was still regaining his balance.

"And you?" Christian asked, leaning a little more on his arms.

"Oh, I'm good," she said with a shaky smile. "I think I may be a little out of my mind, though. I mean this is... What I just saw you do... What I *think* I saw is... I don't even know. I think I'm going crazy." Laughing a little, she glanced back at the body, again pushing at the stray strand of hair that had fallen from behind her ear. She didn't seem aware of the movement, leading Christian to think it was more of a nervous action than anything else.

Christian watched as she blinked a couple times, then quickly looked at him again. He could almost see her going over the past few minutes in her mind, probably trying to convince herself she wasn't losing her mind. He was still a little stunned as he watched her. She wasn't acting like any of the others he had helped, and there have been a few. Instead of fear or shock, she was confused but curious. And the question of his well-being was also a new one he'd never heard before.

I need to get out of here, he thought, looking past her and down the alley. It was too quiet. Someone may have heard or, even worse, seen all the commotion. If anyone saw anything, Darren and the boys were going to have a fit. Not only had he gone out on his own, but he had completely forgotten to enact the shade, a handy bit of glamour he and his brothers had in their bag-o'-tricks to keep the humans from noticing things.

Standing up, he looked down at the woman. "You're not going crazy."

"I'm not?" Shaking her head, she pulled herself to her feet and leaned against the wall. "Okay, I like not being crazy. However, that means I just watched a massive pair of wings sprout out of a grown man's back! Oh, and then there was whatever you just did with the fog that burst from the drunken asshole's body. But I'm rambling. Glad I'm not crazy, though." She paused, a shaky laugh escaping her lips. "So, um... Now what?"

Christian met her gaze and felt himself go still. *Now what indeed*! "Well, I'm going to get out of here, and you... I suggest you head home."

He watched her look around the alley. In a nervous gesture, she pulled on her black knit top, curling the edges with her fingers. She shook her head again. "Just like that?" she whispered. "I get attacked, watch you, um...do what you did, and you're response is that I should just head home? I can't believe–"

"What were you doing out here anyway?" Christian bit out. "What game were you trying to play?"

He watched a sudden flash of realization cross her face, followed by a flash of anger. "I needed to get information. I was told he'd be able to help me."

"Help you?!" he laughed. "Was that going to happen before or after he raped you?" Christian knew his words hit home when he saw her cringe. Good! She needed to realize how bad this could have gone. Grinding his teeth, Christian just glared at her. The level of irresponsibility humans showed never ceased to amaze him. "What information could you have needed so badly that you came to this sleazy bar and purposefully caught the attention of that piece of shit? No! You know what? Never mind. It's none of my business. I think you should just go home."

Closing his eyes, he took a deep breath. *I really need to get out of here*, he thought crossly.

†

Ella couldn't believe it. She had just watched a character out of one of her favorite novels come to life in a rather spectacular and breathtaking fashion, and now she was expected to just head home like nothing happened? Yeah, there was no way in hell that was going to happen.

She watched him as he closed his eyes and took a deep breath. His shoulders weren't shaking anymore, and his hands seemed a lot steadier as he reached up to run his fingers through his hair. Her breath caught in her throat as she watched his muscles tensing. Looking back at his face, Ella wished he would open his eyes. He had the most amazing blue eyes she'd ever seen, and she just had the strongest need to look into them. If nothing more, she wanted to memorize every second of this encounter because, once this moment passed, she feared she'd never see him again.

When he opened his eyes, his bright blue irises almost glowed in the dim light of the alley. With a quick glance her way, he turned his head, looking off towards the street.

"I have to go," he whispered, not looking back at her. He tilted his head to the side, giving Ella the impression he was listening to something, yet there was no one else around.

She just stared at him. He was so tall compared to her, so dangerous, so...manly!

Slowly turning his head, he looked back at her and, for the briefest moment, their eyes met. *Those eyes!* Ella felt the heat building in her, but this wasn't right! How could she feel so attracted to him? She didn't even know who, or what, he was.

Inhaling sharply, he took a quick step back. "I can't be here any longer. I… I need to go." His words sounded forced.

Breathing deeply, Ella watched as he closed his eyes, his tongue slowly running over his lips. *Oh god*! There was no way she could let him leave. There had to be something she could do, something she could say…

"What's your name?" she blurted out.

Yup, that'll do the trick. Great way to keep the conversation going, Ella. Groaning inwardly, she stood there, hoping it didn't sound as lame to him as it did to her.

His eyes snapped open and he just stared at her. Shoving a stray strand of hair behind her ears, she sighed. *Okay, let's try a different approach*. "My name's Ella, and yours is…?"

He tilted his head as if contemplating her question. The act reminded her of her cat at home, always tilting her head as if to say *I have no idea what you're saying*, or *silly human*. In this instance, she would bet he was thinking the latter.

"Christian."

"What?"

"My name... It's Christian."

Ella was surprised because part of her hadn't really expected him to answer. Staring at him, she could just barely see the sides of his mouth turn up into a smile.

A loud bang from the end of the alley caused her to gasp as she looked to the left. A black cat ran from behind a downed trash can, causing her heart to skip a beat or two. Shaking her head, she looked back towards Christian. She was fully prepared to get some answers, find out who and what he was. *He's gone!* She was all alone in the alley.

"Well, shit...," Ella exhaled.

Chapter 4

From the rooftop, Christian looked down at Ella. Why had he told her his name? For that matter, why did he stay and talk to her for as long as he did? He just felt so drawn to her, almost like he needed to be by her. Shaking his head, he watched as she wrapped her arms around herself. With a last look around the alley, she started making her way to the street. Suddenly, he saw her pause and look back over her shoulder.

What the heck is she doing? Curiously, he stared down at her as she started making her way back towards the end of the alley. Christian laughed quietly as he watched her walk up to the dumpster, get up on her tiptoes, and lean over the edge. Giving a little groan, she leaned further into the dumpster, rummaging around with her right hand, holding on for dear life with her left.

Christian heard her give a sound of triumph as she jumped down, holding a little black purse in her right hand. Looking into it, seeming satisfied all her things were there, she slung the strap over her shoulder and began to make her way towards the street. He watched her as she walked farther into the night, finally disappearing from view as she turned the corner.

Christian felt the urge to follow her, making sure she got home okay. The urge came on so strong and so fast, it took his breath away. He squashed this feeling and began to back away from the edge. He had felt the heat coming off her. By the sudden change in her scent, he had known what she had been thinking about, and that was not going to happen. He had done his stint with human women and was not going through that again.

As he stood there, silently cursing to himself, he felt his phone vibrate in his pocket. Pulling it out, he glanced at the screen out of habit since he already knew exactly who was calling.

"What?" he asked gruffly.

"Where in the hell are you?" Darren hissed through the phone. "You were supposed to be back at the house hours ago!"

Massaging his temple, Christian felt the familiar pulse of a headache coming on. "I'm on my way now. I was just... I just got a little distracted."

"You've been getting *distracted* a lot lately, Christian. What's going on with you? You were out hunting by yourself again, weren't you?"

"I'm fine! Just let it go, Darren." Christian could almost feel the tension as the silence stretched on between them. They had always been close. He just didn't feel he had to tell Darren everything...lately anyway. He definitely didn't feel like telling him about Ella. Nope, he wasn't going to mention anything about her to any of his brothers. There wasn't anything to tell anyway.

"Fine, Christian! You don't want to tell me what the hell is going on with you, that's fine. Just get your ass back to the house."

"Yeah, I'm on my way," Christian spit out as he hung up. He had to end the call quickly because, given the chance, he knew Darren would keep the argument going. He was frustrating that way.

He took a last look down the alley. His victim, who would later be found to have suffered a massive heart attack, was lying right where he had dropped him. His Ella... Shaking his head, he stopped that line of thinking. *His* Ella? Where in the world had that thought come from? Anyway, she was long gone, which was for the best.

Giving his head another shake, he looked up at the sky, only slightly acknowledging the heavy clouds beginning to roll in. With a last sigh, he faded away into the shadows, heading for home.

†

Two hours later, Christian could only smile as he listened to the laughter erupting from the poolroom down the hall. They always spent part of the evening laughing and joking over a couple drinks and a game of pool. Tonight's special? Crown Royal and the latest tales of Cyrus' lady problems. There were plenty of both to last the rest of the evening.

So much had changed in the years since they'd been here. It had taken some time but, for the most part, they had all found their paths.

Christian closed his eyes as memories crept in of the first damaged human he had come across. He had instantly noticed the blackness within the man. In his mind's eye, he could see the darkness churning within the human, swirling just beneath the surface. Christian had always been able to sense the darkness in demons, which was what made him so good at tracking them, but a human with that kind of blackness in him caught him completely off guard. And how that soiled soul had called to him, tempting him, begging him to come closer. At first, he had fought it. How could it be right to cleanse a human in the same manner he did a demon?

It had just seemed...wrong. However, once he stopped fighting the impulse to absorb that blackness, he had been surprised by the feeling of rightness that had followed. Well, surprised and disgusted, although that soon faded. Each dark soul since that first one called to him louder, enticed him more. It had become such a natural occurrence, he craved it now, gave into it when the opportunity arose.

They each had found their purpose in that way, one shocking fucking revelation after another. Over the years, they had also discovered that maybe being put here wasn't as devastating as they had first thought. Not that it was a big party or anything, but it was manageable.

A sharp rap on the door quickly brought Christian out of his musings. "Yeah?"

Darren cracked the door open. "So, are we going to talk about tonight, or are you just going to hide in here?"

"There's nothing to talk about, and I'm not hiding," he answered with a deep grunt. Narrowing his eyes, Christian grit his teeth. "Listen... I went out, things ran late, and now I'm home. Period." Glancing down at his whiskey, he felt a dark heat come over him. "Can you just drop it?"

"Fuck, Christian!" Darren came into the room, shutting the door behind him before heading over to sit on the bed. Christian could tell that behind all Darren's aggression, he was truly concerned. "I wish you still trusted me. You used to, remember?"

Christian looked out the window, watching rain hit the glass and slide slowly down. He had always trusted Darren. They had been close and shared everything. He wanted to tell him how tired he was of being here, how lonely he felt, but he just couldn't. It wasn't that he didn't trust him, but he felt like he wouldn't understand. How could he?

Sighing, Christian stared back at Darren. "I'm fine, Darren, and I do trust you." Shaking his head, he looked back towards the window, the sight of the rain soothing to his tattered nerves. "I just... I don't know. I just need some time."

Out of the corner of his eye, Christian watched as Darren slowly shook his head, working his jaw back and forth as he looked around the room. "Sure, Christian," he finally said with a sigh. "If time is what you need, fine." Darren stood and stared down at him, his sapphire eyes glowing in the dimly lit room. "I just hope you know what you're doing."

A flash of Ella's face flew across Christian's mind as he met Darren's gaze. "Of course I know what I'm doing." He imagined the frustration and anger Darren and the others would have if they found out about her. He was sure they all remembered the last time he had been involved with a human female. How could they not? It had not ended well. Arguments had erupted within the house, bruised egos and feelings had occurred and, in the end, the female's mind had needed to be wiped. He had never really felt the same after that. In fact, he hadn't been with a female since.

He really didn't have to concern himself with Ella, though, seeing as he wasn't planning on seeing her again anyway. At that thought, Christian felt a slight pressure in his chest. Rubbing his hand over the spot, he stood up and walked towards the window. The rain was still falling, running down the window in rivers. "Like I said," Christian's voice came out a mere whisper, "I just need some time."

Keeping his back to Darren, he could feel the tension in the air. Darren didn't believe him. Of course, if the shoe was on the other foot, Christian was sure he'd feel the same way. Anyway, he hadn't really given a reason to trust him lately, had he? In the eerie silence that was stretching out, Christian heard him sigh.

"Well... You know where to find me if you need me."

Christian glanced over his shoulder, only giving his brother the slightest nod in response. Darren stayed still for a second before nodding, then turned towards the door.

"Darren?" Christian murmured, turning back towards the window. He could sense his brother pausing in the doorway. "Thank you."

Moments later, he heard his bedroom door shut with a whisper, leaving him lost in his troubled thoughts, images of Ella invading each one.

†

At the other end of the city, Ella let herself into her empty apartment, turning off the alarm next to the door as she tossed her keys onto the table. Looking down, she surveyed the dismal appearance of her purse. It was covered in God knows what and smelled absolutely horrible, but at least everything was still in it. She had not wanted to dig any further down into that dumpster. Hearing a soft, yet demanding meow, she looked over and saw her cat, Holly, standing there, staring at her.

"Let me guess," Ella said as she leaned down and rubbed Holly's head. "You're hungry?" The cat answered with a long meow, followed by her ever-present purring. "Okay. Let me take care of this mess, then I'll get you some food."

With a sigh, she made her way over to the kitchen table, Holly close on her heels, and emptied out the contents of the purse. Setting her gun off to the side, she sifted through the rest...wallet, lip gloss, small bottle of Heavenly perfume, and some loose change. *Well, it's all there*, Ella thought. Making sure it was completely empty, she threw the purse into the trash. Thank god it hadn't been one of her better purses.

Glancing around the kitchen, she suddenly felt very alone. Even though she had always lived on her own, she had never truly *felt* alone, until today. It was probably the adrenaline still coursing through her from this evening's excitement.

Excitement? Yeah, that was one way of describing it. Rolling her eyes, she made her way over to the cabinet and grabbed some cat food.

Emptying the contents onto a plate, she shooed Holly off the counter and set the plate by her water dish. "I told you, no eating on the counter." With only a quick glance over her shoulder, the cat began to devour her food.

Smiling, Ella watched her for a bit before looking back at her belongings on the kitchen table. A sudden image of Christian flashed through her mind. Now that was an impressive man! Maybe *man* wasn't the right term...definitely male, though. None of the men she had ever known had wings, so unless she missed the memo, Christian wasn't human. However, given what she had seen, she was willing to bet the rest of him was. Ella felt heat rush to her cheeks as she put a halt to that line of thinking.

"I keep this up and I'm going to need to take a cold shower!" She exhaled, shaking her head. She reached over and turned off the kitchen light, causing the apartment to go dark. The only light illuminating her way to the bedroom was the soft glow from a single night light in the front bathroom. Ella had always preferred it that way. She knew every inch of her apartment, easily walking down the dark hallway.

Walking into her room, Ella reached over and flipped the switch to turn on the light in her ceiling fan. She leaned against the door jamb, slipping off her left heel and throwing it off to the side. Teetering slightly, she reached for her other shoe. Ella glanced over at her bed as she tossed her heel to the floor. She had forgotten to make it this morning so her many pillows were crushed and the blankets were all tossed off to the side. If anyone else had seen her bed, they would have thought she had left in a hurry after a long night of good sex. Unfortunately, that hadn't been the case for a while now.

With a sigh, she made her way over to the bed and lay down, her hands shaking as she pulled the comforter up. Tonight's events had left her feeling restless and agitated. A hot shower would probably help...or maybe she should sit down and do a little reading...or maybe she should put in a movie? She needed to do *something* to get her mind off of tonight, off of the horrible situation she had put herself and her rescuer in.

A flash of glowing blue eyes and a sexy smile slowly crept across her mind. She lingered on that smile, then slowly slid down over an impressive set of broad shoulders, muscular arms, and solid chest. She could feel her eyelids lower as she began to imagine what the rest of him looked like under his clothes. His impressively wide back, rippling muscles, flat stomach... She could feel her heart start to speed up and a slight shiver ran down her spine.

Ella glanced towards the bathroom as she exhaled a shaky breath. "Okay... Shower it is!”

Chapter 5

"Ella? Ella, did you hear me?"

Blinking a couple times, Ella glanced over towards Cindy. "I'm sorry. What?"

"Ella Roberts, what is going on with you today? I've been sitting here going on and on about what's happening in the office, but you haven't heard a single word, have you?"

Running her hands through her hair, Ella just rolled her eyes. "Like you're saying anything different from any other day. Face it, Cindy. Nothing new ever happens at this office."

Glancing around the room, she eyed the eggshell walls, the bland window coverings, the empty desks. When she had started at this consulting office, working alongside Cindy, business had been good. They had helped the police and the locals a lot in those days, never a dull moment to be had. Of course, it helped that Ella had this uncanny ability to be able to find things and people.

Well, until the recent disappearances, she thought with a sigh. If this weird sixth sense of hers was ever going to work, now would be a great time. Glancing around the dismal office, she couldn't help but give her head a slight shake.

Crap. They used to be so overwhelmed with their paperwork, it had been piled high on the desks. Now, though, they couldn't seem to get a case if their lives depended on it, and with the lack of income coming in, it pretty much did. Sure, she was busy looking into the multiple disappearances around town, but that was on her own dime.

Sighing, Cindy stood up and began to pace around the room. Running her hands through her curly blond hair, she spun and put her hands on her hips. "Listen, I know it's been slow and we're pretty strapped, but something has to turn up soon. It can't stay this slow forever."

"*Pretty* strapped?" Ella said, spreading her arms wide. "I think completely *tapped* would be a better word!"

She watched as Cindy began to pace again. She walked over to the window and leaned forward to peer through the blinds. Ella couldn't help but notice how tired she looked. If she was being honest with herself, though, Cindy had looked worn out for a long time now.

"Listen, Cindy, I'm just not sure if things will pick up again. You know, ever since Grady–"

"Don't say that slime ball's name, Ella! You know how I despise that man, and hearing his name just makes me want to hurl!"

Grady had been the one to start this business with Cindy, the one she had fallen head-over-heels for, the one who had wrecked everything. To say there had been fireworks would be putting the encounter mildly. Things had gone great between the two of them, too...for a while. Their relationship had gone on strong for over four years until, *poof*... It was all over except for the shouting. And, boy, was there a lot of shouting. In the end, Grady had left Cindy to start his own office, to get his life back in order. In turn, he'd taken all the business with him.

Clearing her throat, Ella shook her head. "Fine! Ever since *that man* took up shop and started working with the police as their own personal consultant, things have gone to shit. I mean, it's been ages since they've come to us for anything." She watched as Cindy turned to her, her blue eyes downcast. Ella tilted her head, softening her voice as she continued, "I don't want this to end any more than you do, but I think it's time we got realistic."

"This business is all I have, Ella. It's all I know!" Sitting back down with a loud thump, Cindy just stared blankly at the wall. "What do I do from here?"

"I don't know, Cindy. I'm sure everything will work out, though," Ella said softly, watching her friend blink several times, trying to clear the tears that seemed to be threatening to fall.

After several moments of silence, Cindy seemed to shake herself from her thoughts and looked at Ella. "Well, enough about this. How did things go at the bar last night?"

Wasn't that the question of the day, Ella thought, her mind reeling over the previous night's events. "Um, it went okay. Not much happened."

Cindy raised an eyebrow and leaned forward in her chair. "Not much happened?"

"Well, I found the guy I had been looking for, but he turned out to be of no help." *Mainly because he turned out to be a drunken, aggressive rapist, who was now dead thanks to her...* Ella blinked a couple times. Her what? Hunky savior with wings? Yeah, that'd go over great!

"Ella?" Cindy said sharply. "There you go again, zoning out."

"Hmm?"

"What...did...he...say?" Cindy enunciated each word slowly.

"Oh..." Ella looked over towards the window. "Not much. He really didn't know anything. I think it was a wild goose chase all along." Ella looked back at Cindy, attempting to give her a bored look.

"You seem awfully distracted for having such an obviously uneventful night." Cindy's eyes narrowed as she stared at her. "Did anything else happen last night?"

Yes. "No."

"Are you sure?"

Besides the most gorgeous man on the face of the Earth sprouting wings and killing my would-be attacker by sucking some grey mist out of him...?

"Yup! Like I said, the night was a dead end."

She could tell Cindy wasn't believing a word of it but, like the friend she was, she started talking about something else. They chatted about family, about the best way to try and drum up some more business, and the familiar girly chatter they always fell into. However, no matter how much she tried to force herself not to think of him, Ella's mind continued to turn towards Christian. He was such a mystery to her and a complete delight to her senses, she couldn't *not* think of him. So it didn't surprise her when, once again, she realized Cindy was repeating her name, trying to regain her attention.

"Earth to Ella!! You're fogging out on me! Again!"

"Sorry. Maybe I'm still tired from last night." She glanced over at her friend and, although it was a complete cop out, she was actually feeling a bit on the tired side. The shower last night hadn't helped to calm her nerves as much as she had hoped. Actually, Ella wasn't even sure she had really slept at all. "I just got home late and it took me longer than usual to unwind."

Cindy stared at her, seeming to mull over whether or not to accept what she was saying. After a while, she shook her head. "Well, since nothing is going on here, why don't we just call it a day. You should head on home, get some rest."

Ella nodded. "Sounds good to me. Call me if you get anything and I'll head on back." She got up, stretching her arms behind her back. "Maybe we'll get lucky and get a job soon."

"Yeah," Cindy said with a sad smile. "Maybe."

Ella walked over and gave her a quick hug. "Things will be fine. You'll see."

Looking into Cindy's eyes, she saw the sad acceptance of the truth. Things would, in fact, not be okay.

†

"What the fuck?!" Christian shouted as he fell out of bed. The fire alarm was blaring so loud, his ears were ringing.

Swinging open his bedroom door, Christian quickly made his way down the hall. He reached the end of the hallway just in time to see a billow of smoke come out of the kitchen, one of his brothers yelling out a string of obscenities that would make a barmaid blush. Stepping into the kitchen, he grabbed some random papers to start fanning away the smoke. Staring over at Cyrus, he couldn't help but laugh.

Cyrus was standing at the oven holding a smoking tray in his outstretched arms like some sort of burnt offering. His black eyes were wide, shining like onyx in the midst of the gray smoke. Christian quickly covered his mouth as those black eyes narrowed and turned his way.

"It's not funny!" Cyrus spit out as he tossed the pan into the sink. "All I did was look away for one fuckin' minute and the damn thing catches on fire!"

"What were you trying to cook?" Christian smirked as he walked over, cautious to give Cyrus a wide berth. In this kind of mood, he was liable to catch on fire himself. Leaning down, Christian slid open the kitchen window, immediately feeling the warmth of the summer air rush in. "Really, Cyrus. How many times are you going to almost burn the place down before you realize you don't belong in the kitchen?" Shaking his head, Christian glanced over his shoulder. Cyrus was leaning against the counter, scowling at him.

"I do just fine in the kitchen, thank you very much! It's just... Sometimes I don't hear the timer on the stove, okay?"

"Sometimes?"

Cyrus' scowl depend as he continued to stare at Christian. "Fine, *most* of the time! I'm the only one around here who even wants to try fixing anything. The rest of you would be happy living off of mac and cheese and fast food every day."

Christian began to form a snappy response when their attention was drawn to the kitchen doorway, a very cranky and disheveled looking Nicholas standing there.

"What's wrong with mac and cheese?" he grumbled, running his hand through his hair. His ruby eyes blinked a couple times before scanning the kitchen, finally settling on Cyrus. "And what in the hell did you do to the kitchen?"

Christian watched as Cyrus exhaled noisily, turned back to the sink, flipped on the water, and grabbed a sponge. All of this was done with very exaggerated and dramatic motions, which only caused Christian to want to laugh more. He watched as Nicholas walked past Cyrus, bumping him as he passed, and headed for the coffee pot. Cyrus just growled at him before setting the pan in the rack. Grabbing a towel to dry his hands, he leaned against the counter.

"Maybe if you guys did some cooking around here, I wouldn't feel like I had to," Cyrus remarked as he watched Nicholas prepare the coffee.

"And deprive you of the joy of almost burning down our house? Never!" Nicholas shot over his shoulder.

Christian shook his head as he watched Cyrus' eyes light up. This was about to turn into an argument and it was way too early for him to be dealing with it. Sliding his way past the two, Christian started making his way back towards his room. He was still laughing when he turned the corner and smacked right into Darren.

"Cyrus cooking again?" Darren asked, stepping back, obviously still feeling a little distant from their conversation the other night. It had been two days and they had hardly said anything to each other. Not that Christian had been avoiding Darren, but he hadn't gone out of his way to find him...and it seemed the distant feeling was mutual.

"Trying to," Christian said, attempting to keep a relaxed smile on his face.

Darren stood there, nodding his head as his sapphire eyes gazed at Christian. "Well, he'll probably keep trying until he burns the place down."

"That's what I was thinking," Christian said with a slight chuckle.

Looking past Darren, he could see his bedroom at the end of the hall and wanted nothing more than to duck into the room to escape from this awkward moment.

"Listen, Christian..." Darren stopped and shook his head. "I just wanted to let you know that I'm not upset about the other night. You asked for some space and that's what I've been trying to give you."

"I know and I thank you for that. I just..." Christian cleared his throat as he stood there, looking at his brother. "I appreciate you doing that. I'm feeling a lot better now, though." Hoping Darren couldn't smell the lie as it rolled off his tongue, he smiled and gave a little shrug. "I guess I just needed a little break."

It had hardly been a break, though. He had spent the last two days thinking about Ella, then getting mad at himself for thinking about Ella. Actually, he felt even more tired and depressed now than he had when he and Darren had last talked...if that was even possible! But there was no need to bring his brother into all of the mental crap he had going on.

"Well, I'm glad to hear that," Darren mumbled, still staring at him, the look on his face saying he hadn't bought a word of it. *Oh well*, Christian thought. At least it seemed he wasn't going to push it.

"Yeah... Thanks." Christian ran a hand through his hair. "Well, I'm going to get ready to head out. I'll catch ya later."

"Sounds good. I'm going to head into the kitchen, see what needs to be taken care of in there," Darren said as he began to walk past him. He paused to look at Christian one more time before he finally nodded and headed down the hall.

Christian watched him as he turned the corner. He needed to get his head on straight. He knew Darren was concerned about him, so it was likely the others would also start to notice something was up...if they hadn't already.

Sighing, Christian slowly started walking towards his room. The light mood he had been in from the kitchen fiasco was slowly fading, quickly being replaced by the dark depression which had been following him around.

Stepping into his room, Christian looked over all the bookcases lining his walls, the many photos and paintings he'd collected over the years, and his bed draped with a heavy black quilt he had picked up from a store a while back. The room was so completely him, right down to the dark colors and mixture of old and new items, yet it felt empty! He supposed that was also a reflection of himself.

Chapter 6

Darren moved his cursor around the local news page, scanning through the recently updated articles. *Same shit, different day,* he thought with a groan, reaching over for his coffee. Every morning, he would sit down and look over the latest news, searching for any signs of supernatural or demonic intrusion. This morning, like every morning the last couple months, was showing nothing out of the norm.

He shook his head as he thought back upon the articles he'd read in the past, ones that had been littered with otherworldly causes. It never ceased to amaze him how humans could be staring a demon in the face and write it off as just a "troubled" person. His favorites were the articles where something truly horrible had happened and, when being interviewed, individuals who had known the culprit stated how he/she would have never done something like this.

Well, of course not, Darren would always muse. *People who are possessed never act like themselves.*

Taking a drink of his coffee, he scanned down the list: car accident with two injured, liquor store robbed, teens caught smoking pot behind the local movie theater, et cetera, et cetera, et cetera!

Sighing, he clicked over to look through the local missing person's list. Just as he was scanning through the names, he heard his office door open. Glancing over his shoulder, Darren spotted Nicholas sauntering in and, after closing the door, he promptly plopped himself down on the couch.

"Can I help you, Nicholas?" Darren asked, turning his chair to face his brother.

"I was just wondering something," Nicholas said as he reached over and grabbed a magazine from the coffee table.

Darren raised an eyebrow as he waited for Nicholas to continue. When he finally realized this wasn't going to happen without a little push, he rolled his eyes. "Wondering what?"

"Have you noticed that Christian's been acting a little...off lately?"

"What do you mean by *off*?"

Nicholas set down the magazine and looked straight at Darren, an exasperated look on his face. "You know exactly what I mean by *off*. He hasn't been taking anyone with him on his hunts, he's been getting home later every night, and when anyone starts to ask him how he's doing, he just looks away and changes the subject!"

"And you're coming to me about this why? Do you think I know something you don't?"

"Of course you know something I don't. You always seem to know what's going on around here," Nicholas said with a sigh. He turned his deep red eyes towards the window, blinking several times as he stared into the bright daylight.

Darren stared at him for a while, wondering if he should just tell him what he *knows* is going on, or if he should tell him what he *thinks* is going on. Christian had been so guarded lately, especially the last couple of days, and although Darren tried, he sensed that whatever was going on was going to be something he would have to wait to find out about. Waiting was not one of Darren's strong suits, though. He would normally demand Christian come out with whatever was bothering him but, for his brother, he would put this need of his aside.

He knew everyone in the house had noticed that something was up, and he had wondered when someone was going to come and ask him about it. Though he didn't know very much about what was going on with Christian, he did feel his brothers had a right to know there may be a concern. The last thing they needed was for Christian, or any one of them, to lose it and go AWOL. Rolling his shoulders, Darren cleared his throat, causing Nicholas to look back at him, his red eyes filled with concern.

"I talked to Christian the other night," Darren started. "He told me he just needed some time."

"Some time? Some time for what?" Nicholas stammered.

"I'm not sure..."

"But you have an idea?"

"Yes," Darren said with a sigh. "I think he's getting frustrated with everything. I think he feels lonely and angry, and I think he's trying to decide what he should do about it."

"Lonely? But he has us!" Nicholas said, waving his hand through the air. Darren blinked a couple times as he stared back at his brother. Nicholas, seeming not to notice Darren's incredulous stare, just shook his head. "I mean... What more could he want?"

Turning his chair back to face the computer, Darren just shook his head. "Strangely enough, Nicholas, a man sometimes needs more than just his brothers in his life."

Glancing back over his shoulder, Darren stifled a laugh as he watched the confusion flash across Nicholas' face before finally fading away, his eyes widening in understanding.

"Oh...," Nicholas said. "Well, um... What do we do? I mean, the last female he spent time with turned out to be a real *psycho.*" Nicholas emphasized the last word with his fingers swirling around next to his head. "You do remember her, right? Jessica?"

"Of course I remember Jessica, but that was a long time ago, Nicky. I think we just need to give him his space and hope he figures out how to get himself through this," Darren responded, going back to scanning the missing person's list. "There really isn't anything more we can do, except..." His voice trailed off as he leaned in a little closer to the screen.

"Except what? Darren?" Nicholas asked as he stared over at him. "Darren? Except what?"

"This is weird," Darren whispered to himself, not even hearing Nicholas. He grabbed a pen and paper and began writing notes in a quick, jagged motions.

"What is?" Nicholas asked, getting up from the couch and making his way over to his brother's side.

Darren continued to look back and forth between the computer screen and his tablet. "There's so many missing..." His eyes flickered from one photo to another as he scrolled down the page.

He felt Nicholas lean over his shoulder, gazing at the screen. "Do you see the dates?" Darren asked, pointing at the screen. "Notice how there is a person disappearing every other day?"

"Yeah, but people disappear all the time, Darren. What about these people has you so upset?"

"It's the *way* they've disappeared. One walked out to get the mail and never returned, one vanished while taking the dogs for a walk, one went out for a smoke break, and look at this one," Darren said, enlarging a section of the page. "This one says a woman went into the changing room and never came back out. Witnesses say she just...vanished!"

Shaking his head, Darren reached over and began printing out the pages. As they printed, he picked up the notes he had made on the tablet and, standing, began to pace.

"There's too many of these odd disappearances to be a coincidence."

"How many are there?" Nicholas asked, watching Darren pace back and forth.

Shaking his head, Darren glanced over at Nicholas. "There has to be at least six missing. I mean, one or two could be considered a coincidence, but six? I think we need to get everyone together and take a look at this."

"What do you think could be behind it?" Nicholas asked, walking towards the door.

"I don't know, Nicholas. Whatever it is we need to figure it out before more people vanish."

†

Christian sighed as he glanced around the table. Darren had said there was something strange going on that they needed to discuss. Part of him was hoping it was a demon for him to fight to take the edge off or, in the mood he's been in lately, the devil would suffice. The other part of him wanted nothing more than to go back to his room, shower, and pass the fuck out. However, by the look of the papers Darren was arranging on the table, it didn't look like that was going to be an option...at least not one that he would be able to take advantage of anytime soon.

Christian anxiously tapped his fingers on the table as he watched all of his brothers chatting as they sat down. From his place at the end of the table, he had a great view of everyone as they made small talk. They seemed to be a bit on edge. Seeing that Darren rarely called these meetings, nobody really knew what to expect.

He looked over and spotted Cyrus running his hands through his short, black hair. His equally black eyes held an irritated glint as he glanced towards Darren. Cyrus had never been real big on meetings. All he ever wanted to do was fight and fuck. As crude that sounded, that was Cyrus.

Shaking his head, Christian kept watching as Cyrus unconsciously ran a finger over the scar running down the side of his face. To a stranger, that scar alone would be enough to have them turn and run the other way. To the brothers, though, it was a reminder of what could happen when things went wrong, when the other side momentarily got the upper-hand. That day had been a wakeup call for all of them.

Cyrus, Christian, and Nicholas were fighting against a group of Shadows they had found behind a local bar. It had started off like every other fight they had been in, but things quickly started to go wrong. They had gotten careless and, because of it, the Shadows had gotten the upper-hand. During the chaos, Cyrus had been taken. It had happened so fast. More Shadows had emerged from all the dark corners of the alley, but Christian had never seen anything like that before. Never had the Shadows shown any sense of organization or true intelligence. They were usually just angry, vengeful spirits, driven by rage and an animalistic need for violence. That night, though, they had fought as one! They had ganged up on them, caught them completely off guard, and had quickly taken control of the situation.

They had searched for two days for Cyrus. Those days had been the hardest on Christian and Nicholas because, although the others said they couldn't have known what was going to happen, they blamed themselves.

Finally, they located him about fifty miles outside of the city, chained to a rotted bed in the back room of an abandoned cabin. Beaten and bloody, it had taken him weeks to get back on his feet. In that time, Christian and his brothers had tracked down and killed most of the Shadows involved. None of them had given any reasoning behind what had occurred, no matter how hard they pushed for answers.

That had been two years ago. Cyrus never told any of them what had happened in that cabin, and none of them pushed or questioned him. Christian felt the scar spoke for him.

Mentally shaking his head to stop the direction in which his mind was starting to wander, Christian looked at Nicholas who, much to Cyrus' irritation, sat down next to him. Nicholas, with his smiles and jokes, was always the one who tried to make light of everything. He was also the first one there when anyone needed help. Christian smiled as he watched Nicholas reach over and pretend to pick lint off Cyrus' shoulder. Cyrus responded by rolling his eyes and pushing Nicholas away. Nicholas' red eyes shone as he suddenly burst out laughing at something Manuel said when he walked behind them.

Slowly, Manuel made his way around Christian and pulled up a seat next to him. "So, what's going on?"

"No idea," Christian responded, leaning back in his chair. Tapping his fingers a couple more times, he looked from Manuel to Darren, who was now staring at him. Clearing his throat, he leaned forward again. "I really don't see how there can be much to talk about, let alone have a meeting over."

"Why do you say that, Christian?" Darren asked, looking up from his papers with a sigh.

"There just hasn't been much of anything going on lately, so I can't see how there is anything worth having a meeting about." Christian waved his hands around as he gave a grunt. "I've hardly seen a demon, Shadow, or anything resembling evil in the last couple months. It has been the same thing each night. Nothing! I mean, come on. I feel like I'm going crazy with how little action I've seen." Sighing loudly, he leaned back against his chair, running his hands through his hair. Watching Darren, he noticed a look come over his face, one filled with concern and uncertainty, which immediately caused a wave of guilt to go through him. "Okay, Darren. I'm sorry. You called us here for something that is obviously important. What exactly have you found that has you so worried?"

Darren cleared his throat as they stared at each other for a bit before he looked off to gaze at the others. "I think I may have found a major demonic disturbance. As I was looking over the local news, I came across a high number of disappearances within the area." Everyone shifted in their seats as Darren leaned forward on the table. "All of them happening within a day, if not less, of each other." He sifted through the stack of papers before handing them out.

Cyrus and Nicholas took a couple sheets, then passed them on to Christian. He took a couple and sent them on to Manuel. At first glance, it didn't look like there was anything about this list that was special. It was a list of six names, along with pictures, a description of each person, where they had been last, and who to contact. However, the dates were what stood out. As he started looking at the accounts of their whereabouts right before they vanished, he felt a tingle begin in his shoulder blades. Darren was right. Something was wrong with this list.

Hearing Darren clear his throat, Christian glanced up from the list. "So, now that everyone has seen the list, I'm sure you all can agree there's something...wrong with the disappearances." He looked around the table. "I, for one, can say that I'm not sure what is going on, but there *is* something. The more I look at this list, the more I feel we need to work fast on figuring this mystery out."

"Are you sure it isn't just some crazy coincidence?" Cyrus mumbled as he continued to eye the list. "Maybe this is a case of a group of people... A cult. You know, where they all decide to disappear at the same time or some shit like that."

"One of the girls that vanished was *in a dressing room*," Nicholas growled. "How do you explain a person going into a room, with only one way in and out, and never being seen again?"

"I don't know, but it could happen!" Cyrus hissed back.

"How?"

"I said I don't know!"

"Well, maybe before you start just assuming things, you should–"

"Okay, come on!" Darren barked out as Cyrus started to lean in closer to Nicholas.

"No, Darren, I want to hear what this little shit was–"

"I said, that's *enough*!" Darren yelled, slamming his hand on the table, his sapphire eyes glowing in anger. "Now, can we please continue?" They all stared at him in shock. He looked around at them as he took a deep breath, his eyes slowly beginning to go back to normal.

"Sorry, Darren," Nicholas said, glancing down at the table.

"Yeah...sorry," Cyrus mumbled, staring at the paper in his hands. "I just want to be sure there really is something here to be concerned about."

"I know, Cyrus. I wouldn't have brought this issue to your attention if I hadn't thought it was serious, though," Darren said, leaning back in his chair.

Amused, Christian sat there and watched them all as the silence stretched throughout the room. Everyone seemed to be lost in their own thoughts as they gazed at the list before them. Darren was right. He wouldn't have brought this to their attention if he hadn't felt it needed investigating. Glancing back down at the list, Christian felt that tingle in his shoulders again.

Shit! "Do we have any idea what, or who, could be behind all of these disappearances?" he asked, looking at Darren.

Darren relaxed as he looked at him and slowly shook his head. "Not that I can tell. I mean, if these humans are just vanishing into thin air like it seems, then I'd feel comfortable guessing it's something demonic. I just don't know what."

"Yeah. Most of the demons we deal with are Shadows, lower-level ghouls, and they've never attempted to pull off anything like this," Nicholas murmured, continuing to peruse the list.

"Nicholas is right," Manuel said. "The most they ever do is try to influence people, alter someone's way of thinking so as to turn their souls black. This... This is something on a whole different level."

"That is *if* it's a demon at all," Cyrus said, keeping his tone light. "Until we know for sure, I think we should keep our minds open to every possibility."

Christian nodded as he glanced from one face to another. "I think Cyrus is right. Although it would be easier to pin this on someone or something right from the start, I think we need to get more facts before crossing anything out."

Darren's face was grim as he sat there and stared off into the distance. Slowly, he let out a sigh. "I agree. So, until we know what is going on, no more going out hunting by yourselves."

Christian grunted as Darren looked right at him. He watched his brother raise a single eyebrow, daring Christian to argue. Narrowing his eyes, Christian debated about doing just that, but after realizing everyone else had turned to look at him, he just mumbled, "Fine."

He watched a smile tug at the corner of Darren's lips before he covered it up with a cough. "All right then. It looks like Christian and Manuel are up for tonight." He looked between the two of them. "Keep your eyes open."

Christian saw Manuel smile as he looked at him out of the corner of his eye. "Can't wait," Manuel said with a wink.

Darren *would* team the two of them up. Christian groaned and shook his head. *Just great*!

Chapter 7

Father James shivered as he ran his fingers over the finely written words. Each was in Latin, the sight so beautiful, it almost blinded one to the dark meaning behind them. He had been reading through this book for the past couple weeks, and with each chapter he completed, he felt a little more lost. However, the Being had claimed that, once finished, he would have his faith returned to him. He wanted this so badly that, with little questioning on his part, he had opened the book and never looked back.

Leaning back in his chair, Father James looked around at the calm grey walls and warm wood furniture. His room in the rectory was small, homey, and had everything he would need. Turning towards his bed, Father James gazed upon the crucifix hanging on the wall above it. Ever since he was young, he had felt the call to be a priest, spending most of his days at the local church.

He had such faith in those days. It had been so strong, he had thought there was nothing in this world that could shake it. He had been wrong, though...so very wrong. His faith *had* been shaken. Well, if he was being honest with himself, it had been more than shaken. It had been ripped away.

Father James still remembered the day he began to question his faith. It had happened nine years ago, but he remembered it like it was yesterday.

The day had started off like any other. He woke up early, went to morning mass, and made plans to meet up with the local parents to discuss classes the church was going to start offering. There was nothing strange about the day at all, nothing to give him even the slightest warning that everything was about to change.

But it had!

He had just shown up for his meeting with the parents. The weather was warm and the sun was shining. He parked his Cadillac by the curb and had just stepped out of the car when the first gunshot echoed through the streets. Things happened so fast, he barely remembered running from the car to the entrance of the local youth club. The gunshots had become a constant ringing in his ears and he had lost track of the number of them. Reaching the doors, Father James could hear the yells and cries, the cruel laughing and shots. His mind was screaming for him to run, to get far away from here, but his heart said to go in. The need to be with these people, families he had known for decades, was too strong. He made his way through the halls, unsteadily stepping over bodies, some of them so covered in blood, he wasn't sure if he knew them or not.

As he neared the conference doors and found them open, dread overwhelmed him. Children and parents were crying, some huddled against the walls, others curled on the ground.

In the center of the room was, in Father James' eyes, the very devil himself. The man's dirty brown hair was damp and matted to his head, his shirt was dark with sweat, and his eyes were crazed as they looked around him. His right hand waved wildly as he pointed the gun from one person to another.

It felt like forever before the gunman's eyes landed on him. Father James could tell the man was disturbed. His cruel mouth curled into a sneer as he waved his gun, pulled the trigger, and sent another bullet flying, thankfully hitting just above a mother and her child.

"Please, put the gun down," Father James whispered, holding his hands out in front of him. "Nobody else needs to die."

"Well, of course nobody else needs *to die,* Father,*" the man said with aggression, each word spit out. "But I* want *them to."*

"Why? Why would you do this?"

"Why would I do this? Why not?" He looked wildly around him. "Why do you care so much about these people? What have they done for you to make you want to save them?"

"They are all children of God. For no other reason than that, I want you to stop. Violence doesn't solve anything, my child," Father James said, never looking away from the gunman.

"Well, this is not something I am doing because I had a troubled childhood or lost my job, Father,*" he sneered at him. "This is something I'm doing because I* want *to. Is what I'm doing so horrible?"*

Father James looked around at the parents and children curled around each other, bodies littering the floor, images of the bloodied hallway flashing before his eyes. "Yes... Yes, it is very horrible."

"Then where is your God?"

"What?"

"Where...is...your...God?" The man took a step towards him with each word. "Why would He allow me to have gotten this far?"

"I don't..."

"You don't what? You don't know why He would let this happen? Well, the easiest answer would be that He doesn't care. You're God doesn't care!"

"Blasphemy!" Father James screeched. "That is absolutely not–"

"Okay, if that's not the case, Father, *maybe it's that He doesn't exist! What God would allow something like this to happen to individuals who are so innocent...to children?"*

"No! Please...," Father James whispered as he blinked furiously. By now, the man was directly in front of him, the gun pointing towards a child whimpering against the wall.

"Admit it, Father," the man snarled. "Admit that if there was a God, He wouldn't allow this to happen."

"No... I don't think–"

"Admit it!" *He looked over, smiling, steadying the gun on the child. "Admit that He wouldn't let me hurt this child."*

A light sweat broke out on Father James' forehead as he reached out. "Please... You're right. God wouldn't let you harm this innocent child."

The man leaned back, staring at him. He let out a dark laugh, then took another step forward, now holding the gun at his side. "Would your God let me harm you?"

Flinching, Father James felt a chill run down his spine. "I don't..."

"Would He allow me to hurt...that woman over there?"

Glancing over at the woman, Father James began to shake his head. "Why are you–"

The man leaned towards Father James, so close that he could feel the man's warm breath against his face. "I told you, Father. *I want to. I want to show people that not everything happens for a reason, not every story has a happy ending." The gunman rocked back on his heels as he smiled at him. Father James' stomach dropped as he watched the man slowly raise the gun to his own head.*

"No..."

"Oh yes, Father," the gunman said with a smile. "I want this, too. I want for you to know that there was nothing you...or your God*...could do!"*

Father James didn't remember too much after that, except a lot of crying, screaming, and death. He remembered being surrounded by death.

Looking upon the crucifix now, he felt...nothing.

He used to feel such love and hope when he gazed upon it, but after that horrible day, he never felt the same. So many lives had been lost, so many souls ripped from this world, and for what? For the whim of some deranged individual? How could he have faith in a God who would let that happen?

To know that the God he had believed in for so steadfastly long did not only exist, but gave meaning behind all that he did, would be the greatest gift. It was all he wanted and would do anything to get.

Turning back towards his desk, Father James ran his hand over the leather binding, the worn edges, and the ancient words. His fingers shook as they hovered over the beginning of the next chapter. *Just three more chapters to go*, he thought, taking a deep and ragged breath. *Three more chapters, then everything will be better...*

†

Andras felt the air around him shimmer. Blinking his eyes, he couldn't help the large grin. That feeling could only mean one thing. There was a change in the air and it was time to get the next phase moving.

The Father must be close to finishing.

Everything had been moving right along since he last entered Father James' mind and convinced him to read the book. He had felt the barrier getting weaker and weaker, and he was now sure it was weak enough to start sending some of his demons through to the other side.

Andras went over to his desk and sat down. Tapping his fingers, he began to go over what he needed from the ones he would send over first. He obviously needed them to find as many dark souls as they could to add to his cause, clearing the way for the rest of them. This wasn't going to be easy by any means but, if done right, it would all be worth it.

Andras looked at the five names scribbled across his notepad. Shaking his head, he realized he would have to make sure his men stayed away from these five. It would definitely be unfortunate to come across them before they were ready.

Flipping the page over, his eyes fell upon a single name, the name of someone they definitely needed to stay away from...at least for now. Shaking his head, he knew the order of things. He could sense what *may* happen and what *would* happen. Everything came down to choices. If one individual made the wrong choice, his whole plan would go up in smoke. Coming across any of these individuals would definitely flip things upside down. The demons he sent over first would have to know all of this, know whom to stay away from, and know how to handle it if they found themselves around them.

Andras smiled to himself. He had just the demons for the job!

Getting up, he made his way over to the office door and, stepping out into the hall, came face to face with Agalon.

"I was just coming to see you, sir," Agalon said, taking a step backwards. "I felt the change in the air and wanted to see if it was time yet."

"Actually, Agalon, I need you to do something for me. I need you to go find Braktis and Castigo and bring them to me."

"Of course, sir," Agalon said with a tilt of his head.

Andras watched him turn and walk back down the dimly lit hallway. *Of course Agalon had felt the change*, Andras thought with a shake of his head. It made sense, seeing as Agalon was a powerful demon in his own right. One of the many reasons Andras had to keep an eye on him. Closing the door, he made his way back to the desk.

Once again settling into his chair, Andras closed his eyes as he went over the events that were to follow.

Castigo was a pain to deal with and, if he was being honest with himself, Andras should have gotten rid of him ages ago. But he was an asset! He could get information out of a person that even God wouldn't be able to get his hands on. Being a master at his craft, his torture and punishing of individuals was like a ballet, one Andras never grew tired of watching!

Braktis, on the other hand, was a lot easier to deal with. Regardless of all his strength and power, he could never be a leader. For that reason, he followed Andras' every command. However, he was very deadly. If Andras hadn't had him on his side, he would be constantly watching his own back. Not that Braktis would decide to go after him on his own, but if someone who had his respect and loyalty were to command him to... Well, Andras didn't really have to guess the outcome. He'd seen first-hand what Braktis was capable of.

Rubbing his hands over his face, Andras took in a couple deep breaths. His thoughts always seemed to get away from him. This time, he couldn't afford to let his mind wander, especially into the dark "what ifs" of his life.

Hearing the doorknob turn, Andras glanced up just as the two demons walked in, followed closely by a very annoyed Agalon. Braktis and Castigo stopped in front of his desk, both looking directly at him, awaiting instructions. Out of the corner of his eye, Andras watched Agalon walk over to lean back against the wall.

Glancing his way, they made eye contact for a brief second before Andras looked back at the two before him. Both were wearing all black, which caused their skin to look pale white in comparison. Braktis had his long trench coat on, perfectly hiding the multiple knives hidden on his body. His dark red eyes flashed from behind his long black hair, which covered part of his face. Castigo had a short leather coat on, but that didn't fool Andras. He knew Castigo was just as armed as Braktis, if not more so. His eyes were so silver, they almost glowed, while his hair was cut short, but was just as black as Braktis'.

They had to be right for this job because if he were wrong, it would all fall apart. He looked both of them up and down. There was no way they would blend in amongst the humans. He didn't need them out socializing, though. He needed them to stay in the background, remaining out of sight. Which was exactly why he was picking them. Out of all their skills, their ability to blend in with the shadows was key.

"Sir?" Braktis asked, shifting his weight.

Andras glanced at him, meeting his red eyes as he let out a soft hiss. "I need you two to do something for me."

"Anything," they both answered.

"I am sure you are aware of what I have been working on." He watched as they nodded slowly. "Good. I need you both to go to the other side to start paving the way for the rest of us."

"What would you have us do?" Castigo asked.

"You will need to locate and begin to gather as many dark souls as you can. We need them to not only strengthen the bridge between Hell and Earth, but also to help us fight the Guardians. We must shift the balance in our favor. It has been an even playing field for far too long. It is time for us to take the lead."

This was met with growls of agreement from the other three demons in the office. Andras looked from one to the other, watching the excitement and darkness swim through their eyes. His eyes hovered over Agalon for a moment before shifting back towards the other two.

"However, it is very important right now that you two keep away from the Guardians...and this human female." Holding up a picture of the woman, Andras watched as they both studied it. "Her name is Ella and she is a natural psychic, which means she is more powerful than any of the learned psychics with whom we are used to dealing. Now, I do have plans for this female, but those will come later. So, until the time is right, stay away from her. Do you both understand?"

"Yes, Andras," Castigo answered.

"Yes, sir," Braktis agreed.

"Good," Andras said with a nod. Looking down, he was just about to excuse them when he heard a soft cough. Glancing up, he saw Castigo looking at him, his eyes glinting in the light. "Yes, Castigo? Do you have a question?"

"Sorry, sir. I was just wondering... What should we do if we come up against one of these Guardians of which you speak?"

Andras looked at them for a heartbeat, weighing his options. On one hand, he could just tell them to deal with it, hoping this scenario didn't happen. On the other, he could give them a weapon that would ensure the mission's success, regardless of whom they came up against.

He needed them to be successful!

Getting up from his desk, he walked over to his safe in the wall. Reaching into his coat, he wrapped his fingers around the cool key in the hidden pocket. Opening the safe, he pulled out a dark mahogany box and, making sure the safe was securely locked once more, walked back towards his desk.

He saw Agalon shift slightly as he began to open the box. Andras looked up at Castigo and gave him a slow smile. "If you come across one of the Guardians, you will want to use this." Reaching in, he pulled out an old dagger, lifting it into the air for all of them to see. His eyes traveled down the leather hilt in his hand. The symbols on it glowing as he felt its power flowing down his arm. "This should take care of any problem."

"Where did you get that?" Braktis whispered, leaning forward to get a better look at it. "I did not think there were any of those daggers around anymore."

"I have had it for a long time. In terms of where I got it, that is none of your concern." Andras spun the dagger around in his hand before handing it, hilt first, to Castigo. "I expect this to be brought back to me as soon as you return. Am I clear?" He hissed out the last few words as he held Castigo's gaze, holding onto the dagger until he gave him a slow nod. "Also, I expect you both to do as I say and not stray from your mission. I assume I do not need to say what will happen should either of you fail me."

"No, sir," they both quickly answered.

Castigo gave a small smile, slipping the dagger into the inside of his coat.

"Go and begin to ready yourselves. The gateway is now weak enough for you two to be sent through."

They both nodded and, with a slight bow, turned and left the office.

As the door closed behind them, Andras could feel Agalon's eyes on him. Sitting back in his chair, he placed the mahogany box off to the side and began straightening Ella's and the Guardian's information back into an orderly pile. Andras stifled a growl as he waited for Agalon to say what was on his mind. He could sense the agitation coming off him and Andras had an idea why.

After several minutes, he heard Agalon shift his weight and give a soft grunt.

Andras sighed. "Okay, Agalon. What is it?"

"I do not mean to upset you."

"Yet I have a feeling that is exactly what is about to happen," Andras said as he folded his hands in front of him, turning the chair slightly to better look at Agalon.

"No... I was just going to request to be sent up, too."

Andras sighed. He was planning on sending Agalon to the other side eventually. He would not be the leader he was if he ignored the gifts Agalon possessed. Gifts Andras knew would greatly benefit him and his goal. As they say, though, timing is everything.

"I *will* send you up, Agalon...just not yet."

Agalon looked at him without saying anything for a while. Andras could almost see his mind flipping through arguments about why he should go now. If nothing else, the stubborn look on his face was a dead giveaway that he felt Andras was not making the right decision. After some time, though, it seemed Agalon had decided that not arguing with him was the right action to take.

Very smart move on your part, Andras thought.

"But you *will* send me?" he asked with a slight tilt of his head.

"Yes, Agalon. I have great plans for you," Andras answered with a sly grin. He watched as an evil smile slowly spread across Agalon's face, his icy blue eyes taking on an otherworldly glow as they met his.

"I look forward to serving you, sir. Just say the word."

"Trust me, Agalon. When the time comes, you will find it was well worth the wait."

With that, Andras turned back to the paperwork in front of him, his eyes darkening as the plans started unfolding. With a click of his tongue, Andras couldn't help but feel a deep satisfaction beginning to rise up within him. *Well worth it indeed*!

Chapter 8

Christian was still shaking his head over the last couple of conversations with Darren. He hated not being able to tell his brothers about Ella, and the more he tried to avoid the topic, the more he came across as an ass. Even after their meeting, which had been three days ago, Christian had noticed the questions in their eyes as they all watched him get up and leave the table. Where it had once started as a topic he didn't dare talk about, it had now become one he didn't know how to bring up even if he wanted to!

He always seemed to turn into an angry, grumbling idiot when they started pushing for answers, which caused the rest of the guys to just watch his every move even more. *Just what I need!* he thought with a grunt.

Shaking his head again, he started to make his way over to his closet. Grabbing his gear, he began to prepare for the night. Maybe a night out was what he needed. It was Manuel's and his turn to go out hunting again. The night they went out after the meeting had been extremely uneventful, but it had felt good to get out of the house. There was just nothing like a night of searching for evil souls to take away the blues.

He sighed quietly as he grabbed his boots, pulling them on with a tug. Seeing as he was drawn to evil like a magnet, it wasn't really much of a hunt. Shit, with his gift and Manuel's uncanny tracking ability, hunting was like a walk in the park.

His gift was the reason he was in that bar the other night, how he had met Ella. He immediately realized the lies in that statement. It hadn't been the evil in the drunk that had drawn him there. In fact, for once, it hadn't been evil at all. It had been her. He had sensed her from out on the street, soon finding himself inside, staring at the beautiful woman with the shy smile. Finding her about to lead vile, drunk, and dumb out into the back alley... Well, that was just a happy coincidence. Frowning, he shook his head. This was not the time for him to go over that night...again!

Reaching over, he grabbed his stereo remote. With a push of a button, the sounds of metal roared through the room. He stood listening to the rhythmic pull of the instruments for a while, allowing them to wash over him as he took a couple of deep breaths. Music always seemed to help him relax. Christian smiled as he thought back about the first time he had heard the growling and dark sounds coming from a metal band.

He was walking past a local bar and, as the doors opened, the music poured out into the street, pulling him in without much thought on his part. There was nothing like its powerful instrumental cords and the dark, somewhat sexual vocals.

Shaking his head to clear it of the memories from so long ago, Christian knelt down and began pulling out a large case from beneath his bed. Opening it, he eagerly eyed his hunting knives and two Glocks. Picking each up, he palmed his knives, eyeing the crosses etched into their hilts. Running his thumb over one of the etchings, he felt its power flair in response. His brothers and he all had their weapons of choice, ones that were blessed by an ancient power. The cross on their weapons represented that blessing, represented the power flowing through them. Each weapon was catered to their personal needs and preferences. His were two impressive black knives. Sliding his knives into their respective sheaths and his guns into his shoulder holsters, Christian reached over and clicked off the stereo.

He smirked when he heard Manuel coming towards his room. It was easy to know it was Manuel because he was always humming something. Today's song of choice? Aerosmith's "Dream On". Hearing the light knock on his door, Christian grabbed his coat and turned in time to see Manuel opening the door and walking in. His amethyst eyes blinking a couple times, he grinned.

"Ready to head out? I have a feeling this is going to be a great night!"

This was something he said every time they went out, and always with the same boyish grin plastered on his face. Of course, Christian and the rest of the brothers knew that behind the boy next door exterior was a well of anger and deviousness that would make the most hardened criminal curl into the fetal position.

The thought made Christian grin back as he nodded. "Ready when you are, brother."

"Well, come on!" Manuel smiled, giving Christian a quick wink. "Let's get this party started." Turning, he began to hum as he made his way down the hall.

Christian stood there for a minute, listening to Manuel's soft humming fade. Maybe this was going to be a great night after all.

"You coming?" he heard Manuel yell from the end of the hall.

"Yeah, yeah. I'm coming," Christian yelled back when he walked out of his room, shaking his head as he closed the door behind him.

†

Standing on the street corner hours later, Christian closed his eyes, concentrating on the feel of the rain against his face. It was only a light drizzle, but he could sense a storm brewing. Glancing around, he spotted Manuel making his way towards him. The look on his face was murderous, but Christian couldn't blame him. They had been up and down these streets for the last four hours and hadn't come across a single demon, evil soul, or anything. Well, save for a couple drunken humans crawling from one bar to another. Got to love Friday nights!

Sighing, he ran his hand over his face. This was turning into a very long night.

"Anything?" Christian asked as Manuel came to stand next to him. Even in this dim light, Manuel's amethyst eyes shone bright in contrast to his dark brown hair. His usual boy next door look was gone, replaced with an evil scowl that had overtaken his face.

"Not a damn thing! Maybe we should just call it a night, start making our way back to the house." Irritate, he looked around, wiping some rain from his leather coat. "I was so sure we'd find something here."

"Yeah, it's been pretty quiet lately," Christian said, scanning the nearby streets. "Why don't you give Darren a call and let him know tonight was a fuckin'–" He suddenly felt a familiar itch begin in his back. Narrowing his eyes, he tilted his head.

"What? Something going?" Manuel asked eagerly, placing his phone back in his pocket.

"Something... Hold on."

"Just tell me where, bro. I'm ready!"

Rolling his shoulders Christian shook his head and, turning to the right, felt a sudden pressure. It was like a large magnet pulling against his soul. In that instant, he suddenly *knew* where he needed to be. Slowly, he began to make his way across the street, throwing his senses wide open as he felt out around them. He could feel the humans in the bars, the energy given off by the stray cat to his left as it ran from car to car, and Manuel walking behind him. Without looking over his shoulder, he knew his brother had his Glock in hand, held slightly out front and at the ready. Christian also knew that Manuel's eyes, like his, had now taken on an otherworldly glow, the occasional shadow creeping through them.

A sudden need to move faster had Christian pulling out his own Glocks as he went from a walk to a slow jog. Coming upon the next corner, he could hear a sudden drumming coming from the alleyway. He could just make out a shudder of power vibrating through the air. This power could only mean one thing.

"Demon," Christian whispered over his shoulder as they started to round the corner. Carefully replacing his gun, he mentally reached down into himself, preparing for whatever was in the alley. This was going to suck.

"Crap," Manuel hissed. Silently agreeing, Christian took a deep breath and clenched his jaw.

They took the corner quickly, slowing almost to a halt and hugging the wall. A soft grey glow was coming from around the next corner, and the smell of sulfur began to tickle Christian's nose. He rolled his shoulders. God, he hated that smell! It brought up images of past fights. They were always the same, though, Christian and one of his brothers would come up on some second-level demon, what they referred to as Shadows, a fight would follow, and it would end with them sending the demon back to whatever section of Hell it had crawled out of.

Shaking his head, Christian chased away the images of blood and fire from his mind. Catching a slightly sweet scent hiding just behind the sulfur, he flared his nose. *What the heck?* Leaning forward, he peered around the corner.

"Is it a Shadow?" Manuel whispered.

Christian turned his head slightly, seeing Manuel reach up and grasp the hilt of his sica. Its curved blade hissed as it slid free from the leather sheath on his back. Holding it to his side, the outer edge of the short sword, which was honed to a razor sharp edge, caught the light from the moon. The crosses etched down its blade, similar to the ones Christian's daggers, glowed a soft golden light as it reacted to Manuel's grip. The sight of it momentarily stole Christian's breath away. It was a beautiful work of Roman art and, in his brother's skilled hands, a truly deadly weapon.

"I don't know." Taking a deep breath, Christian looked down, trying to focus on the new scent. "I don't think so. It smells...different," he whispered back, looking up to meet Manuel's eyes.

"What do you mean *different*?" Christian heard Manuel ask right before he inhaled sharply. Christian watched as his eyes lit up.

"Do you smell it? It's a sweet smell, right? Almost hidden by the sulfur."

"Yeah. What is that?"

"I don't know," Christian answered, looking back towards the corner. "I don't like it, though. Do you hear anything?"

"Just some moaning, which I assume is a human. There's also a bit of growling and mumbling, which is probably our mystery demon. Nothing of substance, though I can't make out anything that's being said." Nodding, Christian took a deep breath and closed his eyes. He hated not knowing what they were walking into, but as far as he could see, they didn't have a choice.

The drumming began to get louder. Shaking his head, he glanced back at Manuel to see if he was hearing it, too. "Do you hear that drumming?" he asked, giving his head another shake.

"What drumming?" Manuel asked, tilting his head to the side. "I don't hear any drumming. Did it just start?" His eyes narrowed as he looked at Christian.

"No... I heard it as we were coming up to the alley, but it was a lot softer then." Giving his head another shake, Christian hissed, "It's starting to get louder, though."

Christian could feel his shoulder muscles tightening as the drumming got louder. It was starting to get to the point where he wasn't sure he was going to be able to relax enough to keep his wings hidden. He had never had that happen before and he wasn't liking it. The last thing they needed right now was for him to lose any sort of control.

As if sensing the problem, he felt Manuel lean towards him, concern shining bright in his amethyst eyes. "Maybe we should call for backup," he whispered. When Christian started to object, he held his hands up. "Listen, I know you like to go head first into a fight. God knows, I'll follow you every time, but you've been on this self-destructive path recently. This solo act of yours has us all worried. We've all stepped back to let you do your thing, but I don't like that you're hearing something I can't. I also don't like the fact that it seems to be having some kind of effect on you. Just this once, please, let's wait!"

Every muscle in Christian's body was tightening up, almost to the point of being painful. His warrior side was screaming for him to go charging around the corner and face this unknown creature. His mind, though, was telling him that Manuel was right and they needed to back away. He had a feeling that this was one of those times where going in with a more cautious approach was best. However, his curiosity was begging for just a glimpse.

"I think you're right," Christian whispered. "Maybe holding off and calling for backup is the best thing." He could hear Manuel let out a soft sigh, which was cut short when Christian slowly smiled at him.

"But it wouldn't hurt to just take a peek, would it?"

Before Manuel could respond, Christian crouched as low as he could and edged around the corner. Staying low, he quickly spotted a trash bin and made his way behind it. Past the edge of the bin, he could just make out a faint glow coming from the end of the alley. The drumming was a steady rhythm in his ears now and, rolling his shoulders, he eased his way closer, attempting to get a better look.

†

Ella looked around the dimly lit street. She was still confused on what she was doing here but, about an hour ago, she had started feeling a need to drive to this part of town. She watched a group of college girls spill out of the nearest club's doors. They leaned on each other as they laughed, stumbling past her, a couple dazed and glossy looks thrown her way. *Fridays*, Ella thought with a laugh, scanning the area around her again.

"Now what?" she whispered, shivering. Reaching up, she pushed some of her damp hair behind her ears. This drizzle was really starting to get on her nerves. Since she didn't bring an umbrella, or even anything with a hood, she was getting soaked. Making her way past the club entrance and towards the next corner, she began to shake her head. This was crazy! There was no reason for her to be in this area. She didn't know a soul around here, or even a single person who would frequent these types of clubs. Giving her head another shake, she began to turn around and head back towards her car.

That's when she heard it. The sound was faint, but Ella could definitely make out the beats of a drum. *What in the world*? she thought, looking around. It didn't sound like anything coming out of the clubs. All that was coming out of them was techno and rap, definitely nothing like the steady drumming that was just barely audible to her.

Standing there for a moment, she began walking down the street, away from the clubs and her car. The drumming sound began to get a little louder as she jogged across the street. Coming up to an alleyway, she stopped and peered around the corner. The drumming sound was definitely coming from down there, but she couldn't see anything. The alley went down a little ways, then took a sharp right, leaving anything beyond that completely out of view. Narrowing her eyes, Ella contemplated heading back to her car again. Her brain was telling her this was a very bad idea but every other molecule in her body was pulling her forwards.

Okay, here we go. Taking a deep breath, she cautiously began to make her way towards the next corner. The drumming was getting louder and louder with every step, and she leaned against the wall just before the corner. Looking back towards the street, she was surprised to see just how far she had walked. It felt like she had only taken a couple steps into the alley, but she realized she was a lot farther than she first thought. Being this far from the streetlights, she noticed a light grey glow coming from around the corner.

Leaning around the corner, she had to cover her mouth to muffle her gasp. She couldn't believe her eyes. Crouching down behind a dumpster were two of the largest men she had ever seen. They both had their backs to her, but the width of their shoulders was a dead giveaway as to their size. Just then, she saw the one closest to the wall reach out and touch the other's shoulder. At first, he seemed to shrug the hand off, then quickly spun his head around to face his friend. Ella pulled her head back around the corner, smacking it into the wall as she did.

Slowly her hand fell away from her mouth as she stared blankly at the wall in front of her. She just couldn't believe it. It wasn't possible. Over the last twenty-four hours, she had convinced herself that she had been dreaming, or was drugged, or a million other excuses for what had happened outside the bar the other night. Shaking her head, she slowly leaned back around the corner, just enough to see the edge of the dumpster...

Just enough to see Christian.

"This is crazy," Christian heard Manuel mutter from behind him. "We need to be getting the hell out of here, *not* trying to get a closer look."

Christian felt Manuel reach forward and lay his hand on his shoulder. He shrugged it off. "Your concern is duly noted, my friend, but we *are* going to get a look at this fucker." Being this close, Christian could just start to make out the conversation, as one-sided as it was, coming from beyond their dumpster refuge. The demon was whispering, though, so it was tough to really make out any of the words.

"Christian... This is a bad idea, bro. Let's just get the heck out of here. We'll go call Darren. Maybe he knows what we have here."

Christian turned to tell Manuel to just give him a minute when he caught sight of what looked like a figure behind him. Narrowing his eyes, he stared past his brother, but whatever had been there was now gone. Shaking his head, he looked over at Manuel, who had raised his eyebrow and was looking back and forth between him and the corner.

"Now what did you see?" he whispered

"Nothing." Christian shook his head. "Anyway, I'm just going to take a peek and then we'll go. I won't even wait to see its face."

"Christian..."

"Wouldn't it be better if we have some kind of description of this thing to give to Darren?" When Manuel didn't respond, Christian nodded. Putting all his weight on his hands, he leaned as far as he could around the dumpster.

At first, all he saw was the back of a demon. *An extremely large demon*, he thought as he narrowed his eyes. He was tall with a black trench coat, his black hair was long and glowing with that soft grey light that seemed to emit directly off him. It took Christian a moment for his eyes to adjust before he noticed an individual cowering in front of the demon, his back pressed tightly against the brick wall.

The human was clearly frightened. His eyes so wide that even from this distance, Christian could make out the bright white of them. Tilting his head, he watched as the demon leaned closer to the human, causing the man's mouth to drop open in a silent scream as he lifted his arms up in a pathetic attempt to protect himself. He heard the demon let out a cruel laugh, resonating through the drumming that was still echoing through Christian's head.

Then, without any warning, the demon let out a shrill cry, causing the human to fall to his knees. The drumming in Christian's ears became so loud, he reached his hands up in an attempt to block it, but to no avail. The muscles in his back started rippling and the pain shot through him so strongly, he clenched his teeth to keep from yelling out. It took everything he had to keep himself in enough control so his wings didn't rip right out of his back. After what felt like hours, the drumming began to soften enough that Christian could open his eyes and pull in a deep, ragged breath.

Looking back towards the demon, he saw the human still huddled before him, gripping the sides of his head, his eyes rolling back. Then, to Christian's surprise, he watched as the human's back bowed and a thick blackness poured through his gaping mouth, a blackness Christian recognized as the human's soul. That wasn't right though. Demons didn't take human souls like that. They waited for the human's soul to be damned, to turn as black as oil, and then die before taking them.

Christian took the souls from the living! He was the one who goaded them out of their bodies, pulling them into himself.

Why would a demon even want their souls in him? To eat them? To take them somewhere? Christian's eyes narrowed as he watched the human's soul leave him, as if the demon just yanked it right out of him. As it rose high above the human's body, it took a sudden sharp turn and slammed down into the demon with such force, he had to take several steps back.

"Shit!" Christian exclaimed before he could stop himself. He pulled back around the dumpster and was just about to shove Manuel towards the street when he heard the dumpster's wheels scraping against the ground. They both backpedaled just as the dumpster was thrown to the other side of the alley, crashing against the wall with such force, Christian felt his teeth shake.

He quickly jumped into a fighting stance as he faced off against the demon. He could sense Manuel behind him, crouched low, his blade at the ready. Christian had never been so happy to have his brother at his back.

The demon's blood red eyes, standing out against his pale skin and coal black hair, stared at them. The smile the demon gave him would have sent anyone else running for their life, but all Christian felt was a dark calm come over him as he slowly returned the smile.

"I don't think we've had the pleasure," Christian said with a smirk. He felt his eyes going black as he tightened his grip on his daggers.

"No we have not...*Christian,*" the demon said with a curl of his lips. "Unfortunately, now is not good for me, so maybe next time."

"How do you know my name, demon?" Christian growled.

"Oh, I know a lot about you and your brothers..." He paused, casting a glance over at Manuel. Then, with a raise of an eyebrow, he glanced past the two of them. "I also know about the pretty little thing hiding behind the corner there."

Christian titled his head so he could see where he was looking, still being able to keep an eye on the demon. He let out a hiss as he fully turned to find not just any pretty little thing, but *his* pretty little thing. *Ella*?

†

Ella couldn't believe what she was seeing. Well, she shouldn't have had any trouble believing it seeing as she had just been witness to a similar situation only a week ago. This was different, though. Ella flinched as a loud scream come from the end of the alley. *What in the hell?* Before she could even begin to process what was going on, the drumming began to build, causing a pressure in her head. It grew so strong and so fast, she thought her head was going to explode. Clamping her hands over her ears, she shuddered, blinking rapidly as she tried to clear her vision. The drumming was so loud, she felt her insides tensing up, and it was getting harder for her to pull any air into her lungs. *I'm going to be sick*, she thought, doubling over.

Oh god, make it stop, she thought frantically, her vision beginning to blur. Then, just as quickly as it had built up, the drumming began to fade. Ella took her hands away from her ears and gave her head a slight shake to help clear her vision. Looking up, she watched as Christian's shoulders seemed to relax and he shook his head a bit. The other man, though, seemed completely unaffected. *What the heck?*

The two men suddenly tensed up, both backpedaling away from the dumpster. Their urgency seemed to flow from them, causing Ella to feel an equally desperate need to run. Then, before she could move, the dumpster flew off to the side, crashing into the wall.

Her hand clamped over her mouth as she watched the most evil-looking man she had ever seen sneer down at Christian, his unblinking red eyes flashing bright.

Oh, my god! Oh, my god! she thought wildly, observing the aggressive exchange happening before her. The man with Christian waved his sword around, obviously highly agitated by whatever was being said between Christian and the red-eyed man before them.

She saw Christian's shoulders tighten as he tilted his head to the side. It wasn't until she glanced past Christian that she realized those horrific red eyes were staring right at her!

"Oh, crap..." Ella whispered.

"Hello, Ella," he breathed out, although she couldn't actually say he said it. She saw his mouth move, but it was like his deep voice had just breathed through her mind. Shaking her head, she took a step back, still maintaining eye contact with him.

"How... How do you know my name?" she whispered.

"As I was telling our dear Christian here, I know a lot of things."

"Who are you?"

"That, my dear, will have to wait for another time." He flashed a devilish smile as he looked away.

She saw Christian take a step towards him, a glint of light flashing off the dagger he held at his side. He twisted the dagger around in his hand as he took another step.

No, Ella suddenly thought. *No. Christian needs to stay away from him*!

Her thoughts got frantic as she started to watch everything before her play out in slow motion.

Christian leaned forward, obviously preparing to lunge, just as the being in front of him gave an evil smile. Ella felt her heart begin to race. If she didn't know any better, she would have thought she was on the verge of having a heart attack. She saw Christin take another aggressive step forward. Ella reached her hand out, almost as if she was going to will him to move back. Before she could yell for Christian to stop, the demon vanished in a flash of grey light and a cloud of smoke.

Blinking a couple times, Ella stared at where he had been. Her body gave a violent shudder as a cold breeze rolled over her, feeling like hundreds of little needles relentlessly stabbing into her soft flesh. Pulling in a shaky breath, Ella felt a wave of dizziness wash over her. Stumbling sideways, she leaned against the wall, her knees weakening.

Ella was only vaguely aware that Christian and the other man had come up and were now standing over her. She felt Christian lightly touch her cheek, turning her face to meet his worried gaze. She saw his mouth moving, most likely asking her if she was okay, but there was no sound reaching her ears.

"What was that?" she whispered, or maybe it was in her head. Nothing seemed to be making any sense anymore and, as she stared at Christian, she began to feel more and more lightheaded. Reaching out, Ella placed her hand on his arm. A thick blackness began swirling around the edges of her vision and, with a last breath of air, she passed out.

Chapter 9

With a soft groan, he watched as Braktis dematerialized in front of the two Guardians and, he assumed, the psychic female Andras had been talking about. He had just been scouting out the area when he had sensed Braktis nearby. Curiosity brought him to this rooftop to be witness to the mess below.

Castigo could only imagine the talking to Braktis was going to get when he informed Andras of this little mishap. The one thing that had been drilled into them both as they had been getting ready to leave was to stay away from the Guardians and the psychic. Andras was going to be pissed. Braktis would be lucky to not end up a scorch mark on Andras' wall.

"Idiot," Castigo muttered as he continued to watch the alley.

Castigo just couldn't wrap his mind around what he had just witnessed. Braktis had stayed a while and talked to them. He *talked* to them! All he had to do was take off as soon as he realized they were there, but no. He just had to taunt them. He had to get in his little remarks.

That kind of stunt was what was going to get him taken out of the game. He just didn't listen. What if things had escalated? The Guardians had sure looked like they were gearing up for a fight, both of them aggressively holding their weapons at their sides. Weapons that were etched with wording promising to wipe a demon out of existence. Crouching down, ready to engage the Guardians had waved these weapons out, beckoning Braktis to make a move. If a fight had happened... Well, Castigo could only imagine the outcome of that. Out of all the scenarios that came to mind, none of them ended well for Braktis.

Sure, if things did escalate, he would probably have gone down there to help. Castigo was the one with the dagger, so it would definitely tip the outcome of the fight in their favor. He had even palmed the dagger when Braktis had sent the dumpster flying into the wall. The sudden rush of power from the dagger had given him an instant burst. He had almost rushed down right then to fight the Guardians, but did he really want to help the demon?

He wasn't sure.

Luckily, the time to make that decision had never arisen because, as soon as things really started going, Braktis had retreated.

So here Castigo was, watching as the Guardians went over to aid the psychic. Reaching into his pocket, he pulled out a cigarette and lit it. Taking a drag, he paused as he watched the Guardians below. The real downside to this little meeting was that if they and the psychic had been strangers before, they most definitely weren't now. Meaning they would now be fighting together instead of separately. Which, of course, could cause a major rift in Andras' plans.

Hopefully, Andras has planned for this possibility, he thought, watching the psychic faint into the arms of one of the Guardians. The Guardian gently picked her up, cradling her to his chest. *Yeah, this is not good!*

Castigo watched the males make their way out of the alley, one carrying the psychic. A need to follow them washed through him. *No time for that!* Shaking his head, he pushed the need aside. Castigo had other things to worry about, like completing the mission Andras sent him on.

Sure, Andras had asked them both to find dark or lost souls to add to his growing army but, right before he left, Andras had pulled him aside to talk, asking him to gather information on the Guardians and the female psychic, along with this lovely town he now found himself in. Fhallon Heights. Castigo shook his head. Andras, for reasons unknown, had taken a particular interest in the area, mainly the vacant buildings downtown. So, as much as he wanted to follow the brothers right now, he had actually been in the midst of scouting one of these vacant buildings when he had happened to sense Braktis in the alley.

Glancing one last time in the direction of the Guardians, Castigo put his cigarette out on the bottom of his boot and turned back the way he had been headed. *What a mess!*

As he dematerialized from the rooftop and popped back up at street level, he felt a shudder in the air. Sighing, he pulled back into the shadows and waited for Andras' voice to come to him. Even though he knew what this sudden call was about, it still caused him to cringe when Andras' voice hissed through his head.

Castigo!

Yes, boss, he answered.

Where are you?

I was just heading to the location on Sixth Street that you wanted me to check out. Castigo paused, waiting for Andras to respond. He knew this had to do with what had just happened. The dumb ass probably went right back below, spouting off how cool he was for going up against two of the Guardians.

Were you in the alley with Braktis?

No, sir. He felt a shudder run through him as Andras growled in disbelief. A need to clarify came over him. *I was on a nearby rooftop and saw Braktis in the alley, but I was not with him... sir.*

And were you aware that Braktis was not alone in the alley? That two Guardians, along with the female psychic I had mentioned earlier, were also in that alley?

Castigo licked his lips as he gazed out onto the street. He could feel his anger rising at the thought that he was going to lose favor with Andras because of Braktis' stupidity. *Yes, sir.*

What did I say before you two left?

To stay away from the Guardians and the female psychic. I did not come in contact–

I understand that, Castigo, Andras hissed. *I just want to make sure you heard me and understood what I said.*

Yes, sir. I heard and understood what you said. Castigo took a deep breath when he felt another wave of energy rush through him. He knew Andras was upset. Castigo just hoped his anger was not going to be turned on him. As calm as Andras usually was, he was known to take his aggression out on whomever he wanted, whether they were the cause of his anger or not.

Did they see you?

No, sir.

Did Braktis know you were there?

No, sir.

What did you see?

Taking a deep breath, Castigo closed his eyes. *Braktis must have been collecting a soul when the Guardians and the psychic made their way into the alley. He talked to each of them briefly – one of the Guardians more than the other, then some to the female. Then he dematerialized.*

Andras was quiet for a while. Castigo blinked rapidly and looked down at the ground as he waited for a response. Surely he just wanted a quick rundown and not a detailed description. He was just about say something when he felt Andras sigh. *Did the Guardians and the female show up together?*

I do not believe so, sir. I was not there when they showed up, Castigo said slowly, stopping to lick his lips. *But they did leave together.*

A growl was the only answer he got. Andras was obviously less than happy with the news, and because of the energy pouring into him from Andras' displeasure, Castigo felt his body shudder.

Sir? Castigo quietly whispered.

I want you to continue gathering the information I asked for. I will deal with Braktis.

Yes, sir.

And Castigo?

Yes, sir?

Do not disappoint me.

No, sir. I will not disappoint you.

Good.

With that, Castigo felt Andras pull away. He shook his head as he straightened his shoulders. Not being fond of being questioned, Castigo was relieved when the conversation came to an end.

Damn Braktis for pulling him into this!

Although he was not directly involved with what had happened back in the alley, Andras was still sure to keep a close eye on him. He was not only going to have to get all the information Andras wanted, but he also knew he was going to need to find something else... Something that would get him back into Andras' good graces.

Castigo had spent more time than he wanted to admit getting himself onto Andras' good side. He wanted to be one of his lieutenants, instead of being just another one of his disposable lackeys. Being his third would be great! Second would be even better, although that was unlikely seeing that Agalon was Andras' second...and for good reason. That demon was especially vicious, even by Hell's standards, and didn't get his status for playing nice. Castigo would be content to fill the position as being Andras' third...for now. But he had to prove he was deserving of the title first.

That was not going to happen if he was put in that position again.

Looking up and down the street, he made his way back onto the sidewalk, pulling out another cigarette as he moved. His mind started going over possibilities to get himself off this dangerous ledge, but he knew one thing for sure...

Braktis would pay for this setback.

Chapter 10

As soon as the demon vanished, Christian glanced over his shoulder at Manuel. Wide-eyed, he was staring at the spot where the demon had been just seconds before. Christian knew he felt the same way his brother did, but his mind pushed the anxiety to the side as it was consumed by worry for Ella. As his eyes went past Manuel, he saw Ella stumble a bit, then watched as she leaned against the wall. She was not looking well at all. Quickly making his way past Manuel, he sheathed his blade and walked to Ella. He had barely taken two steps past Manuel when his brother came up to walk with him.

"What the fuck just happened to you? I swear, I thought your wings were going to come flying right out of your back! And if you tell me it was some drumming noise only you could hear, I'm going to scream," Manuel said in a rush. "I told you we needed to wait." He waved his arms in front of him, his voice now coming out in a harsh growl. "And who in the hell is she? Why do I have the feeling you know her already?"

Christian heard him, but chose to ignore all of the questions, giving a slight shake of his head as he came up next to

Ella. Her eyes were unfocused as she looked past them to where the demon had been. Her breathing was far too shallow, and he could hear her heart beating way too quickly.

"Ella?" he whispered, leaning towards her. Her eyes were still staring off into the distance, hardly blinking. "Ella... Ella, look at me. Can you hear me?"

He watched as she took a deep breath, her bottom lip quivering a bit as her eyelids fluttered. Christian reached up and, placing his fingers on her cool cheek, gently turned her face towards him.

"Ella?" he asked again. He watched her lips move, although she made no sound. As he stared into her gaze, he got the sudden feeling she was looking right through him. "Ella, it's Christian. Come on, honey. Talk to me."

He felt her hand against his arm and she started going down.

"Shit!" Christian said, catching Ella in his arms. She was out cold. Maneuvering her limp body in his arms, he felt Manuel's questioning gaze. Deciding to ignore him, he kept his eyes on Ella, concentrating on her breathing.

"Okay, Christian... Who is this girl, and how do you know her?"

"It's a long story," Christian mumbled as he scooped her into his arms, tucking her tight against his chest.

"Well..." Manuel looked at her limp body, "she's out like a light, so I think we have some time."

"Not now, Manuel."

"Is she someone new? A love interest? I mean, it *has* been a while since Jessica." Christian gave him a sideways glance, hoping the scowl on his face would give Manuel pause. It didn't. "So, did you save her? Is she why you've been going out on your own lately? If she is, why have we never heard of her? Were you keeping her a secret for a reason? Because you *know* everyone back at the house will want to know why. I mean, if it's because of Jessica, I totally get it. Hell, I'm glad you're truly over that crazy woman, but you still could have told us...told me!"

"I said not...now...Manuel!"

"Come on, Christian! If she's a conquest of yours, just say so. She is awfully pretty. I'm sure she's a lot different than Jessica. That one was a real bitch. Not that you don't know that. This is just surprising! I mean, I thought Cyrus was the only one out making an impression on the female population around here, but if you decided to start playing around, too, that's–"

"Shut up! Ella is not a *conquest*! She is not like that, and if you think I'm going to let you say things like that–"

Manuel held his hands up, giving his brother a slow smile. "Hey, hey, hey... I'm sorry. I didn't realize you cared for this woman."

"I don't know her well enough to care for her. I just met her last week," Christian said with a scowl. "I just don't think you should talk about her like that, that's all. And stop bringing up Jessica..."

Not waiting for a response, Christian started making his way out of the alley. He didn't know what he was going to do with Ella yet, but he sure as shit wasn't going to leave her by herself.

Coming out onto the street, Christian looked around. She had to have left a car out here somewhere. "Manuel, grab her purse and see if there are any keys in it." *Oh, please tell me she didn't take a cab.*

"I don't make a habit of going through a woman's purse, Christian."

"Make an exception, dammit. We need to get out of here, and we're taking Ella with us," Christian growled, looking up and down the wet street. After a pause, and a little grumbling from Manuel, he heard the sound of a zipper opening. Shaking his head, he noticed the streets were almost completely empty and the slight drizzle had stopped. *When did that happen*, he thought, taking another step, *and how long have we been down there?*

He turned to face Manuel when he heard the sound of keys.

"What kind of car are we looking for?"

Manuel glanced down at the keys in his hand and, after a quick inspection, looked down the street and pointed. "That one down there. The Jeep."

Looking in the direction Manuel was pointing, Christian instantly spotted the black Jeep parked two blocks down and, right beneath one of the only working street lights thankfully. Turning, he began to make his way down the street towards it. "You'll have to drive so I can keep an eye on Ella."

"So why are we taking her with us? I mean, I can find her driver's license and we could just take her home," Manuel stated, falling into step next to Christian.

"We're not just going to take her home. Like I said, she's coming with us."

"Well, I heard that. I just don't understand why."

"Because the demon knew about her...about all of us. So until we find out the why's and how's of this situation, she's staying at our house." Christian glanced out of the corner of his eye towards Manuel. "That's why."

He heard Manuel sigh as he nodded. "You're right. I don't like how the demon knew about us. We need to sit down with everyone and start figuring this out. I'm sure they'll have some questions for your Ella, too."

My Ella, Christian thought. *Not likely*. The way he figured it, as soon as they got all of this sorted out and made sure she wouldn't be in any danger, she would be on her way. It wasn't like he could keep her like some freakin' pet. And after all the crap she'd already witnessed, he doubted she would even want to stick around.

Looking down at Ella, he felt a tightening in his chest. Yeah, best to figure everything out quickly so his life could get back to normal. However, as they reached her Jeep and he got inside, Ella curled up nicely in his lap. He realized getting back to normal was going to be a lot easier said than done.

Pulling up to the front of the house, Christian could feel the uncertainty radiating off of Manuel. They hadn't talked the whole way home. Usually, they joked or bitched about the evening, but the air within the Jeep had been thick with tension. He could almost sense the questions and concerns hanging in the air between them. Looking out of the corner of his eye, Christian watched as Manuel turned the Jeep off and then, with a slight shake of his head, placed his hands back on the steering wheel.

After some time, Manuel cleared his throat and looked over at him. "So... What are you going to do about everyone else? I mean, you're going to have to tell them something."

Christian looked down at Ella, still passed out in his arms. "I don't know. I haven't really gotten that far yet." Sighing, he reached over and began to open the car door. "I guess I'll just have to tell them everything...not that there's really much to say." He looked back over his shoulder, finding Manuel still watching him intently. "I'll take Ella in, get her comfortable, then we'll talk. Okay?"

"Okay, Christian. You know me," he said with a crooked smile. "I got your back."

Christian smiled and, with Ella held tightly in his arms, got out of the Jeep, bumping the door closed behind him. Looking towards the house, his smile faltered a bit. *Here we go*, he thought as he began to make his way to the front door. With every step, Christian felt his muscles tense.

Manuel got to the door before he did. As he opened it, Christian could hear his brothers talking and laughing loudly about whatever they were watching on TV. Stepping through the door, he quickly walked past the room where everyone was, grinding his teeth a bit as he felt everyone turn and watch him. The silence in the house was overwhelming, and he briefly entertained the idea of staying in his room with Ella.

As he went down the hall, he began to hear a low murmur coming from the room behind him. Manuel must be handling everyone's questions. *At least until I walk back in*, Christian thought gravely, quietly opening his bedroom door.

Walking across the moonlit room, he made his way to his bed. Leaning over, he gently lay Ella on the bed, resting her head upon the pillow. She sighed softly, and Christian held his breath as he watched her turn her head into the pillow. *She's so beautiful*, he thought, brushing a strand of her damp hair off her face.

Shaking his head, he took a couple steps away from the bed. Now was definitely not the time for this. Actually, it would never be the right time for this, which was why he needed to figure out what was going on with this mystery demon and his connection to them. The sooner he did that, the sooner he could get Ella home, back to her own life and out of his.

Leaving her in his bed, Christian quietly made his way back down the hall. As he got closer to the front room, he could hear his brothers.

"Who is she?" he heard Nicholas hiss. "And why did he bring her here?"

"It's a long story," Manuel answered. Christian could hear the strain in his voice, which told him they had been grilling him pretty hard. "I told you, we'll explain it all to you as soon as Christian comes back out here."

"Fine, but at least tell us why he needed to bring her *here*." This came from Darren, his voice filled with unease and irritation.

Christian heard Manuel let out a sigh and decided it was time to jump in. He couldn't let Manuel continue to be put on the spot like that.

"Because she was in danger. That's why," he calmly stated, rounding the corner. Everyone turned to stare at him, and Christian took in a ragged breath. "The demon knew her. I couldn't just leave her there."

Everyone was quiet for a moment as they stared at him. Finally, Darren stood up and looked intently at Christian. "Okay, Christian. Why don't you start from the beginning?"

Taking a deep breath, Christian told them everything. He told them about the drunk, the fight in the alley, and the conversation between him and Ella. Christian decided to leave out the part about not being able to stop thinking about her. No need to come across like an obsessed teenager. He watched them all as they listened intently to his account of the other night. When he got to the part about his conversation with Ella, he saw some of their eyes widen. It had been well over a year since he had last talked to a female.

There was a time that Christian, like Cyrus, had been very much into females. Having never been around them, at least not in a way he could interact with them, Christian couldn't get enough when they first began to mingle with the humans. The sexual tension and closeness had been...intoxicating. After a while, though, the interactions began to feel empty and hollow. At that point, Christian had felt that to continue filling his nights with females and sex would be his undoing. He had decided to take a break from it all, which had been working out just fine for him...until Jessica.

That female had taken his world and shattered it. He still didn't know when she had gone from sweet, innocent girl next door to stalking psycho, but when the shit hit the fan... Well, he had been left cleaning it up. And the destruction she had left in her wake had been legendary. Good thing they had been able to clear him from her memory. Crazy female!

Because of that mess, he decided not get involved with females anymore, to just concentrate on himself and what he was there to do. Fight. That was what made him feel alive, what gave his life on Earth purpose.

That night in the alley, though, Christian just hadn't been able to pull himself away from her.

"So you haven't seen her since then?" Darren asked suddenly, causing Christian to jump.

"What?"

"I asked if you've seen her since that night."

"Sorry," Christian said, clearing his throat. "No, not until tonight."

"Okay." Darren glanced back and forth between him and Manuel. Leaning back against the wall, he crossed his arms over his chest. "So what happened tonight?"

Christian glanced over at Manuel and watched as he rubbed his hands together. Deciding he would let Manuel take the lead on this one, he nodded at him, then leaned back against the wall. He listened as Manuel went over the evening, talking about how Christian had sensed something, and how they had ended up in the alley.

Christian felt his mind start to wander to Ella in his bed, her head resting on his pillow. *Maybe I should go check on her*, he thought, glancing over his shoulder. *She's probably still out cold*. Shaking his head, he looked back towards Manuel. His eyes wandered around the room. The events of the night had left him feeling on edge, and he wasn't liking the occasional glances from everyone, as if he had done something wrong.

Grinding his teeth, he glanced down. He knew he was thinking irrationally, but he just felt so aggravated.

"So you're telling me that you both decided to hang back and call for help...*then* decided to take a look anyway?" Darren's voice rang out, interrupting Christian's line of thought.

"Well, we figured–" Manuel started.

"*I* figured," Christian cut in, giving Manuel a quick glance, "that it would be best to have some sort of a description of the demon to tell you guys. Plus...I was curious."

"You were curious?" Darren said, glancing over at Cyrus, who was trying to cover up a laugh.

Seeing Darren's glance, Cyrus sighed. "Come on, Darren. Most of us would have done the same thing." He glanced over at Christian and winked. "Although not all of us would have been lucky enough to go through that *and* come home with a beautiful female."

At this, Christian felt an involuntary growl rumble past his lips, causing Cyrus to laugh again.

"You may be right, but still...," Darren murmured, tilting his head and looking back at Christian. "Next time you realize you're in need of backup, would you *please* call us?"

"Okay," Christian said with a sigh, glancing back over his shoulder. This whole evening felt like it was never going to end. As Manuel started to tell them what happened next, Christian began to zone out. Rubbing his hands over his face, he couldn't help but start to feel the exhaustion coming over him. He needed to get some rest. This realization quickly turned his thoughts back to the female in his bed.

Chapter 11

Ella groaned as she rolled onto her side. Yawning, she brushed her hair out of her face. Her eyes slowly opened and she blinked lazily at the sunlight shining through the drapes. *What a weird dream*, she thought, trying to stifle another yawn. Burying her face into the pillow, she took a deep breath and began to try to force herself back to sleep. Her brain slightly registered the heavy leather and oak smell tickling her nose. Suddenly, her eyes flew open and she sat up, looking around.

Oh, my god! she thought, looking around wildly. The soft morning sunlight coming in helped her make out the dark wood furniture, the shelves of books, and the art lining the walls. Looking down at the bed, she was surprised at the black comforter beneath her, soft and full as it hugged her figure.

Thinking back, she could remember being pulled towards the alley, the drumming, and the dark. Blinking quickly, a flash of the man with red eyes came to her mind and she felt her body begin to shake. The memory of his eyes boring into her, his voice whispering through her mind, caused Elle to momentarily squeeze her eyes shut. Just the thought of him made her feel cold inside. Sucking air in through her teeth, she willed the image of him away, forcing her mind back to the question at hand... Where was she?

Ella remembered the red-eyed man disappearing, then her vision had started to blur. The last thing she saw, before everything went black was Christian standing in front of her... *Christian!*

Her hand flew to her mouth as Ella looked around the room again. This couldn't be Christian's room...could it?

Sliding herself to the edge of the bed, Ella slowly started to stand up. She didn't think she was in any kind of danger, but she didn't really know what to think of anything that had happened the last couple days.

Making her way across the room, Ella reached towards the door, slowly opened it, and stepped out into a hallway. Looking around, she could hear a deep murmuring coming from the end of the hall to her right. The sound of multiple voices flowed over each other, and she couldn't make out a single word. Taking several cautious steps towards the right, Ella held her breath as she slid her hand against the wall.

The closer to the end of the hall she got, the clearer the voices became. Pausing, she listened to the conversation in the next room. The first voice she heard, the one that caused her breath to catch, was Christian's. It was deep, dangerous, and highly agitated.

"I know we don't usually bring humans back here, but this was different," Ella heard Christian say. *Humans*? Hearing him use that term should have surprised her, but he had shown off a pair of pretty impressive black wings the other night. So it really didn't strike her as *too* strange. "We've been over this and over this. Look," Christian sighed, "I didn't do anything wrong... It wasn't safe for her to go home."

"Listen, Christian. Nobody's saying you did the wrong thing by bringing the female here," a deep voice responded, followed by a couple of grunts and mumbles. "We just want to make sure you know what you're *doing* bringing her here."

"I'm keeping her safe. What else do I need to know right now?"

"You're right," the deep voice sighed. Ella leaned closer to the end of the corner. She wanted to look into the room, but wasn't sure if she should interrupt or not.

"Well, now what should we do?" a younger voice asked.

"We need to find out what Ella was doing there," Christian answered. "Then we need to find out who the demon was and how he knows about us."

So it was *a demon!* Ella felt her head start to swim as she leaned her forehead against the cool wall. *This is crazy!*

Taking a couple deep breaths, she realized she wasn't getting any of her questions answered standing there. She could hear the conversation still going as she took a step forward. Walking into the room, her first thought was how large and intimidating all the men were. The next thought was that maybe she should have thought this through a little more.

Ella stopped just inside the room and watched as the conversation continued without them noticing her entrance.

"The fact that the demon knew who we all are is definitely a cause for concern," the tall blond-haired male stated. "And how is the woman involved?"

There was a silence as the four other men seemed to search for an answer to his question. Clearing her throat, she watched as five pairs of eyes shot her way. Glancing around nervously, Ella took a deep breath. "I would like to know how I'm involved, too." Licking her lips, she glanced over and met Christian's stare. "And where am I?"

†

Christian blinked as he stared back at Ella. He had been so wrapped up in the conversation, he hadn't even heard her come down the hall. Looking at her, Christian could tell she was a little unsure and nervous but, all in all, seemed fine. When he didn't detect any fear coming from her, he sighed in relief. The last thing he wanted was for her to be afraid of him or any of his brothers. Everything was going to be tough enough without adding that to the mix.

"You're in our house," Christian slowly answered. He was careful to keep his tone level. No need for his frustration about the situation to give her the wrong idea.

"Okay...," Ella responded just as slowly, never breaking eye contact. "Why?"

Christian shifted his weight as he watched her, debating on whether to go right into the whole demon thing. He started to smile as Ella raised an eyebrow.

"So?" she asked with a shake of her head. "Why did you bring me here? Not that I'm complaining. I'm sure glad you didn't just leave me in the alley after I blacked out, but why didn't you just take me home?"

"You're safer here," he stated, watching her take another tentative step into the room.

"Okay... Well, thanks and all." Ella glanced around the room. "I guess I should be going home now, though, since I'm okay. I'm sure you guys want me out of your hair."

"No, you'll be staying here," Christian said as he watched her head snap back to look at him. She began to open her mouth to argue, but he held his hand up. "At least until we know for sure that you're not in any danger."

"And what exactly am I in danger from?" she asked, crossing her arms across her chest.

"From the demon in the alley."

"Demon? You mean the man with red eyes?"

"Yes, Ella... The man with red eyes," Christian said in exasperation.

"Why would you think I'm in danger from him?"

"He knew your name!"

"Okay... I'm sure he knows a lot of people's names. He knew *your* name, too!" she argued, pointing at him, her eyes flaring as she shook her head. "I think I'll be just as safe at my house."

Christian narrowed his eyes as he looked at her. He couldn't believe she was being so difficult. She was in danger, so she would stay here with him to be safe. It really wasn't a very hard concept to figure out. Sighing, he reached up and pinched the bridge of his nose, feeling a headache coming on. "You'll stay here until we make sure you're not in any danger and that's that."

He watched her open and close her mouth, like she was trying to decide whether or not to continue arguing. With some amusement, Christian saw her eyes narrow. He could almost see the steam coming out of her ears.

"No... I'm going home!"

"No, you're not!"

"But–"

"No! This is not up for debate!" He leaned towards her a bit. "End of discussion!"

"End of discussion?! Who do you think you're talking to?" Ella's eyes were practically blazing as she glared at him. "And who in the hell do you think you are?"

Christian just stared at her for a heartbeat. The nerve of this female! "Who am I? I'll tell you who I am. I'm the one who saved your ass – not once, but twice! And I will continue to make sure you are safe until we figure out what the hell is going on!"

"Well, aren't you just a good little Guardian–"

"*Don't say it*!" Christian ground out. He could hear his brothers around him muffling their laughter in various forms of coughs and grunts. "This conversation is over, done, finished. You are staying here until it is safe for you to leave, until I decide you aren't in any danger."

"Fine! So what am I supposed to do while I'm *waiting* for you to decide if I'm in any danger or not?"

"Well, you can help us figure it out by telling us what you know, and why a demon would know who you are."

"Great. Well, this should be quick... I don't know!"

Christian shook his head as he stared at her. *Women!* He was just about to respond with some sarcastic comment when he heard Darren clear his throat. *Damn*, Christian thought, looking over at him. He had completely forgotten his brothers were in the room. Looking at Ella out of the corner of his eye he watched as a surprised look came over her face. Seems like he wasn't the only one who had forgotten they weren't alone.

"Why don't you two just take a deep breath?" Darren said calmly, looking back and forth between them. He finally looked at Ella. "Ella, right?"

"Yes...," she answered, a little cautiously.

"Hi, I'm Darren. This is Nicholas, Manuel, and Cyrus." Christian watched each of his brothers nod as they were introduced. Then Darren glanced over his way and, with a crooked smile, said, "And it seems you've already met Christian."

Christian rolled his eyes and looked away. He heard Ella greet each of them, then quietly clear her throat. Glancing back her way, he found she was looking at him. "We've met," was her quiet response to Darren.

"Well, it's nice to meet you, Ella," Darren said, smiling at her. Christian could see her relax as she returned his smile. "You have obviously had a long night, so why don't we take a little break. I'm sure you have plenty of questions, probably more as the seconds tick by, and I promise you will get your answers. For now, let's just take a moment."

"Thank you," Ella whispered as she glanced back over towards Christian. He could see relief in her eyes.

"Great!" Manuel piped up, causing everyone to look his way. "Now that we have that all out of the way, can we please eat? I'm starving!"

Christian listened to them all grumble about being hungry. Even Ella shyly made the comment that she hadn't eaten in a while. Standing back, he watched them all start heading towards the kitchen, Manuel leading the way and pulling a hesitant Ella with him. Christian could hear Manuel asking Ella what she wanted, and Nicholas saying maybe she should cook instead of Cyrus, which caused everyone to chuckle. Well, except for Cyrus, who just scowled. Once Nicholas explained Cyrus' habit of burning food, even Ella let out a soft chuckle. As she headed around the corner, he watched her glance over her shoulder at him. The look in her eyes was questioning as she turned and smiled back at Nicholas, who was still talking.

"You comin?" Darren asked him. Christian turned and looked at his brother, whose face was blank except for the curiosity swimming through his eyes.

"Yeah," Christian murmured.

Darren reached over and placed a hand on his shoulder, as if trying to tell him that everything was going to be okay. Right now, though, Christian wasn't too sure about that. Actually, he wasn't too sure about anything. What if he had made a mistake bringing Ella here? What if he had put them all in more danger? After all, he didn't know anything about her. Christian opened his mouth to tell Darren that maybe he had been wrong, that maybe it would be best for all of them if Ella just went home, when he heard her laughter filling the house. He paused, feeling a warmth starting to creep through him as he listened to her happiness.

Seeing a knowing looking come across Darren's face, Christian felt his shoulders drop. "Come on, Christian. Let's have some breakfast. We can figure everything else out later."

"Okay, Darren," Christian said with a sigh. "Okay."

Chapter 12

"What was the one thing I told you *not* to do?" Andras snapped as he stared at Braktis. His temper was getting hotter and hotter by the minute. He knew if he didn't calm himself down soon, he would end up burning up his entire office. Several dark scorch marks already marred the walls behind Braktis. *Bastard was lucky he was light on his feet*, Andras thought as he ground his teeth together. "I told you *not* to come into contact with any of the Guardians, but you did. Then I told you *not* to come into contact with the psychic, but you did. How can I trust you to take care of the things I *do* ask you to do when I cannot even trust you to refrain from doing the things I ask you *not* to do?"

"Andras, they came out of nowhere and–"

"No more excuses! I cannot believe this happened, and on your first trip up there no less!" Andras took a deep breath and leaned back in his chair. Staring at Braktis, he felt a sneer form on his face. "Is there anything good that came out of your trip? For, you see, if all that came out of this was you inadvertently *ruining* all my plans, you will not like the outcome of this conversation."

"Andras...sir... I was able to get some new souls for you," Braktis said with a flinch. Then, as if sensing Andras' coming remark, Braktis quickly continued, "And I noticed something strange about one of the Guardians."

"Strange? What do you mean by strange?"

"It was the one called Christian. He was behaving strangely, like he was not comfortable being around me."

"That is still not telling me anything! Of course he is not comfortable being around you! You are a demon! He is an angel! If we were meant to be *comfortable* around each other, we would be on the same side, would we not?" Andras reached up and pinched the bridge of his nose. *Idiots! All of them!* With a deep sigh he said, "Okay, Braktis. Tell me how he was acting strangely?"

Taking a deep breath, Braktis whispered, "He seemed to be fighting to keep control of himself. Even his companion, Manuel, seemed concerned about him." Braktis looked around, as if trying to find some better way to explain what he had witnessed. Finally, he looked back at Andras. "I do not know what it was, but it was also affecting the female."

Tilting his head, Andras stared at Braktis for a heartbeat. "Interesting," he finally murmured as he mulled over the information he had just learned. Maybe Braktis running into them was not such a horrible thing. Maybe this was going to help. If he could find out what kind of reaction they had, maybe he could use it to his advantage.

He knew the psychic would be able to sense things about the demons, would know what they were, which was why he had wanted them to stay away from her. If they had come upon anyone else, they would be able to hide their true selves without them sensing anything different. However, once any of them got around this psychic, or any of the Guardians, their cover would instantly be blown.

To have both of them reacting to being around Braktis was interesting, though, especially since whatever it was that was bothering them didn't seem to have any effect on the one they called Manuel. The fact that both the Guardians and the psychic were able to sense one of his demons so quickly, to be able to find him so fast, was a huge problem, though. He knew there was at least one Guardian who had the ability to track a demon, to sense him and be able to find his position. This must be the one Braktis called Christian, which made sense since he was the first one to come across him. Andras shifted slightly in his seat. The fact that the psychic had also been able to find Braktis was a little unsettling. She was even stronger than he had feared. Narrowing his eyes Andras had a sudden thought.

"When you came across Ella, did she know what you were?"

"Who, sir?"

"The psychic, Ella... Did she know you were a demon?"

Braktis seemed to think on this for a bit before he slowly shook his head. "No, sir. I do not believe so. She seemed very frightened and confused by what she was witnessing."

Andras smiled slowly as he stared back at Braktis. "So if she did not know what you were, we can assume she does not know what *she* is! That she does not know what she is capable of." He felt excitement start to build as he realized exactly what this meant. He stood up and walked around his desk, stopping in front of Braktis. "Go get, Agalon. I need to speak to him at once."

Braktis gave a slight bow and turned to head out the door. Disappearing into the hall, he closed the door behind him, leaving Andras to his thoughts.

If he could get his hands on this psychic, he may be able to persuade her to work for him. Andras rubbed his hands together as he thought of what he could do with her on his side. For one, the Guardians wouldn't be a problem anymore, and two, getting himself to the surface would be much easier. At first, it would probably be tough to get her to go along with this. He had never been one to shy away from a challenge, though, and he definitely wasn't planning on starting now.

There had to be some kind of weakness of hers that he could exploit, something he could hold over her head to make sure she made the right decision...maybe someone she cared about. He would need to get her away from the Guardians, though. Andras was sure that now that they knew of her, knew what she was, they would keep her with them. *That is where things might get a little tricky*, he thought, striding back to his chair.

Andras knew he was going to need to get her away from the Guardians before he would be able to get to her, but how? Just then, he heard his office door begin to open and, looking towards it, watched as Agalon and Braktis walked in.

Agalon's ice blue eyes flickered between him and Braktis as he made his way over to his usual post against the wall. "You wished to see me?" he asked casually, although Andras could hear a slight level of irritation just below the surface. Agalon's gaze rested on his as he crossed his arms over his chest.

Andras turned his gaze towards Braktis. "Why don't you fill him in on the information you got?"

"Yes, sir," Braktis answered, then went on to bring Agalon up to speed.

Andras closely watched Agalon's face as he learned of Braktis' run-in with the Guardians and Ella. If he didn't know him like he did, Andras doubted he would be able to pick up the small flinches around his eyes and the tensing of his lips as he grew angry.

Andras marveled at how calm Agalon seemed, even though he could tell his second-in-command was itching to rip the other demon's head off. Then there was Braktis, who seemed oblivious to the possible danger, continuing to rattle off his account of the evening.

By the end of the recount of events, Agalon was shaking his head, looking quickly between Andras and Braktis.

He finally looked back at Braktis and, with a low growl, muttered, "This is just great. How could you be so stupid?" Looking back towards Andras, he shifted his weight. "I should have gone."

Although this wasn't said with any kind of anger towards Andras, he couldn't help but feel defensive, and he was going to be damned if anyone put him in that position. "I will have you know, Agalon, that I still stand by my decision to send Braktis. Even though I am pissed about him running into the very ones I told him to stay away from, I think I have figured out a way to use this incident to our advantage."

"I am sorry. I did not mean to insinuate that your decision was wrong. What would you have us do?"

Andras stood there for a minute, then began going over his ideas concerning Ella. He watched as both Agalon and Braktis nodded and grunted their agreement.

After he finished, Andras watched as they both thought everything over. Finally, it was Braktis who asked the question first. "So how do we get to her?"

"I'm sure she is with *them* right now," Agalon commented, gazing down at the floor. Andras watched the demon's eyes narrow in concentration. "We will need to discreetly lure her away from the Guardians, so as not to alert them to what is going on."

"Yes," Andras said, looking between the two of them. "We need to get her away from them and get her here."

"We need to kidnap her," Braktis stated. Looking towards Andras, he tilted his head. "I would do it, but she has already seen me. She would take off the minute I came near her."

"And I do not think I would be good for this, either, sir," Agalon said, looking up at Andras.

Andras sighed and leaned forward, placing his arms on his desk. "We need someone quick, someone who can get in and out without her even being aware of what is happening."

"What about Castigo?" Braktis asked. "He is still out there, and he is quick."

"He is," Andras acknowledged slowly. "But I have him working on something else for me at the moment. No. We need someone else."

"Qual?" Agalon said.

Andras gazed at him for a moment, thinking about everything he knew of the demon. He knew Qual was fast. He was the smallest and the stealthiest of the demons under him. He was also very loyal and would do whatever was needed to get the job done. "Yes...," he finally stated, looking at Agalon. "Qual will do quite nicely." Looking towards Braktis, he spoke quickly, "We need to find him and fill him in. That way, as soon as we have an opportunity to grab her, we are ready to take it."

"Of course, sir," Braktis said with grin. "I will go and locate him."

As Andras watched Braktis make his way out the door, he felt Agalon watching him. Turning his head, he met Agalon's questioning gaze with a sigh. "What is on your mind now, Agalon?"

"I was just wondering what we should do, if anything, about the information Braktis gave us on how the Guardian and the female acted around him."

"I am not sure. We need to find out more information on the matter." Andras waved his hands around. "Is this reaction they had just towards Braktis or all of us? Is this something we can use in our favor?" Shaking his head, Andras fell quiet for a moment. He just wasn't sure what to do with this information. What if it wasn't important and they ended up wasting time on this when they had bigger issues to tend to? *Then again*, Andras thought, running his tongue over his teeth, *if I could get control of a natural psychic... Oh, the hell I could rain down upon any who stand in my way.*

As if reading his mind, Agalon took a step towards the desk, an eager look in his eyes. "If being around all of us affects them to a point they are not able to control themselves, we would have a huge advantage. I believe this is something worth looking into, sir."

Andras nodded slowly as he looked at his second-in-command. After thinking it over for a bit, he finally agreed. "I am going to put you in charge of this, Agalon. Find out what you can about this strange reaction and then, if it will help us, I want you to find a way to use it against them."

He watched an evil grin spread across the demon's face. Andras felt himself smiling in return. He had a feeling this was going to work out even better than he could have hoped for.

Chapter 13

The house was quiet. Ella lay in Christian's bed staring at the ceiling. The day had passed by in a blur and, the next thing she knew, it was night once more. She had offered...no, insisted...that she sleep out on the couch, but Christian hadn't wanted to hear it. He told her she would sleep in his room, he would stay out on the couch, and that had been the end of that.

Of course, that hadn't been the end of it at all. An argument, much to his brothers' delight, had erupted between the two of them. Ella had even made the attempt again to get him to see that she would be fine at her own home. After a bit of going back and forth, she had finally given in. She still wasn't sure it was necessary to remain here, but something about the look in Christian's eyes had caused her to trust him.

Ella remembered the look of relief on Christian's face when she had said she would stay. He had even gone as far as to give her his phone so she could call Cindy. *That had been an interesting conversation*, Ella thought with a smirk. Of course, Cindy had known something strange was going on, but Ella had assured her she was just following a lead about the disappearances and would only be out of town for a short while. Cindy had promised to stop by her place to check on Holly, telling Ella several times to call her if she needed anything. Ella had a feeling she may be taking her up on that offer, even though she fully intended not to get Cindy involved. Ella was the first to admit that sometimes what we intend to do wasn't what we needed to do.

Sighing, she rolled onto her side, gazing at the bookcases lining the wall.

When she had finally retired for the night, much to her new friends' dismay, she had wandered around Christian's room for a bit. He had more art on his walls than she had ever seen, outside of a museum. Although she wasn't a big art person, she just couldn't seem to get enough of them. Some of the pieces were so old, she had to wonder how he had gotten them.

Then there were his books. Just the thought of all of them made her sigh. He had everything from books by Edgar Allen Poe and Shakespeare, to ones on Christianity and the occult. Looking at them all made her head spin.

Turning to lay on her back again, Ella attempted to will herself to sleep. It had been a really long day... Scratch that. It had been a long week, and she really should be exhausted. After another half-hour of tossing and turning, though, Ella sighed and got out of bed. Looked like there was going to be no sleep for her.

Opening the door, she leaned out into the dimly lit hallway. Ella could make out a soft glow coming from the room across from her, but she could hear no noise from within. *Must have the TV on*, she thought, walking quietly out of the room.

Figuring she just needed to get some water or maybe a snack, Ella began to head for the kitchen. Running her hand along the wall, she stepped carefully to avoid running into anything. The last thing she needed was to knock a table over or something and wake everyone up. *They'd probably all come flying out of their rooms, guns blazing, like this was the Wild West or something*, she mused, smirking.

Coming to the kitchen, Ella reached for the light switch. She blinked rapidly as the fluorescent lights flickered before finally bathing the room in their soft glow. Glancing around, Ella quietly began to search through the cupboards for something to snack on. She was sure she would be able to find something because, even though she really didn't know much about any of the men that lived here, she knew they liked to eat. Thinking back to eating with them earlier, she couldn't help but release a soft laugh. They certainly could put away a full feast, and probably still be hungry afterwards, especially the one with the black eyes and the scar. Just thinking of that scar brought a chill to her spine.

What was his name again? Ella thought back on her earlier conversations with the guys... *Oh, Cyrus. That's right.*

He was nice enough when they spoke, but she could tell there was a darker side to him. His very presence was overwhelming. "Not someone I'd like to run into in a dark alley," she whispered, realizing what she had said, Ella couldn't stop another soft laugh from escaping her lips.

"Who wouldn't you want to run into in a dark alley?" a deep masculine voice said from behind her. Ella whipped around to find Christian leaning against the wall, amusement glinting in his steel blue eyes. "You wouldn't be talking about me, would you?"

"N-no!" Ella stuttered out.

"Good, because then I would have to remind you that has already happened."

"Well... Of course, I remember you. I mean, that night is a little tough to forget." Seeing a sly grin spread across his face, Ella glanced away. She could feel her cheeks turning red. With a rush of breath, she shot out, "How long have you been standing there anyway?"

"Just long enough to watch you going through our cupboards, laughing to yourself," he answered with a smirk.

"Oh," Ella responded, her eyes narrowing. "You know, it isn't very nice to spy on people."

"I wasn't spying. I was observing."

"Still..." Ella shook her head as she looked around the kitchen, then back towards Christian. He had his arms crossed over his chest and his head slightly tilted to the side, as though he was trying to figure her out. She felt her pulse rise as she looked at him. Ella had seen sexy, handsome men in magazines before, ones you knew just couldn't be real, but none of them held a candle to this guy. Just the thought of him made her feel hot. He had been invading her thoughts and dreams ever since that night, and to have him right in front of her now... Ella mentally shook herself.

Looking away, she pretended to continue searching through the cabinets. She just couldn't believe how much he affected her. Never before had she had this kind of pull towards a man. Taking a deep breath, Ella forced herself to look back towards Christian. His eyes were narrow as they stared back at her and, with a small huff, he pushed away from the wall and started towards her.

"What were you looking for?" he asked gruffly.

"I couldn't sleep," Ella muttered. "So I thought a snack or something would help."

Nodding, he stepped past her and began going through the cabinets. "Well, unfortunately, we don't really have any snack food at the moment." He paused, reaching into the back of one of the shelves. "How about a bowl of cereal?" he asked, looking over his shoulder.

Ella was just about to say yes when she paused, arching her eyebrow. She grinned. "You guys aren't a bunch of Wheaties lovers, are you?"

Laughing, Christian pulled out the cereal box and waved it in the air. "Nope. More like Lucky Charms kinds of guys."

"Well, in that case...," she laughed. "Yes, I would love a bowl."

"Okay," Christian said, handing her the box. "Why don't you go sit down? I'll get us some bowls and milk."

"Us? You planning on joining me?" Ella asked with a shy grin as she made her way to the kitchen table.

"Of course," he answered with another smirk.

She watched as he went over to a different cabinet and, reaching up to the top shelf, grabbed two bowls. Ella shook her head as she saw his arm muscles flex when he reached up, his t-shirt stretched tight across his shoulders. A sudden image of huge black wings flashed through her mind and she bit her lower lip, looking at the cereal box in front of her. After getting the milk, Christian made his way over to the table, taking a seat across from her. She looked up at him as he poured the cereal and milk into the two bowls, slowly sliding one of them over to her as he glanced up.

She smiled as she took the bowl. Part of her was still on edge with this whole situation. She was staying in a stranger's house...in his bed! Then there were the other men who lived there. They all seemed nice enough, but from what she witnessed the other night, Ella could bet none of them were what they seemed to be. However, she felt safe with them. It was like her sixth sense was telling her this was where she needed to be, regardless of how much she wanted to fight it. Since she had learned a long time ago to trust her intuition, she would stay...for the time being.

"Oh, I almost forgot...," Christian said, quickly getting up.

"What?" Ella said, frowning.

After rummaging through one of the kitchen drawers, he returned to the table. "Spoons." He smiled, handing her one.

"Oh... Thank you," Ella mumbled as she took it. Taking a couple bites of the cereal, she smiled. It had been years since she had eaten Lucky Charms and the moment those little sugar cubes hit her tongue, she was instantly taken back to her childhood. If she was being honest with herself, things had never truly been normal for her, but they had been less complicated. Day to day, all she had needed to worry about was school, boys, and the most recent gossip. Yes, she had her secrets, but who didn't? *Things had been so simple then*, she mused as she took another spoonful. Now she had people missing, strange beings with red eyes, and men with wings.

Yup, not so simple anymore!

Christian watched as Ella slowly became lost in her own thoughts. He wasn't sure what fascinated him so much about her, but he just couldn't seem to help it. He had been lying on the couch when he had heard her walking down the hall. It had been cute that she was trying to be so quiet, especially since everyone in the house was sure to have heard her. Then again, she wouldn't know that, would she?

When he decided to get up and walked into the hall, Christian had planned on finding out what she was doing walking around their house so late, but then he had seen her standing there. Her hair was slightly disheveled, and she had a smile on her face as she quietly laughed to herself.

He had stopped, unable to take his eyes off her.

Christian shook his head as he took another spoonful of cereal. Never before had a female affected him so much, not even Jessica. He just wasn't sure how to handle it. *Maybe it would be best if I just ignored it*, he thought, looking down at the bowl in front of him. With everything that had been going on with him personally, the mysterious demon they encountered, and the strange list of missing people, Christian wasn't sure if he needed anything else in his life.

Looking at her, though, he had a feeling ignoring her was going to be a lot easier said than done.

Christian watched with amusement as emotion after emotion crossed her face. Seeing her eyes narrow, he knew she was thinking about the last couple nights. He could almost feel the weight of the questions swirling around in that pretty little head of hers but, thankfully, she seemed to have decided not to voice any of them. That gave Christian a huge sense of relief, seeing that most of her questions probably revolved around him and his brothers...a topic he wanted to avoid for as long as possible.

"What are you thinking about?" Ella asked, her soft voice shaking him from his thoughts.

"Hmm? What was that?"

"You just seem to be in deep thought, and I was wondering what about?"

"Oh... Just going over what we need to do so we can get you home." Saying this, he felt a sudden twinge in his chest. *What the heck*? he wondered as he looked down at the table.

"Oh, right... Good," Ella mumbled. He looked back up at her, catching her gaze for only a moment before she looked back down at her own bowl.

Christian could feel the confusion and sadness rolling off her as she used the spoon to swirl the remaining cereal around. Suddenly feeling like an ass, Christian cleared his throat. "Of course, you're more than welcome to stay here as long as it takes...or even longer, you know, um...if you don't feel comfortable going home. I just assumed you wanted to get back to your home, your life, as soon as possible." Seeing conflicting emotions once again cross Ella's face as she stared down at the table, Christian quietly added, "It's not that I want you to leave..." Realizing what had just said, his mouth dropped open as he watched Ella look quickly up at him, her eyes wide.

"You don't?"

"No, um..." Christian felt his face heat. *Why the hell did I say that?* He looked around quickly. The last thing he needed was for one of his brothers to pick this time to grace them with his presence. Shaking his head, he cleared his throat. Of course he wanted her to leave...didn't he? His thoughts ran at ninety miles an hour. Maybe he should have left her in the alley. *No*, he thought with another shake of his head. He couldn't even think that without feeling a tightening in his stomach.

Realizing Ella was still staring at him, Christian shoved the rest of his cereal in his mouth. "How was your it?" he asked, swallowing.

"What?" Ella asked. Christian watched her blink rapidly as she tried to make sense of his sudden change of subject.

"Your cereal... How was it?"

"Oh, um... Good. Thank you."

"You're welcome," Christian muttered, watching Ella narrow her eyes. Noisily placing her spoon back into her bowl, she frustratingly bit her lip. Before she could ask him again about what he had said, he rushed on. "Well, it's pretty late. We should probably call it a night." Standing, he cleared his throat. "You've had a long day. I'm sure you're tired."

He stood there for a minute, his hand gripping his bowl to the point he thought he might break it. Christian watched her open and close her mouth a couple times. "Here," he grunted. "Let me get that." Reaching down, he grabbed her bowl and quickly walked over to the sink.

Christian could feel her eyes on him as he began to rinse out the bowls. After what seemed like forever, he heard the chair slide across the floor as she pushed it away from the table.

"Well... I guess I'll just head to bed then."

Glancing over his shoulder, he gave her a small smile. "Sounds good. Good night."

"Night." Her voice sounded a little unsure, as she whispered, "Christian?"

"Hmm...?" He slowly set one of the bowls back into the sink.

"Thank you for...for taking care of me. I know it may not seem like it, but I am really grateful."

He paused, closing his eyes as he nodded his head. Christian listened to her slowly make her way past him and down the hall.

It wasn't until he heard the bedroom door close that he released the breath he hadn't even been aware he was holding. Leaning on the counter, he looked down into the sink and let out a long sigh. "What am I doing?" he whispered.

Turning around, he slowly made his way out of the kitchen and into the pool room. Walking to the little bar, he opened a bottle of whiskey, pouring himself a healthy glass before heading back to the couch.

His thoughts started spinning. He *wanted* her to stay. Taking a drink, Christian's face wrinkled as the warm liquid burned its way down his throat.

Sinking into the couch, he willed the alcohol to work fast. Unconsciousness couldn't come soon enough!

Chapter 14

The next morning, Darren walked in to find Christian quietly sitting at the kitchen table, his head in his hands, his shoulders slumped. An empty glass and bottle of whiskey were sitting next to him. Pausing, Darren briefly contemplated heading back towards his room. Looking over his shoulder, he realized that if he were to go now, Christian wouldn't even know he had been there. However, he stopped in mid-turn because the part of him that wanted to be there for his brothers when they were in need yelled for him to turn back. *It's too early for this shit. Haven't even had my coffee yet*, he thought with a sigh.

Walking farther into the kitchen, Darren made his way over to the coffee pot, silently contemplating on whether he should interrupt Christian's musings or not. It wasn't until he had the pot going that he heard his brother let out a soft sigh.

"Mornin', Darren," Christian whispered.

"Good morning, Christian." He turned around and made his way to the kitchen table. "You look like crap. Sleeping on the couch not working out for you?"

"The couch was fine," he murmured, still not looking up. "I just have a lot on my mind, so I couldn't sleep."

"That what the alcohol's for?"

"Yeah. It didn't help, though. Just made me more confused and frustrated."

"Because of Ella?" Darren asked quietly, although he already knew the answer to that. He sat down across from his brother, taking in a deep breath as he watched Christian slowly shake his head. "Look, Christian–"

"It's not just about Ella. I don't know why I had such a strange reaction to being around that demon. I've never had that happen before and it's bothering me."

"Okay...," Darren said slowly. "Let's talk about your encounter with the demon."

"Okay."

Darren sat there silently, waiting for Christian to start. Sure, he had noticed how off Christian had been lately, but this... This was very troubling. With the appearance of this new demon, the last thing they needed was for one of them to be taken out of the game, especially Christian. With his talent of finding demons and evil souls, it would be devastating to not have him in the right state of mind. As much as Darren wanted to help Christian through this emotional turmoil he found himself in, he needed him to snap out of it. They could go over the emotional backlash later. "Christian?"

"Right. Where do I start?"

"Let's start with when you first sensed something was off."

"Well, I sensed the demon, like I normally do. Manuel and I went in the direction my senses were telling me to go. The closer we got to the alley, I started hearing drumming, but Manuel didn't hear anything."

"So the drumming was just in your head?"

"Yes, but it was so clear. Then my back started tensing."

"Like when your wings are about to come out, or did your back tense like it would from stretching wrong?"

"It felt like it does when my wings are going to come out. At first, I was able to control it, but then it was like... I don't know. I've never had that happen before."

"And this happened when the drumming started?"

"Yes, and the louder the drumming got, the more tense my back got. I was afraid my wings were going to rip out of my body right there. What if that had happened and someone had seen? What if losing control of my wings was just the start? What if whatever was causing me to lose control of my wings caused me to lose control of everything else? I could hurt an innocent person...or one of you! I just don't like feeling that out of control."

"I don't think you would have lost control, Christian. When we first landed here, you were the first one to gain control of yourself. You're like a rock, and I don't believe you would ever allow yourself to get to the point where you could hurt someone else."

"That's the thing, Darren, I would never *let* myself get to that point, but what if I didn't have a choice? What if I'm not strong enough to fight it off next time?"

Darren watched his friend, his brother, who had always been so confident of himself and his abilities. Now, he seemed so shaken by what happened in the alley, he almost looked like he was on the verge of a mental breakdown. It really made him wonder just how close to losing control Christian had actually gotten. Darren realized they had all been on Earth for so long, they had forgotten how powerful they really were.

In Heaven, Christian had been able to literally turn a being inside out just by thinking about it. Darren had seen it first-hand when he had been up against a second-level demon trying to pin him against a wall. Christian's eyes had suddenly gone from their regular ice blue color to a blackness so dark, they seemed like they could swallow someone whole.

Christian had always had the ability to take an evil soul into himself, which was part of how they kept the balance within this age-old war, but this time had been different. With the help of Manuel, Christian would usually go out and easily track these souls. Back then, though, things had been less...complicated. They had not felt the need to concern themselves with the innocents, only with taking care of what needed to be done. Once one of these evil souls was located, Christian would absorb them. In doing so, these souls would be completely destroyed. If any demons got in his way, he would use his ability to send them straight to Hell. Stripped of the ability to resurface, they would become useless to Lucifer.

That day, though, things took a turn for the worst. Darren even remembered thinking that it felt different as he watched Christian and the demon square off. As Christian's eyes had taken on the look of the blackest orbs, he had turned his gaze on the demon. Within an instant, the demon had gone from snarling and spitting to its mouth hanging open in a silent scream. It had seemed like a light had grown inside the demon, spilling out every opening in him. As it had gotten brighter and brighter, Darren had heard a growl come out of Christian that he had never heard...right before the demon was blown apart.

Darren had never seen such a horrible sight. Pieces of the demon were everywhere, and Christian was standing there, his body visibly shaking. At that moment, Darren had found a new wave of respect for Christian. To constantly have that kind of power within you and being able to keep it bottled up tight so that nobody would ever know was true control.

So the fact that something had been affecting him enough in that alley to make him feel like he could lose control of himself, in even the smallest aspect, was absolutely terrifying. Darren continued to remain calm on the outside, telling Christian he was sure everything would be fine. On the inside, though, he was shaking right to his core.

Darren watched Christian run his hands through his hair as he began mumbling, "I just don't know what to make of any of this. I don't even know where the drumming was coming from."

Darren began to shake his head, trying to think of something to say, something to give his brother hope and comfort. Before he could utter a sound, though, he was distracted by a movement at the entrance to the kitchen. Glancing over Christian's shoulder, he watched as a wide-eyed Ella leaned against the wall.

"I heard the drumming, too," she whispered, glancing from the back of Christian's head to Darren.

Darren stared at her for a heartbeat, letting what she had just said sink in. "Well, that's interesting," he murmured. Christian turned around in his chair and stared at Ella. His shock was visible to Darren and he could feel the tension rolling off his body. Glancing back at Ella, Darren noticed her look of confusion. He could only shake his head. "Very interesting."

†

Ella glanced at Christian. She watched a look of shock cross his face as he blinked several times. She curiously regarded the bottle of whiskey sitting by him, choosing to let that go.

"What did you say?" he whispered.

She let out a sigh as she looked past him to where Darren was sitting. "I said I heard the drums, too. At first, I thought they were coming out of one of the clubs, but the farther into the alley I got, the louder they became. I assumed they were coming from that demon thing with the glowing eyes." Ella watched as the two looked at each other, then back at her. "Am I wrong?"

"No... Well... We're not really sure," Christian stated as he gave a slight shrug. "That's as good an assumption as any, though. It did get louder to me the closer I got to him."

"Yes!" Ella exclaimed, thinking back to that moment. "Then when he growled, or whatever that was, it was so loud, it was painful."

"That's right! I forgot about that," Christian said, looking back towards Darren. Ella watched as Darren's eyes narrowed. She may not know him, but she *did* know the look a person got when they thought of something, especially if it was something bad.

"What? Is this a big deal or something?" Ella asked. Darren gave a slight shake of his head as he stared back at her. "I mean, obviously it's a big deal, but... I guess I should be asking *how* big of a deal."

"It's just interesting you and Christian heard the drumming, but Manuel didn't. Has something like that ever happened to you before, Ella?"

"Like what? Hearing drumming sounds in my head?" she exclaimed with a wave of her hand.

"Well, hearing anything strange. Hearing things nobody else around you could hear."

"I don't think so... I mean, sometimes I know things or see things, but I've never heard something someone else couldn't."

Darren tilted his head a bit. Ella watched as he tapped his finger on the table, obviously thinking over what she had just said. Christian glanced at Darren, then turned to her. "What do you mean you know and see things?"

"It's nothing really...," Ella said, glancing nervously away from him. "I just sense things... I don't know. It really isn't a big deal." Ella sighed as she walked over to the coffee pot. She was going to need some caffeine for the rest of this conversation.

"Cabinet to your left, bottom shelf."

"What?" Ella asked, glancing over at Christian.

"You want coffee, right? The mugs are in the cabinet to your left, bottom shelf," he said with a small smile.

"Oh, right. Thanks." Ella gave a soft laugh as she opened the cabinet and grabbed a mug. Glancing back over her shoulder at the bottle of whiskey, then over to Christian, she smiled. "You want some?" His cheeks flushed and he gave her a slight nod. Reaching up, she grabbed another mug.

She was relieved they left her to her thoughts as she fixed the coffee. It had been a restless night. Although she had been able to doze off a bit after her conversation with Christian, it hadn't gone uninterrupted. In fact, she hadn't really experienced any sleep last night at all. She'd just had several really long blinks.

Turning, she slowly made her way to the table and sat down at the end, passing Christian his coffee before taking a sip of hers. Looking between the two, she felt her cheeks start to flush. "What? Why are you two staring at me like that?"

She watched them exchange another glance before Christian turned towards her, a slight frown on his face. "When you say you sense things, what exactly do you mean?"

"I don't know," Ella said with a shrug. "I just get a feeling about things. It's something I've always referred to as my sixth sense." She sat quietly for a moment, looking between Christian and Darren. There were so many instances, too many to mention, where her sixth sense had kicked in and helped her out.

There was one experience, though. The one that started it all, at least as far as she was concerned. She's never spoken of it before...to anyone! However, something was telling her it was time.

Finally, she looked at Christian, gazing into his brilliant blue eyes. "There was one time when I was in high school. A friend and I were at a party, drinking and just being teenagers." Ella smiled as she took a sip of her coffee. "The music was blaring and there were people everywhere. We were dancing and having a good time when my friend, Tina, said she was going to go and get another drink. I went with her into the kitchen, and while she was grabbing a beer, I started talking to some guys. I don't know how, but I suddenly turned around and she was gone. The house we were at was in the woods, so there wasn't a neighbor for miles, and there had to be a hundred teens there. I searched everywhere for her. I just had a feeling something was wrong. Everyone around me was drunk or on something and I-I was starting to freak out..."

Glancing away from them, Ella blinked a couple times as the memories of that night came flooding back. She could feel their eyes on her, but neither said a word. There was a comfort in their silence, one that helped her to continue. "At first, I didn't understand what I was seeing. They were just flashes, like the flickering of an old movie projector, of some guy sneering down at me. A feeling of disgust rushed through me and I felt myself start to gag. It felt so real! I remember running outside. It was cool and the wind had started to pick up. Tears were running down my cheeks as the images started to become clearer. I could see the guy towering over me, then a weight on my stomach, like he was sitting on me." Ella took a couple more of sips of her coffee and took a deep breath. Her hands shook slightly as she set the mug down. "Sorry. I've never told anyone about this."

Christian leaned across the table and placed his hand on hers. "It's okay, Ella. Take all the time you need."

Ella smiled sadly. "I don't even know why I'm telling you this. I just... I feel like you should know."

"Well, we're not going anywhere," Darren whispered, his eyes showing soft kindness. "Whenever you're ready to continue, you go ahead."

Ella smiled and glanced down at her hand still covered by Christian's. The warmth from his touch calmed her and, releasing a deep breath, she let her mind wander back to that night. "I don't remember walking towards the woods. The images were coming so often and so clear, I was having trouble telling the difference between what I was seeing with my eyes and what I was seeing in my mind. I remember the fear I felt as I approached the edge of the woods, and I knew this feeling had nothing to do with the darkness before me. When the images were starting to go in and out of focus, I realized I was seeing through Tina's eyes. She was shaking her head back and forth, fighting against this man pinning her down. I started making my way through the woods, not knowing in what direction I was heading but, the same time, knowing it was the right way. I moved quietly, trying to concentrate on my steps. When the feelings started to overpower me, I began to get short of breath and felt this...pressure on my throat.

"He was choking her, making the images fuzzy. I started to move faster, not even thinking about what I would do once I found them. I just knew that I had to get to Tina fast because he was killing her. I...I found myself at the edge of this clearing and that's when I heard them. He was breathing heavy and grunting. I could almost smell his horrid stench as I came around a couple trees and spotted this vile man straddling my friend. He had his hands around her throat and she was gasping for air. Her feet were kicking beneath him, but I could tell she was starting to get tired. I looked down by my feet and found a thick tree branch and picked it up, not even thinking about it. I just took a couple quick steps towards the man and swung, slamming the branch right into the back of his head.

"There was a sharp crack as the branch connected with his skull and he rolled off Tina. She was gasping and curled onto her side, away from him, fighting to pull air into her lungs. When I started to run to her side, something stopped me causing me to glance at the man...and he was smiling at me. It was impossible! There was blood where his head had hit the dirt. I had hit him so hard, his skull had split open, yet he was smiling, and his eyes... I swear they had a slight red glow to them as he glared at me. I saw his mouth move as he whispered something, something that was too low for me to hear, but I suddenly felt a chill run down my spine all the same. Then the man's body shuddered, violently, and he was gone. Tina had been so out of it, she didn't see anything. Later, she told me she didn't even know the guy or remember leaving the party with him."

Ella paused as she glanced up from her hand, which was still enfolded in Christian's. He hadn't let go once, only rubbed his thumb slowly along the back of her hand. Ella met his steady gaze, swallowing hard. "She said she was behind me one minute, in the woods the next. I never told her how I found her. I just told her and the cops that I had heard her screaming.

"This kind of thing happened to me a couple more times. Images of people or items that were lost flickered in my mind, pulling me like a magnet. That's why I joined Cindy in her consulting business. It's the easiest way for me to deal with this gift and help people at the same time."

"This ability of yours... Is that how you ended up in the alley?" Darren asked, intently staring at her.

She slowly nodded. "I don't know why I was there. I never go to those kind of clubs, and I don't know anyone who would even be there. I was at home relaxing when I just had to go to that spot. It was like something was pulling me there and I couldn't say no. Then, when I was on the street, I lost the feeling. I was actually just about to head home when the drumming started. That's what lead me to the alley."

Ella took another sip of her coffee as she thought back over the years. It had taken her a while to figure out she could use her abilities to help people. At first, she had hated her gift, mainly because she didn't understand it. Sure, it had helped her find Tina, but Ella would sometimes get images of things so fast, she couldn't make heads or tails out of them. It had taken her years to learn how to block them. Almost getting into a couple car accidents had caused her to learn quickly. Once she had gotten a handle on it, though, it became easier to call on her gift when she needed to.

Once she meet Cindy and started working with her in the consulting business, Ella had been able to help people in a way that didn't draw too much attention to her. She hated the questions that would come if someone looked a little too deeply into her searching methods. Ella had a very high success rate, something she was extremely proud of, but with the recent disappearances, she was hitting a wall.

"So if you can sense people, what were you doing in the alley with the drunk that night? I mean, if you can just use this ability of yours, what did you need to get from him? It just doesn't make any sense," Christian said, standing up to get some more coffee.

Before she could answer, Darren let out a soft grunt. Turning, Ella found him staring at her with a strange look in his eyes. "I want to hear more about this ability of yours but, first, I must know... What were you looking for, Ella?"

"Well, there have been quite a few people missing over a short period of time, so I started looking into it to see if there was anything I could find that would help the cops. I wasn't getting into it too much until a woman I knew went missing. When the cops said they had done all they could, I started digging for information." Ella watched Christian make his way back to the table.

"People missing?" Christian asked as he looked questioningly at Darren. "Is that the disappearances you were talking about the other day?"

"I believe so," Darren said, never looking away from Ella. "Did you find anything?"

"No, and that's what's strange. I haven't been able to sense anything from any of the people who have gone missing! Even the woman I knew seems to be completely lost to me." Ella shook her head, letting out a frustrated sigh. "I've never had this happen to me before. I try, but all I get is this cold blackness staring back at me. I just don't know what to do."

She looked up and found both of them looking at her, confusion and concern clouding their eyes. They looked away from her then, each seeming to pull back into themselves as a troubled silence stretched out. Ella watched as Darren rhythmically tapped his fingers against the table as he slowly leaned his head back, obviously lost in his thoughts.

Looking at Christian, she saw that he was also lost in his thoughts, but instead of tapping his fingers or some other sign of concentration, he was sitting perfectly still, staring at the ground. The silence seemed to go one forever before Christian finally looked back at her. "What had you hoped to find out from that drunk at the bar?"

"Well, Dave had said the guy may know who was behind the disappearances, but I don't think he was capable of knowing who served him his last drink, let alone who was taking these people."

"Who's Dave?" Darren asked, getting up to get more coffee.

"He's an informant of mine. I met him a couple of cases back, and he would help me get the information I needed to help me piece together the images I had floating through my mind."

"Well, I have no doubt the smelly drunk was probably aware of multiple different illegal activities, but I don't think the disappearances were one of them," Christian murmured.

Ella nodded slowly as she watched Darren sit back down. "I had really been pushing to get any information I could. I'm sure he wanted to give me *something*, just not information. I should have known he was off."

"Ella, don't be so hard on yourself. Like you said, for some reason, you can't sense anything when it comes to this case," Christian said.

"I know. I just feel like I should be able to do more! I mean, there has to be something else–"

"I think I may know why you're having trouble sensing anything having to do with these disappearances," Darren interrupted without looking up from his mug.

Ella anxiously waited for him to continue. At this point, any kind of information that could help to calm her anxiety on the matter would be greatly appreciated. She watched as he held his mug tightly between his hands, staring down into the coffee as if it would tell him what to say. Ella soon realized Darren wasn't going to continue without a little nudge, so she slowly leaned towards him in an attempt to get his attention. "What's going on, Darren?"

Sighing, he glanced up at her. "I'm not positive, but I think this has something to do with the demon you guys came across in the alley."

"But I was drawn to the alley...to that demon. So wouldn't that mean there's something else stopping me from sensing the missing people?"

"Not necessarily," Darren said, glancing at Christian, then back at her. "Maybe it wasn't the demon drawing you there."

Ella glanced at Christian. *That doesn't make sense*, she thought wildly. Was Darren really hinting that the demon being there had been a coincidence? That *Christian* had drawn her there? Why would she be drawn to the alley because of Christian? She had only met him that one time and, although it was an unforgettable encounter, she wouldn't think it was enough to link them to each other.

He looked at her, as if sensing the questions that were running through her mind. "Maybe it wasn't me, *per se*. Maybe she was just meant to be there."

Ella smiled gratefully. "Yeah... I think Christian may be right." Looking back over at Darren, she noticed a knowing smile briefly form upon his lips before quickly disappearing back into what she had come to know as his usual relaxed grin.

Clearing his throat, Darren looked at her. "Well, whatever the case may be, you were definitely meant to be there. Now we just need to figure out why."

Before Ella could voice her agreement, they were all distracted by a loud grunt. Turning, she saw Nicholas slowly making his way into the kitchen.

"Mornin'," he mumbled, heading straight for the coffee.

"Good morning," they all answered as they watched him grab a mug.

Ella watched as he leaned against the counter with one hand, the other grabbing the creamer. His black hair, messed up from sleep, stuck out haphazardly around his head, his still half-closed eyelids hiding his deep red eyes from view. Her gaze wandered over him, noticing parts of a tattoo on his right shoulder. From where she sat, it looked like a dark cloud with layers upon layers of greys and black, colors that were bold against the edges of his white tank top. Even with only seeing a part of the tattoo, Ella knew it was large, possibly covering a good majority of his upper back. However, even though it was impressive in its own right, it wasn't the cloud that caused her to stare. It was the lightning bolt, dramatically inked upon his skin, shooting from the cloud. Her eyes followed the angry and jagged line running down his arm. Ella couldn't help but gaze at it. Every line was perfect, the shading on the cloud blending so smoothly, it looked real. Her wonder at the expertly created tattoo turned to shock when she noticed the lightning bolt begin to glow ever so slightly. It seemed to take on a life all its own, growing brighter and brighter right before her eyes. *What in the world*? she thought, unable to look away.

Leaning forward in her seat, Ella narrowed her eyes as she took in all of what she could see. Concentrating intently on Nicholas' back, she almost gasped aloud as she saw the edge of the cloud begin to distort, its edges swirling as the different shades began to blend and separate as it moved. Shaking her head, she just couldn’t believe what she was looking at. This was definitely no normal tattoo.

Suddenly sensing movement, Ella tore her eyes away to find Christian leaning towards her. He had a lopsided grin on his face, his eyes twinkling with amusement.

"Amazing, isn’t it?" he whispered, his voice holding an edge of laughter. "Bet this is the first time you’ve seen anything like that."

"I seem to be having a lot of firsts lately," she whispered back, smiling at him, images of his magnificent wings blazing through her mind. She watched a heat take the place of the amusement in his eyes and she felt her smile widening. "That tattoo of his is definitely something else. It's...intense."

Christian smiled and leaned back in his chair. With a slight nod, he looked over his shoulder. "Hey, Nicky?"

"Hmm?"

"Ella was just commenting on how...fascinated she is with your tattoo."

Ella felt her cheeks flush as she glanced from Christian to Nicholas. Nicholas turned from his coffee and looked her way, his red eyes boring into hers as he gave her a friendly wink. "Oh, that old thing..."

Ella smiled back. He grabbed his mug and sat down across from her. "It really is amazing."

"Well, thank you, dear," Nicholas said, gracing her with another friendly smile.

Ella licked her lips, trying to gather the nerve to ask him about it moving and glowing. When Darren cleared his throat, she looked at him and sighed.

"So, what did I miss?" Nicholas asked, looking at each of them.

"Quite a lot actually," Darren responded. "I think we need to wake everyone else up. It'll be easier to go over everything at one time."

"Agreed." Christian began to get up. "I'll go get Manuel. I'm sure he's already up and probably watching one of his favorite crime shows." Smiling, he turned to Nicholas. "Why don't you go get Cyrus?"

"What? No! You know he isn't a morning person. He'll rip my head off as soon as I step into his room," Nicholas whined, taking a gulp of his coffee.

"Nicky," Darren said, his voice sounding serious. When Ella glanced over at him, she could see the amusement in his eyes. "Go on. We don't want to take all day with this."

"But–"

"Nicholas!"

"Fine!" he said, noisily shoving his chair back.

Ella covered her mouth so as not to laugh. He just looked so sullen, she couldn't help it. She watched as Nicholas and Christian headed out of the kitchen towards the rooms, Christian flashing her a quick smile before he disappeared. She sat there for a minute, staring at his seat.

"Everything will work out."

Ella looked at Darren. "How can you be so sure?"

She watched the mixture of emotions flashing through his deep sapphire eyes. He quietly looked back at her and, although Ella could clearly see the uncertainty he was feeling, offered her a sad smile.

The question was left hanging between them, echoing through the silence as they stared at each other, neither wanting to voice their fears.

The silence itself said it all.

Chapter 15

Father James glanced up at the dark sky. Although it was too early for the sun to have set, the clouds gave the impression that night was already upon them. A cool breeze had started a couple hours back and it felt like tiny nettles against his face as he made his way through the gardens. The weather perfectly matched the dark mood he had been in. It seemed that, ever since he finished reading through that horrible book, he had felt a dark presence surrounding him.

Looking around, Father James stopped, dragging in one shaky breath after another. Standing there in the cold, he couldn't help but feel the all-too-familiar numbness.

"What have I done?" he whispered, looking up at the dark, foreboding cloud. He could feel the dark presence swirling around him. With a shaky hand, he reached up and wiped his mouth. *Surely no true damage has been done by me simply reading out of this book*, he thought wildly, feeling a coldness grip his heart.

Thinking back, he remembered the feeling of doom that had come over him as he had read the last line in the book. *Such simple words*, Father James thought, glancing over towards the rose bushes lining the path. All words held some power to them, and Father James was sure the ones he read were the worst of all. They echoed through his head as his eyes began to blur. Latin words bombarded his thoughts as he went back to that last page...

"*Ut verba habent, maxime hoc haberet locum in oblatione animarum, et virtus castitatis destrui — qua velum apériant patitur tenebras exite, et auferetur lance, quo fides erit transeatur. Pestilentiae super omnes... Sic fiat.*"

He remembered these words vividly because he had sat there for hours translating them. Word after word, he had researched and made sure to get it just right. Once he had finished, Father James had looked down at his tablet and recited those last foreboding words out loud...words that should have never left his lips.

"*May the words herein hold true with an offering of the most innocent souls, and may the strength of purity be destroyed – wherein the veil may open to allow the Darkness to come forth, at which the balance will sway and loyalties will shift. A plague upon all... So mote it be.*"

Why did I read them? What did I do? he thought sadly, making his way over to the closest bench. Sitting down slowly, he could feel all his joints cracking. He had never truly felt old until now. Rubbing a hand across his chest, Father James wished he could go back and make a different choice. He had been weak, wanting his faith to be returned to him with little effort on his part. Making that deal had sealed whatever course his soul would take in the afterlife. He had not only allowed this to happen, but he had played a huge part in it.

He had helped a demon. That was surely damning...

Worse yet, if he had translated the text correctly, he had helped *many* demons and brought a plague on his fellow man. He needed to do something!

For the hundredth time since finishing the book, he considered telling someone what he had done. But who would believe him? Living within a church, you would think that if you said you believed you were visited, possibly making a deal with a demon, someone would take notice. However, that just wasn't the case nowadays. Rather than believe him, Father James was sure anyone within the church would be more likely to lock him away.

Leaning forward, he rested his head in his hands. *What I wouldn't give for some peace*, he thought with a sigh. Closing his eyes, he took in a couple deep and steady breaths. Father James felt his mind begin to get foggy, his troubled thoughts swirling around until they became just a constant humming. It was within this consistent noise that he sensed a dark calm.

It was intoxicating and, in Father James' weakened state, he could do nothing against its pull. He wanted nothing more than to silence the constant thoughts running through his mind, so he mentally reached for the calmness, having little regard to the dark surrounding it. He let it envelop him, felt the darkness completely surround him as he let his head fall back.

Maybe I can just slip away...not have to worry about what I have done, he thought, feeling his heartbeat slow. Completely giving in to the darkness, Father James was just feeling his body relax when a voice stirred him from his peace.

"So you are wanting death now, Father?" a deep voice whispered through his head.

Father James' eyes flew open as he gasped. "What?"

"You amuse me, Father. One minute, you are praying for faith and the strength to continue; the next, you are wanting death."

"Yes, I prayed for faith. I offered to do anything, promised everything, and you gave me nothing but darkness. You lied to me!"

"Lied?" the voice scoffed. "I did no such thing! I told you I would give you your faith back. Do you not have faith now, Father?"

"No, I–"

"Oh, come now, Father... Were you not, only moments ago, worrying about your soul?"

Looking down at his feet, Father James let out a shaky breath. "With what I've done, what I've helped *you* do, my soul will never see Heaven."

"See! The fact that you have even thought of where your soul will go shows that your faith has been returned. So you may thank me now."

"But–"

"Is what I said not the truth?"

"Well...yes, but–"

"If what I said is true, I have held up my end of the bargain, just as you have held up yours. Now thank me."

A strangled breath escaped his lips as Father James began to slowly shake his head.

"I said thank...me...," the voice hissed.

Father James felt a chill as tears began to build in his eyes. "You're right... Thank you."

"You are welcome. See. That was not so hard," the voice whispered. "So, do you still wish to die?"

"No... I just want some peace."

"Peace?"

"My thoughts... Ever since I finished that book for you, my thoughts won't quiet."

"Well, seeing that I am in such a giving mood, I can do that for you. I can give you the peace of mind you so crave."

Father James could hear an underlying tone in the stranger's voice. Not opening his eyes, he let out a soft sigh. "And what will you want in return?"

"Just some information."

"In-Information on what?" Father James stammered. Feeling a warmth touch his downturned face, he opened his eyes and looked up. Blinking several times, he made out a hazy figure standing on the path before him. The figure's eyes glowed red as they stared at him.

"Not what, Father, but who."

"Who? You need me to get information on someone?"

"Yes, but not just any person. A woman, Father. A woman who is very important to me."

"Wh-Who?" Father James whispered as he watched the shadowy figure move towards him. Those red eyes stared at him, unblinking, almost daring him to look away.

"Her name is Ella. Ella Rob–"

"Ella Roberts?" Father James finished, his eyes dropping.

"You know her, Father?"

"Yes, since she was just a little girl. Why do you need information on her?" Father James said, his voice shaking. "What do you want with Ella?"

"What I want with her is none of your concern, Father," the figure sneered. "Since you know her, it is going to make what I need from you even easier."

"Wh-What do you want me to do?"

"All I want, Father, is for you to call her up and have her meet with you."

"Meet with me? Why? What do you want me to say to her?"

"So many questions. Just call Ella up and tell her you need to meet with her. Just get her somewhere out in the open, and I will take care of the rest."

Father James turned his head from the figure and looked at the roses around him. He had allowed himself to give in to the darkness before and, in doing so, his soul was surely damned, but could he really give in again, bringing someone else down with him? Shaking his head, his thoughts turned to Ella.

How could sweet little Ella have anything to do with this evil creature? He remembered the first time he meet her. She was only eight and was skipping behind her grandma. She was a curious and sweet little girl, always asking questions and talking to everyone. Yes, he had always thought she was a little odd, but it was nothing to cause any kind of concern. Ella would just stare off into the distance sometimes, lost in her own thoughts.

Shaking his head again, Father James just couldn't wrap his mind around what this demon could want with her.

"I don't want to involve her in any of this," he finally said, looking back towards those horrible red eyes.

"You do not really have a choice, Father. You *will* call up Ella, and you *will* set up a meeting with her. There really is no other option."

"But–"

"No, Father! You will do this. If you do not, you will not like the outcome."

Father James swallowed hard as he stared into the creature's demonic red eyes. He could feel them boring into him and, taking a deep breath, he shook his head.

"No?" the demon hissed. "You are saying *no* to me?!"

"I will not involve an innocent girl in this evil," he replied, sticking his chin in the air in a sign of defiance.

"We shall see about that."

Before Father James could respond, he felt a rush of hot air hit him, sending him flying backwards off of the bench and into the dirt. Gasping for air, he tried to sit up, but felt an unbelievable weight pressing down upon him. Looking up, he suddenly found the demon above him, leaning down towards his face with a look of sheer evil. The creature sneered at him as he leaned in closer.

"Let us make a deal, Father," he hissed, his breath hot against Father James' face. "You do as I ask and I will not only let you live, but I will allow your family to live, as well."

"My f-family?" Father James whispered, his chest tightening.

"Yes, Father, your family. How is little Tiffany? Your niece must be... What? Four now? Such an adorable little child...so innocent...so ripe... "

"No... Please...," Father James pleaded. He felt his stomach turn as images of all the vile things the demon wanted to do to his niece flashed through his mind.

"Do you see, Father?" the demon said, pulling back far enough for their eyes to meet. "Perhaps I should go and pay a visit to Tiffany's house right now." His head tilted off to the side, his red eyes glowing even brighter. "Aww, yes! I can see her now. Sitting with her little toys, wearing the most adorable pajamas... Why, I think she is lonely, Father."

Tears started streaming down Father James' face. He couldn't allow this demon to harm his niece. As the images began to fade, they were replaced by ones of his sister, brother-in-law, and his eldest nephew. Their bodies were twisted in horrifying positions, their mouths open in a silent scream, pleading for the torture to stop. "Okay...okay. I'll call Ella! Just, please... Don't hurt my family!"

He felt the pressure lift as he watched the demon pull away. "Now that we have come to an understanding...," the creature sneered, "I expect this task to be handled quickly."

"How will I let you know when the meeting with Ella is?" Father James asked in a defeated tone.

"I will know, Father, for I will be keeping a close watch on you to make sure you follow through with my request." The demon gazed down at him, his eyes unblinking. Father James gasped as he stared back at him, too afraid to look away. "And if you do *not* do as I ask...," the demon hissed, not bothering to finish because Father James was all too aware of what he would do.

"I will do as you ask," Father James said as he finally looked away, his eyelids fluttering closed as a sob escaped his lips.

"Yes, you will... "

Father James felt another sudden rush of heat and he reached his right hand up to shield his face, fear gripping him. Then, just as suddenly as it started, the heat subsided and he was left with the cold night air again. Slowly pulling his hand away from his face, Father James looked around to find himself alone. Slowly getting up, he was only able to stumble as far as the bench in front of him before he was overcome by a wave of dizziness.

Gripping the back of the bench until his knuckles were white, he gulped in air, releasing each breath through his teeth. When the dizziness faded, he sobbed loudly, glancing down as his trembling hands. "Oh God, what have I done?"

Chapter 16

Ella quietly sat in the living room, curled up on the couch and looking at the printouts Darren had given her. *So many missing*, she thought sadly, flipping from one photo to another. Darren was right, though. The way they had all just vanished was mind-boggling. For instance, the girl she knew supposedly disappeared while in a changing room! That was ridiculous. Feeling a pang of guilt in her chest, Ella shook her head. Even with concentrating on her friend, picturing her in her mind, she still couldn't see anything. Sighing, Ella set the papers on the table and looked around the empty room.

It was so quiet in the house compared to earlier. The meeting Darren wanted went on forever and, as it is in most meetings, everyone had something to say. Cyrus had been the most skeptical. As the meeting had gone on, Ella noticed the curious glances sent her way by all the men. While each tried not to be too obvious, Cyrus' stare had been direct and challenging. She couldn't blame him, though. She was a stranger who had been tossed into their lives, their home, and no matter how Christian and Darren had tried to make them understand, it was still an intrusion. In Cyrus' case, it was an unwanted intrusion.

Getting off the couch, Ella attempted to stretch her back. Sitting hunched over the papers for so long had caused it to lock up. She was sure the stress of the past few weeks wasn't helping, either. Messaging her back, Ella began to slowly walk around the room.

There wasn't a whole lot in the room besides the couch and table, a couple lamps, and an old maple hutch. Walking to it, she marveled at the many tiny statues and intricately decorated boxes that were lining the shelves. Some of the pieces seemed quite old and hard to come by. These, like some of the older items decorating Christian's room, only further showed her how little she knew about them.

Listening to the silence, she decided that now was as good a time as any to snoop around. Smiling, she made her way from the room and, passing the kitchen, slowly walked down the hall.

She hesitated at the first door she came to. Part of her felt bad for going through their things. *Maybe I should wait for them to get home, then just ask them about who they are,* she thought, eyeing the shiny round doorknob. Then again, if she was going to be staying there, shouldn't she know who she was staying with?

Gently biting on her bottom lip, Ella narrowed her eyes. She knew what she saw Christian do that night. She didn't know what he was, but she definitely knew he wasn't human, so it seemed safe for her to assume the rest of them weren't, either. Her mind drifted back to the strangeness of Nicholas' tattoo, the cloud swirling along his shoulder as if it were alive, the lightning bolt glowing.

Definitely not human!

Taking in a deep breath, she reached down and turned the knob. The door opened with a soft whisper, and Ella was instantly greeted with the smell of leather. Breathing deeply, she smiled. *Books*! Stepping into the room, she reached next to her and, after some searching, found a light switch.

A soft click was the only warning she had as the room was instantly illuminated by a soft yellow glow from the light overhead. Ella couldn't believe her eyes. The room was wall-to-wall bookcases, each shelf stacked full. There was a huge fireplace on the far wall, lavishly decorated with hand-carved wood siding and mantle. The detail was astounding.

In the center of the room was the most comfortable-looking couch and chair set she had ever seen. The soft brown leather looked so inviting, the cushions looked so plush, she was sure she would just melt right into them. The set was complemented by a small wooden table, the carvings in it matching the fireplace mantel.

"Amazing...," she whispered, turning her attention back to the bookcases. Thinking back on the books in Christian's room, Ella just shook her head. This house must hold tens of thousands of books, each one older than the last. Leaning towards one of the shelves so she could read the bindings, she felt her jaw drop. *All first editions*?! This place would make the most avid book collector melt.

One book caught Ella's eye as she was scanning the shelves. It was a darker leather than the rest, with worn binding and a single gold letter, *G*, stamped on the side. She ran her hand over the edges, her fingers tingling as they hovered over the spine. Pulling it towards her, Ella heard it brush against the other books as it slid off the shelf.

Turning the book over in her hand, Ella marveled at the elegant gold lettering on the cover. The word *Tutores* caught her attention and she felt a pull on her memory as she stared at it. Slowly making her way to the couch, she sank down into the cushions, never taking her eyes away from the cover.

"*Semita de Tutores*," Ella whispered, saying the entire title aloud as she lightly ran her fingers over each letter. Gently opening the book, she began to slowly turn the pages. What she originally thought of as an old printed book turned out to be more of a journal...an archive. Each word tugged more and more at her senses, causing her eyes to narrow in concentration as she looked over one page after the next. Three pages into the book, Ella paused as the chapter title, "*Mensam Contenti*", practically jumped off the page at her. She felt her breath catch as old memories came flooding back.

"This is in Latin," she whispered, feeling a sense of excitement. At a young age, Ella's grandmother had taught her to read Latin. She had never understood why and, for the longest time, Ella had fought her during every lesson. Her grandmother, who had the patience of a saint, had always told her that, in time, she would understand why she needed to learn it.

Ella had forgotten all about those lessons with her grandmother...until now. A smile spread across her face as she, once again, looked at the words written across the top of the page – *table of contents*. "I can read this!"

Glancing down the page, Ella noticed the book was separated into four sections: *defenders, aggressors, absolution,* and *balance*. Each section title had several notes under it. She read everything from demon, to Heaven, to Hell, to learned psychics, to natural psychics. Shaking her head, she ran her eyes down the list again.

"Natural psychic, huh?" she murmured. As she looked at the title, she began to feel a tingle of excitement. Although, she had never heard that term before, it seemed to hold some importance, some familiarity. Gently leafing through the pages, she turned to that section, the first few lines immediately catching her eye...

Those born as a natural psychic will have wondrous capabilities and can be an important force in retaining the balance, but only if said psychic is capable of harnessing their power. Beware, though. A natural psychic's power, if left unchecked, can turn dark.

Ella reread the lines a couple times. Though much of it was really confusing to her, there was that underlying feeling she had read it before.

"That isn't possible, though," she said, shaking her head. "Where in the world would I have read something like this?" Looking around the room, she was suddenly overcome with a memory of sitting in her grandmother's library.

Seeing as she had been abandoned as an infant by her mother and never knew her father, her grandmother had raised her. In her house, she had a small room filled with old books – nothing like this room, though. *She would have loved this room,* Ella thought with a sad smile. It had been five years since her grandmother had passed on, yet Ella still swore she could hear her from time to time, telling her everything would be okay.

Thinking back to her grandma's own little library, she had to smile. Ella could remember sitting there day after day, reading through all the old books. Most of the books had been in Latin, so she could only really understand certain ones. It had taken her a long time to learn Latin but, with much insistence from her grandma, she finally had.

Closing her eyes, she could see her grandmother's bookcases lining the walls. Nothing was kept in any order...at least to anyone but her grandma. Ella could feel the carpet beneath her, soft and plush, her hand running over it as she sat on the floor with a book open in her lap. In her mind, she looked down at the book. It was one of her grandma's journals, filled with scribbles and sketches of her thoughts and things she had seen. Those journals had been Ella's favorites growing up. They were to her what fairy tales were to most children. Looking at the book, she noticed a couple words standing out, bold against the light sketching around it – Angelus Lapsis.

"Angelus Lapsis," she whispered, her head resting back on the couch as she allowed her mind to delve further into her memories.

Looking back down at the words, she felt a presence in front of her. Glancing up from the journal, she found that not only was she now truly back in her grandmother's library, but her grandma was leaning quietly against the door frame. Her short silver hair shone in the afternoon light, her eyes gentle as she gazed down on her. "Hello, child," she said with a smile upon her lips.

"Grandma!" Ella exclaimed, the book in her lap landing with a thud as she leapt to her feet. Stepping quickly, Ella made her way across the small room and into her grandma's arms. The smell of fresh linen and soap engulfed her as she held on tightly.

Never in her wildest dreams did Ella think she would ever find herself once again in the comfort of her grandma's embrace, let alone back in the house she grew up in. Leaning back, Ella looked up at the kind eyes and warm smile she had been missing. For five long years, she had wished for her grandma's love, her guidance. Now she was here!

"I knew you would find your way back here," her grandma said, her eyes twinkling as she gazed down at her. Ella felt tears slide down her cheeks as she looked back.

"Find my way? What do you mean, Grandma?" Ella asked.

"Why, to this moment, my dear," her grandma answered, pulling her into another tight embrace before leading her back into the room. "You see, sweetie, this is not a memory of yours."

"It's not?" Ella asked, a slight sense of uncertainty washing over her. "Well, if this isn't a memory, what is it?"

"This is a vision, of sorts," her grandma said, easing herself into her favorite chair.

"That doesn't make any sense, Grandma. How can I be having a vision, and how can I be in your house, talking to you? I don't understand," Ella said with a shake of her head, sitting on the floor in front of her grandma.

"I know, child, and even though we don't have much time, I will try to explain it to you." Ella watched as her grandma sighed, running a hand over the arm of the chair, seeming to be searching for where to begin. Finally, she looked at her and smiled. "Oh, my darling Ella. You're just so special. Not just to me, but to the world. You, my dear, are what's called a natural psychic."

Ella's eyes went wide as she stared back at her. She could feel questions building within her, but was stopped from voicing them as her grandmother raised her hand, a knowing smile playing upon her lips.

"I know you have questions but, as I stated, we don't have much time. Let me say what I need to and hope it is enough." She paused. Ella had the feeling she was waiting for her to do or say something, so she gave a quick nod. Her grandma smiled and continued, "Let me start by saying that the only reason I never told you any of this before was that I was unsure if it would be necessary. You see, although you have always shown signs of your psychic abilities, I didn't know if your powers would ever be fully awakened."

"Signs?" Ella asked.

"Yes, signs. Like your ability to find items or know certain things right before they happen. But, you see, your true powers are just starting to come to light. This could only have happened because you came in contact with a being, an individual of similar or greater powers."

Ella's eyes widened as an image of Christian flew across her mind. Feeling her cheeks redden a bit, she bit her lip and looked towards the floor.

"Yes... Your dark angel," her grandma said with a chuckle. Ella glanced up at her.

"Dark angel?"

"That, my child, is a whole different conversation, but just know you can trust him and his brothers. The two of you crossed paths for a reason, and we can only trust that the powers above know what they're doing. But let's get back to you." Her grandma shifted slightly in her chair and clasped her hands comfortably in her lap. "Now that your powers are waking up, you must learn to control them. *Do not* let them control you. That will not only get *you* into trouble, but it could hurt those you care about."

"I still don't understand, Grandma. How could I be a natural psychic? What *is* a natural psychic?"

"You're right. I *am* getting a bit ahead of myself. Let's see... A natural psychic is someone who is born with a natural connection to the Earth, Heaven, and Hell, and all of the powers they hold. Not being one myself, I can only tell you what I have learned over my years. I'm sorry. As far as what your powers will entail, I cannot help you. You will have to learn as you go." A sadness crept across her face. Ella could see that she was upset at not being able to help more. The last thing she wanted was for her grandma to be sad. To feel she had, in some way, let her down. Opening her mouth, Ella started to assure her that everything would be fine when the look of sadness that was in every line of her grandma's face slipped away, replaced by a wistful, loving calmness. "Oh, how I wish I could be there with you but, there again, you are in great company. Don't be afraid to trust in them. The boys, although rough at times..." She paused, her eyes twinkling as she chuckled, "and maybe a little wild, truly do mean well."

"You talk as if you know them, Grandma," Ella murmured.

Ella's grandma smiled sadly and looked off towards the bookcases. Her eyes were distant for the briefest moment as she let out a soft sigh. "In another life maybe," she whispered.

Then, as if awakening from a dream, she looked back at Ella. "Now for the how. Understand, this is not a topic to be taken lightly. There is a reason why there are not many natural psychics anymore. The only way a natural psychic can be born is if a woman has either slept with an angel, or was raped by a demon. Even then, this only means the child will have the *potential* to be a natural psychic. Although, the chances do seem to increase if the baby is spawned from a demon and not an angel." Her eyes seemed to darken more and more each time the word demon passed her lips.

Ella gasped as she stared at her grandma. "Does that mean...?"

"I'm afraid your mother fell victim to a truly evil demon. She came to me one stormy night, covered in mud and blood, crying hysterically about a man with red glowing eyes. The sight of her was horrific! I immediately knew what had happened and quickly took her in. When she found out she was pregnant, she had wanted to get an abortion and, although I understood her misgivings, I insisted she carry you to term, telling her that once you were born, I would take care of you."

"Weren't you afraid I would be evil or something? I mean, my dad's a demon!" Ella cried out, her eyes welling up with tears.

"No. I never once thought that and I'll tell you why." She leaned forward in the chair, tenderly running a hand over Ella's face, wiping away her tears. "The day you were born, the weather was beautiful, the flowers were blooming, and a calmness fell upon me. There is not an evil cell in your body. Whatever that demon thought he was going to accomplish from forcing himself on a mortal woman was stopped by God himself. I know it! As further proof, if what I just said isn't enough, your powers were awakened by an angel...not a demon. There is such love in you, Ella. Don't let knowing the truth overshadow the good in you, in your life."

Nodding slowly, Ella felt more tears begin to slide down her cheek. Looking back at the book lying on the floor, she leaned over and picked it up. Setting it in her lap, Ella looked down and noticed that her tears had landed next to the bold Latin words scrolled beautifully across the page. The letters slowly blurred out and, as they came back into focus, were replaced by their English translation – *fallen angel.* Looking up at her grandma, she saw she had a very satisfied and proud look on her face.

"Our time is almost up, child, so listen closely. You must learn to harness your powers, exercise them any chance you can and, most importantly trust yourself. Trust Christian. Trust his brothers." Her grandmother stopped then. A grim look spread across her face as she reached down and took hold of Ella's left hand. "There will be a time when everything you believe will come into question and you will not know where to turn. You must listen to your gut...your sixth sense, as you've come to call it."

"What will happen?"

"I do not know, dear. All I know is that the more powerful you become, the closer the darkness moves towards you. There is a change coming. Some will come who wish to upset the natural balance between good and evil, and they will stop at nothing to get what they want. You must remain vigilant, Ella!" her grandma said, tightening her grip on her hand.

"I will, Grandma," Ella responded, squeezing her grandma's hand in reassurance.

"No, don't just say you will. Promise me you will be careful. That you will take care of yourself and allow the boys to watch out for you. You will become an important part in this upcoming battle, and you will have to stand against those who wish to harm not just you, but the world. You will have to fight."

"I promise, Grandma." Ella looked at her and, with a shudder, took a deep breath. "But I'm scared. What if I'm not as powerful as I need to be? What if I fail?"

"You are so strong Ella. I have faith in you just like I always have. When the time comes, you will not only be strong, but you will be a force from God, his will guiding you. I love you, Ella, and although you may not be blood to me, you will always be my child. I'm so proud of you and the woman you have become."

"I miss you so much, Grandma," Ella choked out. Another tear rolled down her cheek. "I wish you were here to help me."

"I do, too, but even though you can't see me, I will always watch over you. I'll always be with you." Her grandma leaned forward, placing a kiss upon her head.

Ella, tears flowing freely down her cheeks, looked up at her grandma. Her vision began to blur. Blinking rapidly, she found it only continued to get worse. She saw a sad smile spread across her grandma's face before the need to close her eyes became too much.

A sob escaped her and she felt her body shudder. Ella suddenly sat up straight and, after taking in several breaths, she realized she was back in the boys' library. Reaching up, she found her cheeks were wet. Letting out another soft sob, she glanced back down at the book in her lap, running her fingers over the section's title. "Oh, Grandma," she whispered, slowly closing the book.

Closing her eyes again, she rested her head in her hands. Ella could feel more tears begin to fall as she thought of her grandma, of the moments they had shared, the times she had missed since her passing.

"Ella?"

Startled, she glanced up to find Christian standing in the doorway, concern covering his face.

"Are you okay?"

Ella looked at him for a minute, thinking over that question. *Was* she okay? She knew she shouldn't be. After everything she had just learned, everything she had yet to figure out, she should be a wreck, running right for the door. She wasn't, though. She actually felt calm, as if everything in her life had just been put right into place. A feeling of peace came over her.

"Yes, Christian," she said with a small smile, reaching up to wipe away the last of her tears. She stood up, glancing down at the book she held tight in her hands. She sighed softly before looking back up at Christian. "I believe I am."

Chapter 17

Christian had been standing there watching Ella for some time.

He had watched her lay her head back, resting it comfortably on the back of the couch, an old book open and forgotten in her lap.

He had seen the tears slide down her face, and heard her soft whimpers as she dreamt. When she had finally answered him and said she was okay, it was obvious she was lying. How could she be okay?

He had gone with it, though, casually walking into the room. After seeing her eyes travel around the shelves, he offered to show her around the library. It had been obvious to him that Ella had found something in the old book on her lap, because after she got up, she held onto it with an iron grip.

Christian had offered to take it from her, hold onto it for her since it seemed to be slightly heavy, but she had just smiled and politely declined. Eyeing it when he could, Christian could only make out a faint gold emblem on the side. It had been ages since he had looked through any of the books in this room, so he couldn't remember what book it was. It hadn't been until Ella had leaned down, shifting the weight of the book in her arms to get a better look at something that had caught her eye, that Christian had seen the title.

Semita de Tutores.

Crap!

In English, that meant "The Path of Guardians" and it was filled with notes on everything – from his brothers and himself, to what they have been doing there, to all of the beings they have come across. Each of them had written in that book at one point or another, taking turns writing their experiences. It was not only a reminder to them of what they have gone through, but of the fight that was still to come. Realistically, it was more like a giant journal than a regular book...and it was supposed to remain hidden! Which one of his brothers had left it sitting out in the open for the world to see?

What is the chance she can't read Latin? He had thought as he'd watched her unconsciously run her hand over the binding.

That had been a couple hours ago and, still sitting in the library watching Ella go through the books, he couldn't shake the sight of her holding their journal. *What to do? What to do?* This become more like a mantra, running through his head until it was almost one continuous hum.

Darren was going to freak when he found out Ella had found their journal. *If he doesn't know already*, Christian thought. Darren had this uncanny ability of knowing when something happened *before* it happened. Even if he didn't know already, there was no way Christian was going to be able to keep this from him. He could try but, in the end, Darren would find out...then the rest of his brothers would find out. Rubbing his hands over his face, Christian inwardly groaned.

"What's wrong?"

"What?" Looking up, Christian saw Ella staring at him from across the room. She was holding the journal tightly in her left hand, her right delicately resting on the closest shelf. With the late afternoon light coming through the blinds, she had an almost celestial glow about her. At that moment, Christian could only stare, completely at a loss of words.

"Christian? Are you okay?"

Christian gave himself a mental shake. "I'm fine," he said, glancing down at his hands. "I'm just a little tired."

"Are you sure? It's just... You seem pretty upset."

Christian looked back up at Ella. The concern in her eyes touched him in a way nobody ever had before, and he felt warmth begin to grow in his chest. Frowning slightly, he rubbed his right hand over his chest.

"It's just, well... You don't seem okay, Christian. Maybe we should continue this later, go and relax for a bit," Ella said with a shake of her head. "I'm sure you couldn't have been comfortable sleeping on the couch last night, then you and the guys were out for hours early doing...whatever you were doing." Christian watched as she took a last glance at the books on the shelf and stepped away. Stopping, she looked down at the journal in her hands. "Um, Christian...?"

He licked his lips as he watched her. Christian could tell she was having trouble asking him about the book. She kept glancing down at it, her eyebrows bunching slightly. "What is it, Ella?" he asked softly.

"Can I ask you something?" Ella asked. Looking up at him, Christian could see the uncertainty in her eyes.

Here it comes! he thought anxiously, leaning back on the couch. "Sure. What's up?"

"This book... The title... What does it mean, Path of the Guardians?"

Whistling softly, Christian stood up. "So you can read Latin?"

Lifting an eyebrow, Ella smiled, "Yeah. My grandma taught me when I was younger." She took a step towards him, and Christian felt a sudden need to get some air. "So... What does it mean?"

He stared at her. He had never tried to explain to anyone who or what he was. Hell, he had never had to! This was bound to come up eventually, even if she hadn't found that stupid journal. He knew she would have questions. After the other night in the alley, he was sure her head was full of them. After reading through their journal, though... Christian shook his head. He wasn't even sure what she had read in that book. Had she read about them? Had she read about the different demons they had come into contact with? Maybe there was something in the journal that touched on what was going on with her. This was bad. This was really bad. He couldn't just tell her nothing, could he?

His head spun with different explanations he could say, but he wouldn't tell her everything...at least not yet. That would be a little much for anyone to take in. First things first. He needed to find out what she knew, or what she *thought* she knew. Clearing his throat, he did know one thing for sure. He needed to get out of this damn room. Air... Air would be good!

"Why don't we step outside? Have you seen the backyard yet?" Only pausing long enough to see her give a slight shake of her head, Christian took four quick steps and pulled open the door. "Great... You'll love it! It has a nice patio, tons of space, flowers... " *And some much needed fresh air*, Christian thought as he stepped out into the hall.

†

Ella trailed behind Christian as she followed him through the house to the back porch. It was a warm afternoon and, although she hadn't realized it, the fresh air *was* a welcoming feeling. Smiling slightly, she glanced around, delighted to find several gorgeous rose bushes surrounding the yard, each one filled with rich, red roses. Christian had been right. She loved it.

Turning towards him, she stopped short. He was standing on the edge of the porch, gazing up at the sky, a look of worry etched on his face. Maybe she should have waited to ask him about the book. Ever since he had stepped into the library and saw her holding it, she knew he had been looking at it in her hands. There were just so many questions. And, although she really didn't know him, Ella felt he would tell her the truth.

Spotting a comfortable chair, she walked over and settled down in it. Curling her legs beneath her, she waited patiently for Christian to turn around. Ella knew she had brought up something he may not be ready to talk about, but she couldn't shake this sudden feeling of urgency. There were things going on she needed to know about.

Looking down at the book in her hands, she slowly opened the cover. Flipping past the title page and the table of contents, she came to the first entry concerning the Guardians themselves. Being so out of practice with reading Latin, she slowly began to decipher the first couple of entries. Ella became so involved with it, she wasn't aware that Christian had turned around.

Feeling herself being watched, Ella glanced up at him. A deep frown marred his handsome features. She felt restless as she waited for him to say something...anything. Finally, she heard him sigh.

"I don't really know where to begin," Christian said, his voice strained.

Blinking, Ella looked down at the book in her hands, slowly closing it. "I just want to know what's going on." Shaking her head, she got up, leaving the book on the chair, and walked over to the closest rose bush. "I mean, a couple months ago, things were so normal. Well, as normal as they can be for me. I got up every day, took care of my cat, went to work, then went back home. Suddenly, people start vanishing, then I meet you..." Glancing over at him, she felt her pulse quicken. "You have *wings,* Christian!"

He turned his head away from her. Ella could see the muscles in his cheeks tighten as he clenched his jaw. "Listen, Ella, there really isn't any easy way for me to explain this. I mean... "

She waited as he paused and ran a hand through his hair. *Why doesn't he just say it?* she wondered. Her need for answers was causing her frustration to grow. She watched Christian begin to slowly shake his head. Immediately, Ella got the feeling he was going to change his mind and decide not to tell her anything. She could almost feel the nervous energy flowing off of him, his eyes flashing as he gazed out over the yard. Looking towards the ground, he let out a low sigh.

No, you don't, Ella thought, clenching her fists.

Determined to get the answers she needed, Ella straightened her shoulders and, turning to face him, cleared her throat. "Listen, Christian–"

Suddenly, the side door flew open, banging against the side of the house. "What the hell's going on out here?"

Spinning around, Ella found a very aggravated Cyrus standing in the doorway, his coal black eyes glinting in the light as he looked back and forth between her and Christian. Finally, his glare landed firmly on Christian. Ella could swear she saw something move beneath his skin. She narrowed her eyes but, whatever she had seen or thought she saw, was gone.

"Nothing," Christian snapped as he looked back out towards the yard, his own blue eyes glinting in the sunlight.

"Nothing? From my *room*, I could feel the emotions rolling off you like a tidal wave!" Cyrus took a step out of the doorway and glared at Christian. "I don't know what the hell's going on, but you need to get yourself under control."

"You're overreacting, Cyrus! I'm fine," Christian growled, running a hand through his hair.

Ella glanced between the two men, feeling she needed to say something, but not sure exactly what.

"Overreacting, my ass. Your vibes are off the chart, and you need to get a handle on it." Cyrus shook his head, then looked over at Ella. His glare was so intense, she unconsciously took a step back.

"We...we were just talking," she stammered, staring back at him. Cyrus was an imposing man and the irritation coming off him was unnerving. "I mean, I just wanted to know..." At a sudden loss for words, she looked anxiously at Christian.

"Wanted to know what?" Cyrus cut in, his eyes narrowing as she spun her gaze back towards him. "What could you *possibly* want to know that would cause him to...?" His voice trailed off as he glanced down at the chair.

Ella's eyes went wide. She watched Cyrus reach down to pick up the book. Christian had turned back towards them and let out a low moan. Cyrus looked again between the two of them and then, waving the book in the air, turned to Christian.

"What the hell is this doing out here? Please tell me you didn't let this girl look through it, Christian." Cyrus waved his free hand over towards Ella as he continued in a rush, "This is not for anyone outside this house and you know it. It doesn't matter that she can't read it! You...shouldn't...have...this...out...here!"

"This girl?" Ella exclaimed, feeling her cheeks redden. She was about to go into a tangent of her own when Christian answered, as if she hadn't said anything at all.

"For your information, I didn't show her anything. She found it on her own. I would never just bring this book out to show anyone."

"How the hell did she find it then?"

"How do you think she fucking found it? She went into the library and found it on her own."

"Well, why is it out here?" Cyrus waved the book in Christian's face. "Why didn't you take it from her?"

By now, their voices were both filled with anger, and Ella could feel her body beginning to shake as the negativity swirled around her. Taking a couple steps back, she reached out to lean against a nearby pole. Drops of sweat had begun to make trails down her back and neck as she attempted to calm her chaotic nerves. Their arguing grew even more intense as she watched the two brothers get into each other's faces.

"You know what? Why don't you go back inside and mind your own damn business!" Christian hissed into Cyrus' face. "Did you ever stop to think maybe this doesn't concern you?"

"Anything that happens with *any* of you concerns me! The sooner you get that through your thick skull, the better!" Cyrus yelled back. "And no, I'm not going to mind my own business because whatever is going on out here has you completely off-kilter!" Taking another step towards Christian, he shook his head. "I don't know what the hell has been wrong with you lately, whether it's this girl or something else, but this keeping to yourself and handling shit on your own needs to stop!"

"Get out of my face," Christian warned. Ella heard the growl in his voice as his eyes narrowed at Cyrus. The air began to vibrate around them, and Ella had to gasp as she fought to pull in a breath.

"Or what? What the hell are you going to do?" Cyrus' own eyes narrowed as he tossed the journal back onto the chair. "You want to fight?" His hands forming into tight fists, he grinned at Christian. "Come on then...

Ella watched Christian's chest heave as he sucked in air, his eyes now glowing wildly. She shuddered as a blackness slowly began to swirl within them. Christian gave a slight roll of his shoulders and, as if sensing the move, she saw Cyrus lean down a little, like a cat ready to pounce.

This was all getting to be too much for her. The air was so thick around them, Ella was having trouble breathing. Her body suddenly stilled as she felt tension beginning to build within her. Shaking her head, she tried to yell for them to stop, but no sound came out. Gripping the pole tighter, her vision wavered, then everything around her turned red. Blinking several times, she opened her mouth to yell, scream, something, but it was like any sound she tried to make was trapped within her. Ella's mind screamed for help as the tension within her grew, building to the point of being painful.

The boys were now inches from each other. A definite shifting had begun beneath Christian's shirt, and Cyrus' skin had begun to take on a soft glow. His veins were visible, flowing like neon strips beneath his skin. She watched as a blackness began to build behind Cyrus, as if he was calling on the shadows. If her world wasn't going on a sudden downhill slide, she would be in awe of what was taking place before her.

Ella suddenly buckled as the pressure in her caused her muscles to spasm. Her vision blurred in and out, continuing to hold a red hue. Her insides began to feel like they were going to explode. She pressed her hands into her abdomen as she tried to will the pain away. *Oh, make it stop. Please, make it stop!* she cried silently.

Suddenly, just as Ella saw Christian make a move towards Cyrus, she felt the pressure within her release. A scream finally escaped her lips, and she felt the air around her shudder. The sound of glass breaking and yelling meet her ears as she fell to the ground. She could feel her heartbeat begin to slow as her lungs pulled in the air she had been needing so badly.

Blinking, Ella slowly realized her vision had now cleared and Christian was standing over her. All the anger in his eyes was gone, replaced by uncertainty and concern.

Ella wanted to ask what had happened. She wanted to know what glass had broken, and about the pressure she had felt within her. How and why had her vision gone red? But as she opened her mouth, she felt her head get heavy. For the second time in only a few days, she passed out.

Chapter 18

A moan escaped his lips as Andras felt the air around him shudder. Closing his eyes, he breathed in deep and smiled. He could feel the wave of energy that had burst from Ella just minutes ago still vibrating through the air. She was so powerful. At the thought of all that power, Andras felt a thrill go through his very core. He needed to own her, to control every part of her. She would be his!

Opening his eyes, he looked out over the crumpled buildings that surrounded him. All of them were old and weathered, as though they had been built ages ago. However, the truth was they had always looked that way. Broken windows were surrounded by blackened bricks, most chipped and cracked around the edges. Beyond this tattered city were deserts and swamps, burnt forests and dried up fields...each inhabited by demons of one level or another.

All, though, were blanked by an ever-present red sky.

Looking up, Andras gazed upon the sky, much like he had done ever since he could remember. Its burning red glow was almost blinding to the eye. The harsh redness, with brilliant yellows and swirls of black, was constantly moving, as if the sky itself was on fire. This gave everything below an eerie red hue. He smiled as the images he had seen from Earth flashed through his mind. Images of Hell on fire, burning constantly and engulfing everything within it.

They weren't too far off, were they? he mused, looking back out over the city.

Andras wasn't really sure which level of demon dwelled within the lands beyond because he had never been past the ratty buildings within the city limits. He had never needed or wanted to venture out there. Demons of one level rarely, if ever, even thought to go where another level demon lived. It just wasn't something that was done. And, up until now, Andras had been perfectly fine in his office, holding command over his demons here as well as surveying the Shadow demons that were sent above.

Not anymore, though!

Now he wanted more... Hell, he wanted everything! He could taste the remnants of Ella's power still hanging in the air. If he could feel her power down there, he knew others did, too. Others who would also want to harness that power and use it for their own.

He needed to move fast.

Hearing heavy footsteps behind him, Andras looked over his shoulder and saw

Braktis. The demon stopped dead in his tracks and, standing perfectly still, tilted his head down, waiting for Andras to address him. With a last look at the sky, Andras turned, offering a small smile to the demon.

"Sir," Braktis said, his red eyes glinting as he raised them to meet Andras' gaze. "You wanted to see me."

"Yes, Braktis. I have recently heard from Castigo, who says he knows the location of two of the Guardians. And, although I am still not happy with your earlier defiance, I feel it is time to give you a second chance. I want you to join him. Aid him in whatever he needs."

"Of course, Andras. I shall leave right away. I will not disappoint you again!"

Andras nodded and stood there, watching Braktis as he disappeared into the building. After receiving the news from Castigo, he had immediately decided to send Braktis to aid him. There were four Guardians Castigo had gathered information on: Christian, Manuel, Nicholas, and Darren. Castigo had mentioned a fifth Guardian, Cyrus, but he didn't know much about the angel as of yet.

The information on the buildings had been very satisfactory. Andras felt he had found the building he wanted to put to use in the near future...once more of his demons could make it topside. Everything was starting to come together nicely. A smile tugged at his lips as he contemplated the future.

Andras turned back towards the city. Now the plan was for them to locate two of the Guardians and learn whatever they could from them. Of course, he knew that Castigo was only looking to watch them, learn what he could while keeping his distance, but Andras also knew how compulsive Braktis was. He would want to get any information he could out of the Guardians, especially since he was trying to redeem himself from his earlier failure. So, if all went well, he would have all the necessary information on the Guardians by day's end. Castigo had promised him as much. Andras, though, felt he would get more information concerning this little venture if Braktis were there. Castigo was always one to keep things to himself until it suited him. This time around, Andras couldn't take the chance of being left out of the loop...on any level.

This plan had to work so they would be able to move forward. It really was too early in this game of theirs to try and take them on, but, if one of the Guardians were to die during this little impromptu meeting... Well, as some of the humans like to say, *c'est la vie*!

Andras laughed softly to himself as he looked out over the city, his mind wandering back to Ella and what he would do with her once he had her.

Soon, he thought wistfully. *Very soon!*

†

Castigo leaned back against the cool brick wall. Reaching up, he ran a hand over his forehead. His fingers came away wet from the sweat that broke out after that sudden power surge had washed through the city. It had been intense! Glancing around him, he watched as cars passed by, and humans ran up and down the streets, completely unaware.

Just like rats, he thought with disgust. Reaching into his pocket for his cigarettes, Castigo shook his head. Who or what in the hell could have possibly given off that kind of power? It had shot through the air like a whip. A need to investigate washed over him. To have that kind of power, to get control of whoever harbored it, would be a solution to many of his problems.

But, like a good soldier, he knew that now was not the time. He needed to concentrate on the task at hand. He needed to prove to Andras that he could be trusted, that he would take care of what needed to be done...and, right now, they needed information.

All of this waiting was driving him crazy, though. However, if what he heard was true, he shouldn't have to wait much longer.

Over the past few days, he had been gathering quite a bit of information on the Guardians. Finding out information on four of the five had been easy. Anything beyond that had become a real pain in the ass. Information on the fifth Guardian was definitely turning out to be harder to find. Sure, he had heard whispers from some of the Shadows about the scarred Guardian, but nothing worth repeating. So, with little to no information on him, Castigo didn't know what to expect if or when he came across the male, which could turn into a big problem. Growling low at the thought, Castigo took out a cigarette and tapped it lightly on the case.

The information he had dug up on the buildings had been much easier. *If only everything could go so smoothly*, he thought with a sigh.

Castigo had some decent information on the other four Guardians, but to get the real dirt, he was going to have to follow them, listen in on a conversation or two.

Any extra information would be great, especially since he was trying to get in good with Andras again. That bastard was harder to get close to than Lucifer himself. The last conversation he had with Andras, Castigo had received nothing but short responses. He knew Andras was happy with what he had found so far, but he could feel his boss no longer held him in his favor.

Such bullshit!

Castigo shook his head again as he lit his cigarette. Inhaling deep, he felt his lungs expand. He watched the grey smoke rise into the air as he released a breath. It swirled before him, twisting and twirling before disappearing into the air.

Seeing movement out of the corner of his eye, Castigo turned and, letting the rest of the smoke slowly roll from his lips, watched as Braktis walked his way, the demon's red eyes noticeable behind his darkly tinted sunglasses. Castigo barely held back a growl as he watched him get closer. *Ass is walking around like he is top dog*. Castigo couldn't wait to knock him down a notch...or six.

"Castigo," Braktis mumbled.

"Braktis. What the fuck are you doing here?" Castigo hissed, even though he was pretty sure he knew the answer. *Damn Andras!* he thought, waiting for Braktis to answer.

"Andras sent me," he responded with a frown. "Why the attitude? He said you found out some good info on the Guardians and asked me to come help you."

Realizing that Braktis wasn't aware he not only knew about what happened in the alley the other day, but had talked to Andras about it, caused Castigo to take a deep breath. "I know some information about them, yes. I am still working on it, though," he said, taking another long drag of his cigarette.

"Is that what you are doing now?"

Castigo's eyes narrowed as he heard the unmistakable hint of sarcasm in the demon's tone. "Yes, actually. I was able to find out that two of the Guardians will be in this area shortly, and I am waiting for them to show."

"And are you planning to just watch them...or are you going to actually talk to them?"

"I was planning on watching them. Why?"

"It is just... With two of us here now, I was thinking it may be quicker to get the information we need by getting it out of them."

"Oh, is that what you were thinking?" Castigo sneered. Although he did see the logic in it, the fact the idea came from Braktis made him want to tell the demon to piss off.

Then again... Castigo thought as he looked away from Braktis. *If I could get some solid information out of the Guardians, maybe even get some information on the sudden power spike, something Andras could really use, it would definitely help me get closer to him.* Just because Braktis thought of it didn't mean he was going to be the one to deliver the information. Hell, there was always the chance Braktis wouldn't make it out of this little meeting he wanted to have with the Guardians alive. Accidents did happen, after all. It would be like taking care of two birds with one stone...getting information to get back on Andras' good side, and getting Braktis out of the way.

Looking back at the demon, Castigo pulled his lips back in a sly smile. "Maybe you are right, Braktis. Maybe the best way to go about this is to confront them, get the information directly from their lips. Who knows? Maybe we can get some info for Andras on that female psychic while we are at it."

Braktis smirked. "Of course I am right, Castigo. Now, when are they supposed to show up?"

Castigo took another long drag off his cigarette as he stood there for a minute, quietly watching Braktis, eyeing him as he relished the plan forming in his mind. He stared for so long, he saw the other demon's smirk slowly begin to fade. Castigo couldn't help but snicker at Braktis' sudden discomfort. "Soon, Braktis... They will be here soon."

Chapter 19

"What the heck was that?" Nicholas asked, rubbing the back of his neck and shoulder. His tattoo was throbbing, sending wave after wave of shivers through his whole body. Nicholas gritted his teeth, trying to calm his nerves. He didn't need to look down to know his lightning bolt was glowing, and he was positive the clouds on his shoulder were now swirling around like some crazed storm. Tugging at his sleeves, Nicholas glanced over at Manuel.

"I don't know," Manuel responded. "But it was powerful, whatever it was, and it's still vibrating through the air."

"I haven't felt anything like that in... I don't know...ages." Nicholas shook his head as he looked around. They had just stopped downtown to get some things for the house when it had felt like a bomb had gone off. Leaning back against the truck, he could still feel his skin crawling from it. Thankfully, his tattoo had finally started to calm down. *And thank God for that*, he thought. The last thing either of them needed was for his little "gift" to start acting up. Things could have gotten really bad, really fast. There's nothing like a good lightning storm or tornado to really set the pace for the rest of the day. "Maybe we should head back to the house," Nicholas muttered as he mentally shook those thoughts from his head.

"Maybe... Maybe we should call... " Manuel's voice slowly trailed off. Nicholas turned towards Manuel and noticed his brother staring off towards the end of the street. Following his gaze, he spotted a shadowy figure walking towards a nearby alleyway. The figure was tall, even from this distance, and was sporting a rather impressively long trench coat.

"Who is that?" Nicholas asked quietly, watching the figure pause right before turning the corner. Hearing Manuel take a deep breath, he turned. Manuel stood there, perfectly still, taking in one deep breath after another. Nicholas watched as his brother tilted his head back and narrowed his eyes.

"Do you smell that?" Manuel asked, licking his lips.

Nicholas was about to say he didn't smell anything when the wind shifted. Curling his lips back, he let out a soft growl. Sulfur. He hated that smell. Once Nicholas got that smell in his nose, he could never seem to get rid of it. Unconsciously, he reached to his side where his bow and arrows should be, only to remember he had left them at the house. *The one time I don't have them!*

Letting out another growl, he turned towards the alley where the figure had disappeared. He was about to make a comment about the foul odor when another smell hit him. This one was sweet, but not in a conventional sense. It was more like the sweet smell that hangs in the air after someone uses an air freshener to try to cover up a stench.

"This is the same smell Christian and I came across the other night when we ran into that demon... The one who knew about Ella...about us," Manuel hissed out, making his way to the back of their Hummer, opening the hatch where he had stashed his blade.

"Shouldn't we call Darren and the others?"

"No! We need answers, and we need them now. We can't wait for the others." Manuel slammed the hatch shut and turned towards the alley, his sword glinting in the afternoon light.

"What if that demon was the source of the power surge we just felt?" Nicholas asked, mentally preparing for a confrontation. Although he may not agree with Manuel's need to rush in and get answers, there was no way he would allow his brother to go in alone.

"I don't think that was from him," Manuel said with a shake of his head. "What we just felt had a sense of purity to it. I don't know what it was, but it wasn't evil."

Nicholas stood there for a moment, watching as his brother took a couple more deep breaths. He could feel the ground beneath his feet shudder as his brother's eyes began to softly glow black, his own tattoo tingling in response. "Well, let's get goin' then!"

Manuel looked at him and, with the slightest nod, began moving towards the alley. Nicholas followed close behind, occasionally looking from side-to-side. He always felt where there was one demon, there was probably another, and the pressure running from his shoulder and down his arm was echoing his concern.

The closer they came to the alley, the stronger the stench got, until Nicholas was attempting to breathe through his mouth to stop himself from gagging. His throat burned from the effort.

As they came to the entrance to the alley, they both stopped and looked around. Listening for a moment, Nicholas was only able to make out a sharp hiss coming from within. The alley was rather long and, in the shadow of the surrounding buildings, it was hard to see to the very end. *Why does it always have to be an alley?* he thought with an internal groan.

"Let's go," Manuel whispered, slowly stepping into the alley. Nicholas let out the breath he had been holding and began to follow his brother, calling upon the shade. This encounter may turn into nothing or it may turn into a true battle. Either way, there was no need for any mortal to stumble upon them right now.

They walked cautiously down the center of the alley and, once they were a little more than halfway in, Nicholas was finally able to make out the figure in the trench coat.

The demon stood there staring at them, his red eyes glowing as he gave them a sly smile. His trench coat moved slightly as he shifted his weight.

"Well...well...well...," he murmured, looking from Manuel to Nicholas. "Look what we have here."

"We...?" Nicholas said as he felt a sudden rush of power come from behind them. His body tensed as he glanced over his shoulder. Trusting that Manuel would remain facing the one before them, Nicholas began to move. Turning, he came face to face with another demon. This one sported a set of chilling silver eyes.

"Yes... We!" the silver-eyed demon snarled.

"And you two high class, pieces-of-shit would be?" Manuel hissed.

"How rude of us," silver eyes said with a crooked smile. "My name is Castigo, and my friend over there is Braktis. We have been looking forward to meeting you."

"And why would that be?" Nicholas asked as he watched Castigo shift his weight. Castigo glanced to Manuel, then back. They stared at each other for a heartbeat before Nicholas let out a low growl. "Answer me, demon! Why would you be looking forward to meeting us? Do you even know who we are?"

"Oh, yes! We know quite a bit about you both," Castigo answered, taking a small step towards them. Nicholas watched as his silver eyes began to glow.

"If you really know anything about us, you know this is a bad idea. It's not like you can win this fight," Nicholas bit out.

Castigo smiled at him, slowly drawing a dagger from behind his back. Nicholas watched as the edge of the dagger flashed. It was an old weapon with a leather hilt, covered in ancient, demonic symbols telling a tale of death and destruction.

It was both beautiful and deadly, especially in the hands of a demon. It was the only weapon they knew of that could kill a Guardian... That was the rumor anyway. Whether it was true or not was a long-standing debate, but there was no way in hell Nicholas was going to let this demon get close enough to him or Manuel to find out.

"Do not look so worried, Guardian. I do not want to kill you...yet!" Castigo sneered.

This did not help to ease Nicholas' mind as he watched light glint off the blade. There had to be some way to get it away from him. The muscles in his back twitched as he stood there, deciding what to do next.

"What is it?" Manuel asked, never taking his eyes off of Braktis.

"He has the dagger," Nicholas replied through his teeth. He felt the pressure in his back begin to grow.

"What?" Manuel hissed, visibly tensing next to him. The ground gave a slight shudder beneath their feet. Nicholas turned his head slightly so he could see Manuel, still keeping Castigo in his sights. Manuel's eyes were glowing as he glared dangerously at the demon across from him. "This is not good," he whispered.

Nicholas couldn't agree more as he watched his brother roll one of his shoulders.

To bide some time, Nicholas put his attention back on Castigo. "So, if you're not here to kill us, what do you want?"

"Just to talk. I thought, with everything that has been happening, we should finally meet."

"Consider us acquainted. Now, what are you talking about?"

"Oh, do not act dumb, boy! Surely you did not think the bizarre disappearances were just a coincidence. "

"What? Are you telling us you two lowlifes are the cause?"

Castigo growled at him, losing his calm for a moment, before offering Nicholas another one of his sadistic smiles. "We *personally* were not the cause of them, no. But we are a part of the outcome of those lost souls. Such a shame the way they were removed from this world, too." His voice was dripping with mock sadness.

"Why those souls? What was so important about them?"

"They were special," Castigo stated simply. "They were meant for such greatness, such accomplishments. What they would have done..." Castigo placed a hand across his chest, his eyes glinting. "They were destined to save so many... It truly is a shame."

"What have you done?" Manuel whispered.

Nicholas heard Braktis give a light chuckle. "Oh, we haven't done anything...yet."

"You see, boys," Castigo said, "it *needed* to be those particular souls. They needed to have that extra spark to them, that extra hint of righteousness, to be of use for this particular...venture."

"And what venture would that be?" Nicholas asked as he felt a tingling in his fingers. His anxiety was growing.

"With each of these special souls removed from this tragic world, that veil you angels installed all those many years ago has begun to crumble." He snickered. "With each piece of the veil removed, we are able to travel a little farther into it. Now that the veil is almost completely down, well... Here we are." Castigo stretched his arms out to his side.

"What do you mean by the veil being almost down?" Manuel asked, his voice coming out strained. Nicholas glanced to the side and saw Manuel's body shaking slightly.

"How do you think we got here?!" Braktis spoke up. "Not that we are here just for you two, though. We do not need you thinking you are that important."

"Fine," Nicholas spat. "If you're not just here for us, what else are you here for?"

"Oh, there are many reasons for us to want to be here. In *this* instance, though, we are here for information."

"Information? On what?" Manuel growled.

"Who, Guardian. Did you not feel that power?" Castigo asked. Nicholas watched as he turned his head slightly, sniffing the air around him. "That power is part of the reason we are here or, more accurately, the *source* of that power. That power will help us not only tip the balance you Guardians have so annoyingly held, but take our claim on this wretched Earth once and for all."

"Why do you think we would know anything about the source of that power?" Nicholas asked.

Castigo shrugged, smirking. "Just a shot in the dark."

Nicholas stared at him for a minute. "Well, I hate to burst your bubble, but we have no idea. I wouldn't even know where to start..." He paused as an image of Ella flashed across his mind. He saw Castigo's eyes narrow and quickly finished his thought. "There's nobody here with that kind of juice."

"Maybe...maybe not," Castigo drawled. "But even if you don't know where that power surge came from, I'm betting you know where this other mystery person we're searching for is."

"Who?" Manuel asked over his shoulder.

"Oh, I think you know who I'm talking about, Manuel," Castigo sneered.

"Weren't you with her the other night? You know, when we had that little run-in?" Braktis chimed in. "Anyway, while I'm truly enjoying this little chat, I must insist we get to the point. Where are you keeping that pretty little female?"

"What female?" Nicholas asked. He stared at Castigo, seeing something pass over his face. Getting the sudden impression that Braktis had said too much, Nicholas narrowed his eyes. "Exactly who are you two looking for?"

Castigo glanced past him, Nicholas assumed at Braktis, before shaking his head. "Now that is the question."

"That's why I asked it."

"True," Castigo said with a smirk.

"Listen, we know it is Ella. Just like we both know she's with you, or you know where she is. So you can stop this evasive bullshit," Braktis hissed.

Nicholas tensed as another images of Ella went through his mind. *Damn!* He needed to let Christian and the rest of them know right away. Hearing Manuel let out a low growl meant he had just had the same thought. "Well, we don't know what you're talking about. Yes, I heard there was a girl in the alley the other night, but she took off."

"Yeah, she was in the alley one minute, then we turned around and she was gone," Manuel said. "Didn't think she was anything important so we didn't look for her."

"So," Nicholas chimed in, sliding his left foot back into a fighting stance, "if that's the information you were hoping to get out of us, I'm afraid you're shit out of luck."

"I figured you would say that," Castigo said. "That is why I pulled this little baby out." Waving the dagger in the air, his eyes flashed as he met Nicholas' stare. "A little persuasion to get the job done."

"You don't think we'll tell you whatever it is you want to know just by waving some little dagger around, do you? That we'll magically have the answers you're looking for?"

"Of course not, but this is not just... How did you put it? 'Some little dagger', is it?"

Nicholas watched as the light glinted off the dagger's sharp blade, almost blinding in its whiteness. One way or another, this was leading to a fight. *Guess I might as well get the party started*, he thought with a roll of his shoulders. Feeling the pressure begin to build, he let out a growl as he hunched his back, allowing his wings to rip through his skin in a flash. His black and red feathered wings curled around him, the tips brushing across the ground.

Nicholas heard Manuel echo his grunt as he allowed his own dark brown wings to flow out around him. Standing there, staring into Castigo's cool silver eyes, Nicholas felt his own eyes begin to glow.

"So... I guess we are done talking," Castigo said with a laugh.

Nicholas watched as his silver eyes glowed and a dark shadow began to spread from beneath him. Knowing Manuel was dealing with an equally threatening response from Braktis, Nicholas couldn't help but relish in the moment. They hadn't been able to fight like this in ages. Slowly smiling at Castigo, he began to feel a warmth growing inside him.

"Well, if I did not know any better, I would say you are enjoying this, my dear Nicholas," Castigo said, taking a step towards him. Crouching low, he held the dagger out, seemingly getting ready to attack. The shadow that had been growing from Castigo was now climbing up the alley walls and creeping towards where Nicholas stood.

"Oh yes, I am enjoying myself very much...although I'm afraid this will not be as fun for you," Nicholas sneered as he sent waves of his power out, sensing the air around him charge in response. He could feel his tattoo tingle as it came to life upon his skin, the clouds crawling across his back, the lightning burning with flashes of heat that traveled across his skin, feeding into his growing power.

"We will see, Nicholas. We will see," Castigo responded. "I am sure... " He paused as the sun became blocked by thick, angry clouds. Nicholas watched as he glanced up briefly before looking back at him, his eyes glinting. "Is this your doing, Nicholas?"

"Yes...," he whispered. "It's all me." He clenched his teeth, mentally reaching for the clouds. He could feel them in his mind, swirling around, lightning surging within them. Nicholas felt his anger building and, with a growl, pushed that anger into the clouds, feeding the air with his inner darkness. His wings rose above his head as he reached his hands into the air.

At the same instant Nicholas sensed the lightning building above them, he felt Manuel pushing his energy into the ground. The Earth beneath them began to growl as it shuddered violently. With a quick flick of his wings, Nicholas lifted into the air. Hovering above Castigo, he smiled, "Something tells me you don't know us as well as you think you do."

"We shall see!" Castigo yelled over the growing wind. He jerked his hand and Nicholas watched as the shadows began to reach towards him, seeming to take on a life of their own. They pulled away from the walls, beginning to break down from the pull of Manuel's anger. Looking at the shadows, Nicholas called to the air around him, instantly feeling the wind begin to blow, throwing debris through the air towards the shadows. As their attack slowed, he glanced back at Castigo. The smile on the demon's face faltered as Nicholas let out a howl of anger.

He could hear growls and grunts coming from behind him. Bursts of energy hit his back as Nicholas sent a quick glance over his shoulder. He saw Manuel crouched down, his dark wings glowing as they shivered around him. His power was coming off him in such violent waves, it shimmered through the air. Braktis was swirling his hands above his head as red balls of light flew towards Manuel, who threw his energy out before him, sending the red masses back towards the demon with such force, they exploded in mid-air.

Sensing movement, Nicholas turned just in time to see Castigo make his move. The demon jumped into the air, riding the shadows as he went. He moved quickly, soaring towards Nicholas with such speed, he almost didn't have time to react. Pulling his wings in, Nicholas lifted himself higher, mentally calling to the lightning above him.

The walls around Nicholas bowed out as he felt Manuel call to the Earth. A crack ripped through the wall to his right, the bricks beginning to crumble and give way. *He's going to bring the walls down around them*, he thought with a smirk, *and I'm going to light it up*!

With a last shudder of power, he felt a sudden release just as two bolts of lightning streaked down, scorching the ground in front of him. The power of them sent Castigo flying backwards, slamming into the wall behind him. He hit with such force, it caved in. Nicholas watched as he lost his grip on the dagger, sending it skidding off to the side. His eyes narrowed as Castigo began to pull himself up, his face contorting in anger as he snarled and growled. Nicholas continued to call the air, the wind forcing Castigo back as more lightning slashed its way to the ground.

Suddenly, a scream, mixed with anger and despair, cut through the air behind him. Nicholas knew it was Braktis because he felt wave after wave of Manuel's energy flowing around him, the walls themselves growling as they crumbled. The sound grew louder and louder until Nicholas couldn't hear the screams – then everything behind him became silent. Nicholas watched as Castigo's eyes widened for the briefest moment before he sent another sneer towards Nicholas. When his eyes darted to the right, Nicholas realized he was going to retrieve the dagger and felt a sense of urgency come over him.

"No, you don't...," Nicholas breathed out, sending all the power he had left towards Castigo. Lightning bolts lit up the alley as they struck repeatedly, chasing

Castigo further and further from the dagger.

Growling, he looked towards Nicholas. His short black hair ruffled in the wind as he narrowed his gaze, his silver eyes cutting into him. "This is not over!"

Nicholas moved towards him, pulling at the air, causing it to enclose them in an angry cyclone. "Oh yes, it is," he hissed, reaching towards the clouds, throwing his power into them. He held the demon's angry glare as he called to the lightning.

Castigo smiled and, just as the lightning reached the spot where he crouched, he vanished.

Nicholas landed next to the scorch mark, panting harshly, his body shivering. The air around him began to calm as he reined in his power, pulling it back into himself, concentrating on calming his nerves. Nicholas' wings curled slowly as, in a flash of light, they disappeared back into him.

He rose slowly, making his way to the dagger, finding it partially hidden by paper and dirt. The demonic markings on its hilt still held a soft glow as Castigo's power finally began to fade from it. Reaching for it, Nicholas felt a tingling run through him as his fingers wrapped around the hilt. Looking at the blade, he rested it against his forehead as he pulled in air through his teeth. *This could have gone so wrong!*

Hearing a grunt, Nicholas turned. Sliding the dagger into his belt, he began to make his way to Manuel. His brother was bent over, his hands on his knees, visibly shaking. Looking at Nicholas, Manuel gave a shake of his head. His wings were no longer out, and Nicholas could just make out a line of blood traveling down his arm.

"Are you okay, brother?" Nicholas asked, placing his hand on his back.

Manuel chuckled as he slowly straightened himself. "Never better," he groaned, glancing over his shoulder. Nicholas watched as his eyes fell to the hilt of the dagger. "How the fuck did that demon get his hands on that?"

"I don't know. I'm just glad I got it from him...even though the little bastard got away."

"I'm glad you got it, too...," Manuel said with grunt. He glanced behind him, Nicholas following his gaze to the shifting pile of rubble. Nicholas started to move forward, but Manuel held up his hand, stopping him.

He watched as his brother stepped forward, reaching to his back for his blade. It hissed through the air as he drew it. Hearing a growl, Nicholas glanced down. The air shivered just as the pile of bricks shook, then blew outward. They both threw their hands up, covering their heads.

"What the fuck?" Nicholas rasped as he glanced back towards where the pile had been, seeing an angry, bleeding, panting Braktis standing there.

"You really thought you could...," Braktis started. A sudden coughing attack interrupted him as he leaned over and spit blood onto the ground. Its black thickness hit the cement like tar, smelling like shit.

Nicholas felt his stomach roll.

"What? Kill you?" Manuel hissed, waving his sica through the air. His power moved through it, causing the sword to take on a golden glow.

Braktis' eyes widened as he glanced at it. He snarled as he began to move towards Manuel. "You will *not* win this!"

"Oh, I think we will," Manuel said with a smile. "Sadly, though, you won't be around to see it."

Braktis started to say something, but just as he opened his mouth, Manuel swung his short sword through the air, slicing cleanly through Braktis' neck, sending the demon's head flying into the wall, his body crumpling to the ground.

Looking down, Nicholas watched as more of the tar-like substance poured out of the body, spreading out across the ground. "Well, that's gross," he said.

Manuel nodded. Nicholas stood back as his brother crouched down by the body. He held his sica out to the side, black blood dripping off the edge. He could hear Manuel muttering under his breath, saying an ancient prayer to make sure Braktis was not only sent back where he was supposed to be, but banished from coming topside again!

The air shivered as black smoke engulfed the area before him. It became so thick, it was impossible to see the demon's body. It curled around itself before slamming back into the ground, taking any remnants of Braktis with it.

"I see you got yours," Nicholas said, glancing around the now empty alley.

"Yes...," Manuel breathed out, a slight smile playing across his lips as he slid his sica back into its sheath. "He put up a pretty good fight, but I got him."

"They weren't just here for us. They were here for Ella."

"I know. We need to tell Christian."

"Do you think that power, the energy we felt earlier, was her?"

"Yes, and she's in danger because of it. A power like that needs to be protected, nurtured. We can't let them get her."

"No, we can't... "

Quietly standing there, they stared at the spot where Braktis' body had been. The dust around the scattered debris was now settled, leaving a disturbing reminder of the fight that had just occurred.

Nicholas listened to the sounds of cars and people as they traveled past the alley. Thanks to him and his brothers' special "gift", the humans lived completely oblivious to the dangers occurring within their world. Looking towards Manuel, he met his tired stare.

With a sigh, he pulled out his phone. *Time to give everyone the good news.*

Chapter 20

"So tell me again, Castigo," Andras sneered, leaning forward in his chair. "How did you end up losing the dagger *and* getting Braktis sent to the Nether Realms all in one day?!"

Shit! Castigo shifted his weight as he stared down at the ground. He had decided to treat this situation like removing a Band-Aid. Just grit his teeth and rip it off. Unfortunately, the aftermath was getting worse and worse by the minute. "I did not *get* Braktis sent anywhere, Andras. One of the Guardians got the best of him. *They* sent him to the Nether Realms." Taking a deep breath, Castigo waited for Andras to respond. He knew his boss would be angry, but the look in Andras' eyes was telling him it went beyond anger.

"And my dagger?" Andras hissed out from between his teeth.

Castigo opened his mouth to respond, then closed it. Fucking Guardians! Everything had been going great until that little piss ant decided to start trying to throw him around like a fucking ragdoll. In a single moment, all hell had broken loose and the dagger had gone flying. Damn it! He knew that was the real source of Andras' anger, not the loss of Braktis. Sensing movement, Castigo glanced out of the corner of his eye, not daring to lift his head.

Double shit!

Agalon had silently moved up next to him. *Hadn't he been on the other side of the room?* He hadn't even heard the demon move. Castigo felt his stomach drop. Obviously, if he wasn't satisfied with his answer, Andras was preparing to have Agalon take him out. Sure, Andras could do it himself...Castigo had seen him take care of a "problem" demon more times than he wanted to recall...but he had a feeling Andras was going to enjoy watching Agalon work him over. *Maybe that will be better for me,* he thought. He definitely didn't want Andras to–

"Castigo?" Andras whispered, jerking Castigo from his thoughts.

"I will get your dagger back. It all just happened so fast. I...I will get it back for you," Castigo stammered. He hated coming across as weak, but he knew if he raised his voice or got angry, he wouldn't stand a chance. "I swear, Andras."

"Do not make a promise you may not be able to keep, Castigo."

"I will keep this promise. If I can find out where they are staying, I will be able to get it back." Castigo swallowed, his throat suddenly tight as he felt Andras' power starting to build around him.

"I am very disappointed in you, Castigo. And you *know* how I hate to be disappointed." Castigo felt his movement as he stood from his seat. Andras' power was moving with him when he came around the desk to stand right in front of Castigo. "I sent you both up there for very simple tasks. Obviously, I was wrong in my assumption you were capable of taking care of this. Was I wrong, Castigo?"

"No, sir. I got the information you asked for and..." Castigo paused as Andras' shiny dress shoes came into his vision. Licking his lips, he pressed on. "I not only found out the information you asked for, but I found out the female psychic *is* staying with the Guardians. I mean, they did not say it out loud but, by the way they reacted to my questions, I just know! I was going to press them to tell us, but their powers... They caught us off guard. It will not happen again."

"No, it will not," Andras hissed. He was close enough now that Castigo could feel his warm breath on his face. He wanted to step back, but he felt that showing more weakness than he already had would only anger Andras more. "I feel your time above has come to an end...for now. You will stay here for the time being."

"Yes, sir," he said, watching Andras' shoes move slightly. The thought that maybe Andras was going to let him off with just this warning was quickly squashed as he felt a sudden shift in his boss' power. It started off as just a prickling against his skin, like tiny needles repeatedly stabbing over every inch of his body.

With a rush, those needles quickly turned into knives. Stumbling backwards, he slammed into the wall. *No!* Taking in a deep breath, Castigo felt his muscles tense as Andras' power seared through his veins, the pain spreading like wildfire. The sound of tearing flesh reached his ears as his old wounds began to be ripped back open. Buckling over violently, Castigo felt his body shudder as wave after wave of Andras' power washed over him.

Sweat and blood began to pour steadily down his body as Castigo ground his teeth together. "Andras...please...," he gasped...or he thought he did. His mind was starting to become nothing more than a constant scream...or maybe he *was* screaming.

A roaring had begun in his ears as Castigo fell to the floor. Curling into the fetal position, he willed the pain to stop. Gashes, which had opened across his body, were pulsing. He could feel them growing wider, tearing deeper. A warm liquid began to trickle down his face, running over his lips and seeping into his mouth as he gasped for air. The strong metal taste of his own blood hit his tongue. He couldn't die like this! He just couldn't!

Just as it felt like his mind was going to break, the pain eased. It did not completely dissipate, but it eased enough that he could breathe once again. Gasping, Castigo looked up through a haze of bloody tears.

Andras sneered as he leaned over him, his multi-colored eyes glowing darkly against his pale skin. "Now, I expect you to remember this moment. Remember what you feel right now and *who* made you feel this way. Do not disappoint me again, Castigo."

"Yes, s-sir," Castigo stuttered, his body shuddering slightly as he tried to regain control of himself. The pain was still evident in every twitch of his muscles.

Closing his eyes, Castigo was only faintly aware of Andras telling Agalon to get him up, his body being partially lifted off the ground, and being roughly dragged from the room. There was no sense in pretending at this point. Pretending to be strong. Pretending not to feel the pain still coursing through his body. Just before he gave in to the numbness, Castigo swore to himself he would never again be on this end of Andras' anger.

Chapter 21

Ella let out a soft groan as she rolled onto her side. She waited for a headache to come, but all she felt was tired. Opening her eyes, Ella had to blink a couple times to clear her vision. Everything seemed blurred, fuzzy at the edges, and the room was a little too bright. Propping herself up on her elbow, she was finally able to make out what was around her. The familiar sight of the boys' living room came into view, along with a rather disheveled Christian.

"You're awake."

Meeting his gaze, she watched him let out a sigh. "What happened?" she asked in a shaky voice.

"Well... Which do you want to hear first? What I *know* happened, or what I *think* happened?"

"Let's start with what you know." Ella had a feeling she knew what he was going to say, but she needed to hear it out loud.

"Cyrus and I were arguing...loudly. When you screamed, I tried to get to you, but a wave of...of energy came off you and pushed me backwards, shattering all the glass behind Cyrus and me at the same time. By the time I got to you, you were lying on the ground. I guess you fell. I don't really know, but as I knelt down, you passed out."

"Glass broke? Because of me?" Her eyes were wide as she stared at Christian. *How could that be*? she thought, thinking over the events of the afternoon. She remembered being outside with Christian, asking him about the book she had found. He didn't seem very eager to talk about it, though... Then Cyrus had come out. Ella remembered him mentioning something about feeling Christian's vibes coming through the house. Shaking her head, she pulled herself up into a sitting position. "I remember you and Cyrus fighting..."

"We were arguing over the book you had found...our journal," Christian said, leaning forward in his seat.

"You were both so angry with each other, almost to the point of being violent, and..." Suddenly, images of Christian and Cyrus arguing flashed through her mind. She remembered the feeling of pressure that had begun to build up in her. She had tried to yell for them to stop, but she hadn't been able to get anything out. Sucking in a deep breath, Ella shuddered. "Okay. How about you tell me what you *think* just happened to me."

"Okay... I think you had a reaction to our arguing."

"A reaction?"

"Yes. I think something in you reacted to the...the negative energy in the air... Maybe drew it into you. When your inner core filled up with the energy, you released it back out, like in self defense. Since it's obviously never happened to you before, the shock to your system from that release made you pass out."

"How do you figure it was in self-defense?"

"You released the energy right when our argument was about to get ugly because I don't think you wanted that to happen."

Ella shook her head as she stared at him. Everything he just said to her made sense, but it still seemed so far-fetched. This couldn't be what her life consisted of now, could it? Filled with angels, demons, and strange supernatural powers... All of which seemed to cause her to want to pass out at every turn. Images from earlier continued to interrupt her thoughts, and each one came with a little more clarity. "I remember... I remember..."

"What do you remember, Ella? I need to know what happened so that we can help you."

"I remember feeling the pressure building inside me. It was a horrible feeling, one I couldn't seem to control or stop, and I tried to call out to you, but nothing would come out. Maybe I *was* pulling the energy in." Ella began to shiver as she thought back over that feeling. Looking down at her hands, she curled her shaking fingers into fists. Willing her head to clear, Ella continued in a whisper, "The pressure… It just kept building. I was so scared because I didn't understand what was happening. I still don't. Then the pressure just suddenly released, like a breath I was holding. I don't know how or even why, but it was just suddenly gone. What you said, what you thought happened, makes sense. It really does, but I still feel scared." She looked at Christian. Ella saw the concern on his face as he gazed quietly at her.

"Do you remember what happened once that pressure released?"

"I remember hearing the glass breaking, yelling, you leaning over me, then everything went black."

"Yes, that's when you passed out…"

"Well," Ella said with a sigh, "I hope that's not going to become a habit around you." She felt a slight heat in her cheeks as she watched Christian smirk at her.

"I hope not…" He paused, glancing over his shoulder.

Ella was just about to ask what was wrong when she saw Darren come around the corner. His deep sapphire eyes held her gaze as he walked over to her. Ella pulled her feet in so Darren could sit down on the edge of the couch. His broad shoulders and muscular frame took up her view as she watched him settle. "How are you feeling, Ella?" he asked, his eyes never leaving hers.

"A little confused, but I'm okay," she said, glancing at Christian. He just smiled at her reassuringly and leaned back in the chair.

"We were just going over what she remembered," he told his brother.

Ella watched the two exchange a look before turning back towards her. Glancing between them, she couldn't help but feel a tinge of unease pass through her. "What?" They looked at each other again. Ella let out an exasperated sigh as she waved her hand in the air. "What? What's with the looks?"

"It's just... That kind of power... It goes far beyond normal psychic abilities," Darren explained, calmly looking at her.

Ella chewed on her lip as she glanced back and forth between the two of them. They both seemed so calm, but she saw a bit of concern peeking through Christian's posture. "There was something in the journal about natural psychics. Do you think that's what I am?"

Darren glanced at Christian before answering. "We think there is a chance, but there hasn't been a natural psychic born in ages. That's because of many reasons, but mainly because it would take a human either sleeping with an angel or..." He paused, trying to gather his thoughts.

"Or being raped by a demon," Ella continued. She gave a slight shrug to her shoulders when Christian and Darren both turned to look at her, eyes wide.

"How did you know that?" Christian asked.

"Well... My grandma told me when she came to me in my vision."

"What vision?" Darren asked, leaning a little closer.

"Today, shortly after I started reading through your journal. One minute, I was sitting in your library; the next, I was in my grandma's." Ella shook her head as she thought back on it. "It was so real. I felt like she was right there with me. She passed away about five years ago. I've never had a vision like that before, but that's what it had to have been, right?"

"I'm so sorry," Christian murmured, seconded by Darren.

"Thank you," Ella said softly, watching Christian stand up and walk over to the window, which now had a plastic sheet covering it.

On the other hand, Darren was watching her very closely. Ella could almost see the wheels turning in his head as he thought over what she had just told them. "More than likely. What else did she tell you?"

"She told me she knew what was going on right away because of how my mom, a complete stranger to her at the time, had shown up at her house."

"So your grandma isn't your family through blood?" Christian asked over his shoulder, leaning against the windowpane.

"No," Ella answered, suddenly finding herself considering just how much to tell them. "My mother took off when I was born, leaving me there. Ever since I could talk, I called her my grandma. She's the only family I've ever known." Pausing, Ella sucked in a deep breath as some of her buried emotions threatened to surface. This was going to be harder to talk about than she had thought. Her grandma's voice telling her to trust them echoed through her head as she looked between the two men in front of her. "She was all the family I needed, teaching me everything I needed to know. It seems she was teaching me things I didn't even know I would need." She laughed a little.

"What did she tell you about your mom?" Darren asked softly.

"Just that a woman showed up at her house one night in pretty bad shape. My grandma said she instantly knew what had happened to the woman. When she found out she was pregnant, the woman wanted to get rid of the baby, but my grandma convinced her to carry me to term and told my mother she would take care of me." Ella smiled slightly at Darren. "She left shortly after I was born."

Hearing a soft growl, Ella turned and found Christian staring at her. His eyes were filled with a quiet anger, and he kept shuffling his feet, like he wanted to move towards her. Ella watched as he finally decided against it and just gave a sharp shake of his head. "How could she just leave you?"

Sighing, Ella tilted her head a bit, gazing back at him. "I don't know, Christian. That's a question I asked myself over and over as I grew up. It's one I'll probably never know the answer to. My grandma gave me a good life, though, and I'm thankful for everything she did for me." Shaking her head, she glanced over towards Darren, then back at Christian. "Let's get back to what it says in that journal, hmm?"

She waited for Christian to respond. He seemed to want to ask her more questions, then thought better of it. Nodding slowly, he sighed. "So, what did your grandma have to say about...everything else?"

"She said she taught me Latin at such a young age because she knew I would need it. Well... She actually said she hadn't known for sure, seeing that the only way for all of my powers to truly wake up would be for me to come into contact with a supernatural being, but she had a feeling I might." Ella smiled, remembering, when she saw Christian for the first time. She leaned back against the arm of the sofa. Glancing down at her hands in her lap, Ella felt her cheeks start to get warm as she remembered looking at those insanely beautiful wings protruding proudly from his muscular back. Clearing her throat, she went on, "It seems that the powers in me, which had been dormant my whole life, are starting to make themselves known. I have to figure out how to control them before they start to control *me*. If I lose control of them, they could turn dark... Oh, and now that they're awake, other supernatural beings, like demons, are going to start looking for me. At least, that's what I got out of what she told me."

Christian shook his head. "No demon is going to be getting near you, that's for fuckin' sure."

Darren nodded, his eyes taking on a light glow. Ella felt herself smile. She was about to tell them that nothing in life was certain, something her grandma used to tell her all the time, when the front door burst open with such force, the pictures on the walls shook. Jumping, she glanced towards the hallway. Darren and Christian had both moved towards the center of the room, shielding her. She watched as their bodies tensed in anticipation, their hands balled tightly into fists. She saw Christian tilt his head slightly and, in an act that reminded her of an animal scenting the air, took in a deep breath. His shoulders suddenly relaxed as he glanced over at Darren. "It's Nicholas," he said, seconds before they heard Nicholas yell out.

"Hey, where is everyone?! And what the hell happened to the windows?! And why isn't anyone answering their phones?!"

"We're in the living room!" Christian yelled back.

Nicholas and Manuel came rushing into the room. Ella wrinkled her nose as a strong sulfur smell rushed over her. She noticed a look of disgust, then anger come over Christian and Darren as they both took in a deep breath.

"We didn't hear the phone ring. What happened? Manuel, you're bleeding. Are you okay?" Darren asked, his eyes flashing with concern.

"I'm fine. I got injured during the fight, but I'm already starting to heal."

"Fight? What in the hell happened?"

Nicholas shook his head, glancing towards Manuel. "We thought there was only one demon, so we followed him."

"Why didn't you call us?"

"That was *my* call," Manuel muttered, looking at Christian. "It was the same demon we confronted in the alley the other night."

Christian seemed completely taken aback as he stared at Manuel. "What did he say? Who is he? Did he give you his name?" The questions were leaving his mouth so fast, Ella was getting dizzy trying to keep track of them all.

"Just hold on, Christian. Let them talk," Darren whispered, never taking his eyes off his brothers.

Christian glanced over at her. "Ella, do you mind waiting in my room? We'll only be a minute."

Before she could object, Nicholas stepped forward, shaking his head. "This involves her, too."

"What?" Christian snarled.

Ella glanced over at Manuel and Nicholas. By the looks on their faces, whatever they had to say was not going to be good.

After a short pause, Manuel began to describe what happened. Ella listened intently as he described the smells that alerted him to the demon's presence, spotting him as he disappeared into the alley. When Nicholas started to talk about the second demon, Ella could feel her pulse beginning to quicken.

They were both taking turns, filling in details of their encounter. She listened closely as Manuel started to recount what the demon, Braktis, had said. Ella noticed that, throughout the conversation,

Christian would occasionally look her way. She couldn't tell if he was looking at her out of concern, curiosity, or both. *Probably curiosity*, she thought, glancing his way. She knew she'd seen concern in his eyes before he really knew her, but there were so many other things going on with which to be concerned. Then again, the guys were saying they thought the demons were looking for her...which made sense given what her grandma had told her.

"Are you sure Braktis is dead?" Christian asked, interrupting Ella's musings.

"Oh, yeah," Nicholas said with a smirk. "Manuel brought the walls down around him, then removed his head clean from his body. I'd say that's pretty dead."

"Wait," Ella broke in. "How do you kill a demon? Aren't they already dead?"

"Technically...," Christian said slowly. Ella turned and looked at him, her eyes narrowing in confusion. "When a demon comes to Earth, their body becomes vulnerable, like ours did when we...landed here. We can get injured and bleed, but it's tougher for us to die. The same goes for them. So when we 'kill' one of them, we are essentially sending their souls back to Hell."

"Can't they come back?"

"No," Manuel spoke up, drawing Ella's gaze away from Christian. "When they get sent back because of us, they get sent somewhere different." Shaking his head, Ella could see he was trying to figure out a way to explain. "Let's say you get into trouble, and the police...exile you to an island. You can't get off of that island and nobody can get to you. You're stuck there. That's kind of what happens to a demon when we kill them. They get sent back to Hell, yes, but they get sent to their own section of Hell, where they're stuck.

"The demons refer to this spot as the Nether Realm. It's a place they fear and want to avoid at all costs." Manuel shrugged. "They just kind of disappear. The only sure way for *us* to be killed, at least to our knowledge, would be to get stabbed by a cursed dagger."

"Yes, a very old dagger," Darren said slowly. "There hasn't been one of those daggers around since–"

"Today," Nicholas said with a sigh.

"What?" Darren and Christian said together, everyone turning towards Nicholas.

"One of the demons, Castigo, had a dagger."

"Why didn't you–" Christian started.

"I got it," Nicholas rushed out. Reaching around his back, he produced a large dagger, one unlike any Ella had ever seen. The leather handle was engraved with an inscription that seemed to take on a power all its own as it glowed in Nicholas' hand. He took a couple steps farther into the room, slowly handing the dagger to Darren.

She watched Darren look down at it, uncertainty clouding his eyes. "They were all supposed to have been destroyed. Did he say where he got it?"

"No."

"Did he say if this was the only one?" Christian asked, staring at the knife in Darren's hand.

"No," Nicholas said quietly. "I don't know if he has another one."

They all stayed quiet for a while, lost in thought over this unsettling news. On one hand, Ella was relieved Nicholas had been able to get the dagger away from Castigo, and that neither him nor Manuel had been hurt or killed in the process. On the other hand, the thought of there being another one out there, that she could possibly lose Christian or any of them, had her wanting to cry. She couldn't lose him after just founding.

"So if something were to happen to one of you, if you were to get stabbed by one of these cursed daggers..." Ella's voice trailed off as she glanced around the room, her eyes landing on Christian. "I mean, would you just disappear, too, never able to come back?"

Christian remained quiet as he looked at her. Ella saw a sadness pass through his eyes before he looked away. Hearing a soft sigh, she glanced towards Darren, who was steadily watching her.

"We don't know...," he whispered, his fingers absently smoothing over the gold cross around his neck. "None of us have ever had to deal with that before...but we believe it would be the same for us."

Chapter 22

Ella watched patiently as the light on her cell phone finally changed from red to green. She had been waiting for it to charge for a while as she sat quietly in Christian's room. She had gone out to her Jeep earlier to look for some items that had fallen out of her purse, but also to be alone and think for a bit. She was still shaken from early when she'd found out that not only were demons after her, but that they could possibly kill one of her... Her what?

She assumed she could consider them her friends. It seemed weird to call them her "acquaintances", or to refer to them as just some strangers. If she was being honest with herself, she felt more comfortable with these five men than she had been with anyone for a long time. *Except for maybe Cyrus*, she thought with a sigh.

Then there was Christian. A smile played across her lips at the mere thought of him. Every time she saw him, she felt a warmth growing within her, but her heart just wasn't sure what that warmth meant. *Can an angel even have feelings like that for a human*? Ella wondered as she looked at her phone on the nightstand.

After the conversation in the front room had grown uncomfortably quiet, she started looking for her phone. Nothing like some bad news sprinkled with a dash of more bad news to really darken the mood. She had used the need to find her phone as a reason to get up and, although she knew the boys all saw through her feeble excuse, none of them had questioned her sudden interest in her purse's contents...or lack thereof. After deciding the best place to continue searching was out in the Jeep, Ella headed outside and discovered that when the boys were bringing her unconscious self into their house, her purse had fallen over, cell phone conveniently landing beneath the passenger seat, where it had quickly died.

Bringing it inside, she had been relieved to learn that Christian had a charger that would work for her phone. *An angel with a cell phone...*, she thought with a small laugh. *Who would have thought*? Sighing, she sat up on the bed, scooting back to rest against the headboard and pillows.

Reaching over, Ella turned her phone on, watching the screen light up with bright swirls before it quickly began to beep at her, one notice after another displayed across the screen.

"Five emails, three text messages, and two voicemails," she muttered.

"Sounds like a version of 'Twelve Days of Christmas'."

Sifting through her emails, which didn't take much time, she found the usual – junk. The text messages were all from Cindy, mainly asking what was going on, wanting info on who Christian was, and saying that Holly missed her. With a smile at the obvious concern, Ella quickly sent a text back to let her know she was okay. She promised to call her soon, thanking her again for checking on Holly. Thinking of the little furball, she decided she was going to need to go home soon because she really missed her.

Not waiting for a reply, Ella clicked through a couple screens and dialed her voicemails. The first one was from Cindy, letting her know she had picked up a case and, with any hope, would be able to save the business. Although Ella still had her doubts, she hoped everything would work out. Cindy went on to chat a little about friendly gossip, ending by saying she missed her and hoped everything was okay.

After deciding to save the voicemail to listen to again later, Ella waited for the second message to start. She released a soft gasp when she heard Father James' voice.

"Ella... It's Father James. It's been a while since I've seen you at church and I...I just wanted to check up on you. If you could, call me when you get a chance. I

would really like it if we could meet up and talk. We used to have such great conversations. I know things in your life got hectic after your grandmother passed, but I would sure like to see you. Call me."

Ella sat there and listened to the message a couple times. It was true that Father James had always been there for her when she had needed a friend, but this was the first time he had reached out to her. Ella's grandma had instilled in her the importance of faith and trust. When Ella was young, she began to take her to church, and Ella had always felt safe and calm there. After meeting Father James, Ella had latched onto him like a Grandfather, someone else in her life she could trust. After her grandma had passed, though, Ella had distanced herself from the church...and Father James. Feeling guilty for not visiting, she immediately began to dial him back.

After several rings, she heard the familiar voice come over the line.

"Hello. This is Father James."

"Hi, Father. It's Ella."

"Ella! How are you, child? It has been far too long."

"I'm fine, Father," Ella said, glancing around Christian's room, releasing a soft sigh. "Just busy. I'm, um...I'm sorry it's been so long. Once grandma passed–"

"There's nothing to apologize for, Ella. I'm just glad you returned my call." Ella could hear his voice quiver a bit.

"Is everything okay, Father?"

"Of course," he quickly replied, clearing his throat a bit. "It's just nice to hear from you."

"It's nice to hear from you, too."

"We have so much catching up to do. However, I'm afraid I was on my way out. Would you be able to meet up with me tomorrow perhaps?"

"Tomorrow?" Ella repeated as she thought about everything that had been happening. She knew she had told Christian she would remain in the house until they figured out how to keep her safe, but surely none of the brothers would be opposed to her meeting up with Father James. It would only be for a little bit anyway.

"It would mean so much to me if you would," Father James said, cutting into her thoughts. "I know you are busy, as most young people are, but why not humor an old man?"

She could almost feel him smiling as he talked. Feeling a faint smile cross her own lips, she decided the guys would understand. "I would love to meet up with you for a bit tomorrow, Father."

"Oh, I'm so glad!" he stated, his voice filled with a mixture of happiness and what sounded to Ella like relief. That caught her a little off guard, but she shrugged it off, assuming it was from him not being sure she would want to meet him. After all, it had been a few years. "We should meet in the garden, by that lovely statue amongst the rose bushes. Do you remember the spot?"

Ella smiled. "Of course, Father. I think that is a great spot."

"Fantastic. How does noon sound?"

"That sounds good to me. I will see you then, Father."

"Yes, yes... In the garden..." She heard his voice quiver a bit. "I will see you then. Goodbye, Ella."

"Goodbye, Father," Ella said, hearing the line go dead. Hitting the END button, she paused for a minute. She felt a slight pressure begin to build within her chest. The thought of meeting with Father James should not bring on this kind of nervous feeling, this sense of uncertainty.

Rubbing her hand across her chest, she laughed at herself. Settling back on the bed, Ella took a couple deep breaths to calm her nerves. *There's no reason for me be nervous,* she thought, fiddling with her phone. She had known Father James for as long as she could remember, and they were meeting in the church gardens... What could go wrong?

Chapter 23

"You planning on going out to buy us a new set of dishes, brother?"

Christian sent a nasty look Nicholas' way as he slammed another dish into the dishwasher. Leaning back to the sink to grab another stack of dirty dishes, he let out a grunt. "Why are you sitting there anyway?"

"Because watching you is more entertaining than picking on Cyrus."

Christian rolled his eyes as he glanced back over his shoulder. "Right."

"Okay, picking on Cyrus is *really* entertaining, but I'm more interested in watching you abuse our plates right now. Plus, I have no idea where he is," he replied with a wide grin.

"I don't know how you can be so...so..." Christian waved one of his hands through the air, "so *you* with everything that's going on."

Nicholas just gave his usual shrug. "Look, what's happening is extremely...shitty, to put it mildly, but I have to have faith that we'll figure it out."

Christian just stared at him, watching his brother give another shrug. "Faith?"

"Yeah, faith," Nicholas said, leaning his elbows on the table. "Come on, Christian. You can't say you feel like all hope is lost. I mean, we've dealt with demons before." Christian opened his mouth, but Nicholas raised his hand. "I know these demons are different than the ones we've dealt with, but we will figure it out."

Christian slammed his mouth shut as he shook his head. Nicholas just didn't get it. Christian couldn't just relax or put faith in them figuring everything out. He just had too much to worry about, too many things that could go wrong if the demons got the upper-hand. Sure, Nicholas and Manuel had been lucky with Braktis and Castigo. Nicholas getting that dagger away from Castigo was a blessing, but he had been lucky. If that dagger had pierced his heart... Well, Christian didn't want to think about that. So much was riding on them getting *lucky*, just like he and Manuel had been that night in the alley, but what if they weren't so lucky next time?

Then there was Ella. He had a connection to her that he just couldn't explain, and when he had learned the demons were after her, it took everything he had to not lose his shit right there. He felt like everything around him was spinning out of control and he couldn't stop it.

"How am I going to protect her?" Christian whispered to no one in particular. He heard Nicholas scoot his chair back.

"Christian, I know that Ella means something to you. I can see it in your eyes every time you look at her and, even if I didn't know anything else about her, that right there is enough for me to want to protect her." Nicholas paused as he came to stand right next to Christian. "We *will* protect her."

Christian turned slightly to get a better look at Nicholas. He wished he had even a drop of his confidence in the matter. He knew he was capable of protecting Ella, protecting his brothers, but there were just so many things that could go wrong. So many different variables. No matter how he looked at it, he couldn't see a light at the end. Was feeling like this helping, though? Would it really hurt to feel hopeful, to believe things would work out? Taking a deep breath, Christian realized maybe Nicholas was right. Maybe he just needed to put a little faith in them and their abilities to handle tough situations, beat the odds...even against the unknown. Yes, he needed this. If he didn't believe they could win, that he could protect Ella, he was going to go mad.

Nicholas must have seen a change come over him because he nodded his head and opened his mouth to say something, stopping and looking towards the kitchen entrance. Christian heard the footsteps and also turned to watch Cyrus come sauntering into the room.

He paused for a minute before continuing into the room, a slight frown on his face. "What have I missed?" Cyrus asked, reaching over and snatching an apple out of the basket on the counter.

Not bothering to answer his question, Nicholas folded his arms across his chest and gave a huff. "Where the hell have you been?"

Christian just stared at Cyrus, his brother's coal black eyes scanning Nicholas, then slowly sliding back to him. "I was out blowing off some steam," he casually responded. "I'm not sure if you noticed, but there was quite a scene here a while ago. I needed to go and clear my head."

Christian saw Nicholas start to send a nasty remark back to him, one he was sure was going to start an argument, but he raised his hand to silence him. "There was an incident," he simply said. Christian knew Cyrus was not one with whom to mince words so, after getting his full attention, he told him about what had happened. Cyrus listened intently and, after Christian was done talking, just quietly stood there, rolling the apple from one hand to the other.

Finally, after some time, he nodded his head. "What's the plan then?"

"Well, Manuel is going to do some more research, and the rest of us are planning on going out hunting," Christian said with a slight smile. "Care to join?"

Taking a bite of the apple, Cyrus smiled darkly as he finished chewing. "So let me get this straight. You want me to join you all in a hunt for a demon we don't know a thing about, have no idea where to even look, and could very well end up injured or killed if we find him."

"Yup," Nicholas said with a grin.

"Well, since you asked so nicely..." He grunted as he began to head back out of the kitchen. "When do we start?"

Christian smiled and gave off a soft chuckle. "Tomorrow morning. I want to get an early start to see what we can find."

"Cool. What's Ella going to be doing?"

"I asked her to stay in the house until we figure things out."

Cyrus paused and glanced over his shoulder, his black eyes twinkling with amusement. "And, how did our little Ella take this request?"

"She was fine with–" Christian started, only to get interrupted by Nicholas.

"Yeah, she was after a while. At first, though, you'd have thought Christian had just told her she would never see the light of day again." Nicholas laughed.

Christian's eyes narrowed, and Cyrus began to laugh softly. "She'll be fine," Christian grunted, turning back to the sink. This, of course, only caused Cyrus to laugh harder.

"Of course she will, brother...," Cyrus said. Christian could still hear the humor in his brother's tone, but chose to ignore it. He was still looking away when he heard Cyrus clear his throat to try to cover his laughter, promising to see them in the morning.

Not turning around, but still giving a quick nod of his head, Christian put the last dish into the dishwasher. Glancing over, he found Nicholas still standing there, grinning. "What?" Christian mumbled, reaching for a dry towel.

"Why don't you go see her?"

Christian just blinked at him a couple times. He had been thinking along those same lines, but still... "See whom?"

"The queen of Sheba," Nicholas said sarcastically. "Ella... Go and see Ella."

Christian sighed, throwing the towel back on the counter. "She said she was going back to the room to charge her phone and check her messages."

"So?"

"Well... She's busy," Christian muttered, turning his head sharply as he heard Nicholas groan in response. "What?"

"Just go back and check on her. I know you want to see her, so just go." Nicholas turned his head to the side as he smiled. "Anyway, she seemed a little shaken up when she learned we can be killed. Plus, with all her psychic gifts developing, and the demons being after her..." His voice trailed off, leaving Christian to just stare at him impatiently.

"And? What are you getting at, Nicholas?"

"It's just... I'm sure she wouldn't be opposed to a little...distraction," Nicholas said, his red eyes lighting up. "Having help to get her mind off things."

Christian let out a low growl. "I doubt that."

"Oh, ye of little faith!" Nicholas said with a click of his tongue. "Just go talk to her. She's probably lonely being in a strange house, surrounded by strangers..."

"What has you so concerned for her all of a sudden?"

"I know she's important to you. Anyway, she's nice. She laughs at my jokes," Nicholas said with a smile. Christian saw the warmth in his eyes and had to smile back.

"But–"

"Go, Christian! For the love of..." Nicholas let out a low laugh and waved his hand around. "Look, I know you want to know more about her. When she's not looking at you, I see you trying to figure her out. Plus, I know you're drawn to her, so just go."

Christian stared at him for a minute, wondering how Nicholas could possibly know any of that seeing as he hadn't mentioned anything. He *did* want to see her. Hell, whenever he was away from her for even a short amount of time, a need to see her would wash over him. Since he didn't feel she had the slightest clue about his feelings, or had any towards him, Christian didn't really see the point in even trying.

On top of all that, he was an angel, for Heaven's sake. A fallen one, yes, but still an angel. Were they even supposed to be drawn to a human female? He was sure it was written somewhere that this wasn't supposed to happen. Christian had gone through his share of female lovers, but none of them had affected him like this, made him really feel anything. Before he and his brothers were cast down, he had heard rumors of angels sleeping with human females, falling in love with them, staying with them, but those had just been rumors, right?

He should just tell Nicholas to mind his own business, go pour himself some whiskey, and call it a night. Then again, would it really hurt anything to just go see how she was? If worse comes to worse, he just wouldn't have to see her again after she was able to leave. Since this would probably be the case, he would just not let her in, not let her really get to him. That could work. *But, what if she* does *like me*? he thought. Could he, like the angels he'd heard rumors of, be with her?

Nicholas, as if reading his mind, just nodded.

Frowning at him, Christian made up his mind and, turning, began to make his way towards his room. Not really knowing what he was going to do when he got there, Christian found himself slowing down the closer he got. He could see the faint glow emitting from around the door frame, and he could hear a soft clicking sound as Ella went through her phone. Walking up to the door, he paused, his hand hovering over the doorknob, again questioning himself on just what he was doing. He had never been the indecisive type, so the inability to make up his mind was grating on him. Christian knew this stemmed from Ella. He just didn't know why.

Pulling his hand back, Christian heard Ella let out a soft sigh. To his ears, that one sigh held all her frustrations, fears, and doubts. Leaning his head against the door, Christian just listened. Ella's breathing was slow and steady, and he could hear the sheets rustle as she made herself comfortable on the bed...*his* bed.

Closing his eyes he could picture her running her fingers through her hair, curling into the covers, burying her face into his pillows. Licking his lips, Christian placed his hand quietly on the door's smooth wood frame, feeling the warmth coming from within the room. His fingertips tingled with the need to open the door. After another moment's hesitation, he lifted his hand and gave a light tap.

"Yes?" Ella asked. Christian could hear the uncertainty in her voice.

"It's Christian. Can I come in?"

"Um, yeah... Come in."

Christian slowly reached down and opened the door. Stepping in, he noticed Ella had pulled herself up and was sitting on the edge of the bed. She was eyeing him curiously as he stood in the doorway. Taking a deep breath, he stepped into the room, quietly closing the door behind him. He was instantly stunned when he realized Ella was wearing one of his favorite t-shirts. His heart began to beat rapidly as he watched the material move across her chest when she took in a deep breath. His eyes, probably lingered longer than they should have because Ella suddenly shifted under his intense stare.

Giving his head a little shake, he tore his eyes from her chest and forced them back up to meet her eyes. "H...How are you?"

"I'm okay."

He looked at her, raising an eyebrow as he tried to figure out if she was telling the truth or just telling him what she thought he wanted to hear.

"Really, Christian," Ella said, brushing a strand of hair behind her ear. "I'm fine."

Christian watched her fingers shake slightly as she rested her hand back onto the bed next to her. Ella's body shuddered as she released the breath she had been holding. The air in the room became warm as he stood there. He could feel her emotions, even from across the room, as they rushed over him.

Christian licked his lips as he glanced at the door, then back at her. His eyes closed slightly as he breathed in her scent. Christian could smell the vanilla from her lotion lingering in the air, and he savored it as he took in one deep breath after another. His senses were becoming more and more heightened as he stood there and, feeling a slight tingle in his fingers, he unconsciously began to rub his hands against his jeans.

"Christian?"

Shaking his head, he blinked several times as he looked back at her. Ella was sitting there, leaning forward slightly. He could tell she had been watching him and, by the slowly deepening shade of pink on her cheeks, he knew she had an idea of what he was feeling. Clearing his throat, he took a couple steps closer to the bed. "I just wanted to come check on you, make sure you were doing okay. I know this has been a lot to take in."

Ella chuckled as he watched her eyes sweep around the room. "A lot to take in... That may be the understatement of the year."

"I was just..." He paused, looking down at the ground. "I don't know. I just figured if you needed anything...someone to talk to or sit with." Looking up, he met her gaze. "I want you to know I'm here for you." She was quiet for so long, Christian began to feel silly. *Nicholas was wrong*, he thought, watching her fidget with the sheet. He shouldn't have come in here. Turning towards the door, Christian let out a sigh. "Well... I'll let you get some rest." He reached for the doorknob.

"Can they find me?" Ella whispered.

"What?" he asked, turning back towards her.

"The demons... Can they find me here?" Ella asked, her voice shaking more and more with each word.

The fear radiating off her made him move away from the door, the need to pull her into his arms so overwhelming, it was making it hard to breathe. "No, I will not let them get you." Stopping at the foot of the bed, he reached down, running his fingertips along the edge. "I promise. I will keep you safe."

"Why?" she asked. "Why would you promise that? We hardly know each other."

Shaking his head, he walked around and gently sat on the bed. "We may not have known each other long, but I feel like I've always known you. I feel it here." Christian said, touching his chest. "I know you are a good person, Ella, a pure soul, and I refuse to sit back and do nothing, allowing you to fall victim to those demons." Christian felt his pulse speed up at the thought of them hurting her. He glanced down at his feet as he fought to calm himself. "I can't lose you to them...," his said, his voice dropping to just above a whisper.

Christian felt the bed dip a bit as Ella slid closer to him. Out of the corner of his eye, he saw her shake her head. "You're not going to lose me Christian," she whispered.

Christian closed his eyes as he felt Ella's fingers slowly slide down his spine.

Shivering, he pulled in a hiss of air through his teeth. *This is not a good idea!* With everything going on, he should be finding out information, concentrating on protecting Ella, not allowing her to get this close to him.

Shifting his weight, Christian leaned away from Ella, putting some space between them. He heard her let out a soft sigh as her hand fell back to her side. Christian instantly felt a loss from the disconnection and, looking up, he was not surprised to find Ella staring at him. "I should go...," he muttered, standing up.

"You don't have to..."

"No, I–I should go." Christian made his way to the door. Every cell in his body was screaming at him to go back, while his mind was telling him he was doing the right thing. He reached down to open the door.

"Okay," he heard Ella mutter behind him. "Thank you, though."

"For what?"

"For coming to check on me...for caring." He heard her voice quiver. "Nobody has ever promised to take care of me before."

Christian stood there, staring at the door. He could hear every breath she took, the sheets moving as she slid across the bed, the faint whisper as she placed her feet on the floor. Turning slowly, he found her standing by the bed. A shiver ran through him as he looked at her standing there in his t-shirt...and *only* his t-shirt. Her hair cascaded around her, framing and accenting her gorgeous face and slender neck.

The look in her eyes caused his knees to buckle, his legs threatening to give out from beneath him. His throat went dry as he watched one emotion after another swim through her beautiful honey-brown eyes. Needing...longing...trust... Watching her lightly bite her lip, he felt a warmth begin to grow within him. He gave a slight roll of his shoulders as he felt every muscle tighten with his own needs, his own wants.

Suddenly, as if his body had a mind all its own, he was across the room. Wrapping his arms around her, he pulled her body to his. She gasped as she curled her arms possessively around his neck. Every curve of her body fit perfectly against him.

"Christian...," she sighed.

He slid his hands down, wrapping them around her thighs as he lifted her up. With one smooth motion, he lay them both down on the bed. He felt a rush run through him as their lips finally met, her fingers running through his hair, pulling him closer. Christian could hear her heart speeding up as he took hold of her bottom lip, pulling it lightly between his teeth. In a sudden need to deepen their kiss, he ran his tongue over her already swollen lips, encouraging her. She parted her lips, allowing him the access his greedy tongue was longing for. Her arms wrapped around his neck again, urging him on.

Fighting his sudden need to devour her, Christian forced himself to pull back. They were both panting as they met each other's gaze. Christian felt his breath catch as he noticed a soft light shining within her pupils. The light began to grow, swirling slowly around. It moved over her irises until it was mixed within the natural color. They were hypnotizing. Christian couldn't take his eyes off them as they began to gradually pulse, seeming to match the pace of each of her shuddering breaths.

"You're eyes...," he whispered.

"What about them?" Ella panted, gazing up at him as she tilted her head.

"They're beautiful. *You're* beautiful."

Ella's eyes scrunched at the ends as she stared back at him, smiling. Staring down at those illuminating eyes, Christian got the feeling that if he allowed himself to, he could completely fall into their brilliant light.

Suddenly, Christian realized that falling into her was exactly what he wanted to do. And not just her eyes. He wanted all of her.

Smiling, he leaned back down, placing his lips hungrily upon hers. There was no more thinking, no more wondering if what they were doing was right. All that was there was the warmth engulfing them. It was this warmth that took hold of them, bringing their senses to new heights, causing their very being to crave more.

More caressing...

More kissing...

More shudders...

They fumbled with the other's clothes as they fought to keep their lips connected, only parting for the briefest moments when Christian had to fight to pull his t-shirt over Ella's head. She moaned from the loss of contact and, as soon as the shirt was thrown to the floor, Ella moved to him. He leaned down, kissing his way down her throat as he ran his hand over her bare chest. Christian's right hand gently played over one of her nipples, his mouth hungrily finding the other. He kneaded and teased until he felt her shivering beneath him. Each pass of his tongue over her brought gasps of pleasure from between her lips.

Christian pulled back when he felt her lightly push against his chest. With a single motion, he yanked his shirt over his head and dropped it to the floor. He closed his eyes as he felt her fingers travel down his chest, his muscles rippling under her touch, lightly tickling his sides as she ran her fingertips over his flat stomach. His teeth clenched when he felt Ella's fingers running along the top of his jeans, teasing as she made her way to his zipper.

A rush of air left him as Christian reached down to help her with her task. She looked up at him, her eyes glowing brighter than before. This time, he was sure his eyes matched her heated light. Pants finally off, he watched her eyes travel down his body, a smile playing upon her lips as she moaned her appreciation.

That one moan pushed Christian over the edge. He shifted slightly, placed his fingers along the sides of her black lace panties and, with one swift motion, yanked them off. Ella gasped as the cool air rolled over her skin. She watched as Christian's blue eyes devoured every inch of her, causing her skin to blush beneath his unwavering gaze.

Suddenly very aware of her lack of clothing, Ella moved to reach down to shield her most private parts...until she reeled from the feeling of Christian's hand gliding down her thigh. As he reached her center, Ella's head flew back, her breath instantly coming out in shudders as she silently willed him on.

Seeming to sense her growing need, Christian caressed and worshipped her until she was shuddering beyond her control, her fingers twisting in the sheets around her, her body arching into his hands.

Christian watched as Ella ran her right hand up and down her body, playing lightly with her nipples as she reveled in the feel of his intense playing. Slowly sliding a finger into her, he heard her let out a throaty moan. The warmth building in her was now visible to Christian not only by the wondrous sheen of sweat covering her body, but also by the glow that had begun to shine around her.

The light on the nightstand flickered as Christian heard her breathing change. He knew she was close and, as he leaned over her, he used his lips to capture the scream that erupted from her lungs as her climax raced through her body. Her lips quivered beneath his as he placed several slow, teasing kisses upon them.

He then moved to kiss along her jaw and neck as she lay beneath him, shuddering as wave after wave washed over her. Her eyes fluttered open and, still holding onto their steady glow, she looked up at him. Panting, Ella reached up and pulled his mouth to hers, wiggling beneath him, her body demanding more.

Positioning himself between her creamy thighs, Christian slowly began to enter her. She was so tight, he had to grit his teeth to keep from moving too fast. Ella's fingernails dug into his arms as she arched her back, pulling him farther into her. Once fully in, he began to move at a steady rhythm.

They slowly moved together, greedily taking in every shudder, every feel of their bodies against one another. Christian's body was now covered in the same sheen of sweat as hers, his back muscles straining as he began to pick up the pace. Ella locked her legs around him as she arched her back, encouraging him to thrust into her at such a pace, Christian was sure they would break the bed. All the lights in the room were flickering now as the very air around them pulsed. Her skin began to glow brightly beneath him, and he felt her power grow. Her fingers, running down his arm and chest, left his skin tingling. The feel was like nothing he'd ever known and he wanted more. He shuddered above her as he felt her power wash over him. The lights around them suddenly began to glow so bright, he was sure they were going to explode.

None of this startled Christian or Ella. All either of them knew was the sheer pleasure rolling over their bodies from each thrust of Christian's hips.

Ella ran her fingers down his body as she sought for something to hold onto. Finally putting them above her head, she curled her fingers around the edges of the pillows, pulling them closer to her head, turning her face into them. Moaning Christian's name, Ella's eyes closed as the heat between them began to build.

Christian jerked slightly as he felt himself nearing his peak. Gasping loudly, he fought to remain in control, demanding his body hold on until he knew she was ready. The bed shuddered beneath them as he looked down into her eyes. He watched her pupils grow wide as she stared back up at him. Biting her bottom lip, she groaned.

Ella moved beneath him, causing him to grind his teeth as he met each roll of her hips. Then, as her eyes widened and flashed a brilliant white, she gasped, "Now!"

With that one word, Christian grunted and drove into her. Two thrusts later, he felt her tighten around him. There was no covering her screams this time as she arched wildly into his body. Her climax riding her, Christian felt himself shudder violently from the sheer strength of his own. In that instance, he was dimly aware of her power washing over him, calling to him as it covered every inch of his being. And his own power answered back, surrounding her as a flash of light lit up the room.

Yelling out her name, Christian threw his head back as every one of his muscles tightened. Rolling his hips with one last grunt, he dropped his head.

Gasping for air, Christian felt the shudders begin to subside as he leaned over Ella, propping himself on his arms, attempting not to crush her. Blinking slowly, he watched as Ella smiled. Her skin, no longer glowing, held a faint pinkness. Her swollen lips slightly parted as she took in one deep breath after another. Groaning, Christian rolled onto his side, curling his arm beneath him, resting on the pillow. Turning her head, Ella ran her hand along his face.

"That was amazing," she whispered.

Christian smiled lazily at her. "*You* were amazing." Leaning forward, he placed a gentle kiss upon her lips. He heard her sigh and couldn't help but smile at the sound of satisfaction whispering from her every movement. Ella let out a small yawn as she curled onto her side, facing him. He watched as she fought to keep her eyes open. "Rest now, Ella."

Finally allowing her eyes to close, she reached up and took one of his hands in hers, curling her fingers around his. "You'll stay, won't you?"

Christian pulled her hand to his lips and, placing a kiss upon each of her fingers, smiled at her. "I will not leave you. I promise."

He stayed that way as he watched her body relax, her breathing steadily slowing as she began to drift off to sleep.

Christian marveled at her beauty. Every curve of her was sheer perfection. She had opened herself up to him tonight, allowed him to get closer to her than he had ever dreamed she would and, trusting him one step more, asked him to remain with her as she slept.

A feeling of protectiveness washed over him as he watched her lying there, so innocent and vulnerable. The warmth in him now, although not as wild as what he had felt while they were having sex, felt comforting and...right. Christian knew what he felt for her now wasn't going to go away, no matter how much he thought he would be able to just let her go. His heart whispered to him that would never happen.

He needed her in a way he'd never needed anyone else, even his brothers. They had a bond, and he basked in the feel. Christian's very soul sang from the joy, a feeling he hadn't felt in a very long time.

Watching her, he reached out and brushed a strand of hair behind her ear. "What have you done to me?" he whispered with a smile. She turned her head slightly into his hand before nestling back into the pillow. Reaching for her hand again, Christian brushed his thumb over hers. It was not until he was sure Ella was asleep that he allowed himself to begin to drift.

Murmuring a final promise to keep her safe and never leave her, Christian fell into a deep, relaxing sleep, his fingers still comfortably intertwined with hers.

Chapter 24

Ella stirred from her dreams. Stretching, she yawned lazily as she tried to figure out what had awakened her. The answer to that came suddenly as her thoughts were interrupted by a knocking at the door. Blinking a couple times, it took her a moment to remember where she was. Hearing a soft groan beside her, Ella felt a smile quickly spread across her face. Rolling over, she saw Christian still asleep on his back, an arm flung over his face.

She watched his chest move with every breath, her gaze wandering down to where the sheets were bunched across his waist, her eyes devouring every visible inch of him. Her cheeks flushed as the memories of her hands roaming over his warm skin flashed through her mind. Lying here now, though, the soft morning light filling into the room, Ella was able to truly enjoy him.

His skin was taut and firm, splayed over well-formed muscles. Her eyes slowly traveled up his prone form until finally landing back on his face, taking it all in as she mentally pinched herself.

Don't let this be a dream, she thought, biting her lip. That would just be too cruel. Last night had been amazing, better than she could have ever imagined, and the fact that she got to wake up with him lying next to her was mind-blowing.

Her thoughts were interrupted as yet another round of sharp knocks echoed through the room. Christian shifted next to her, raising his arm from his face. His blue eyes were hazy from sleep as he blinked rapidly. As he squinted a bit to adjust to the light, Ella watched him turn his head towards the clock and let out another groan.

"Christian! I can hear you moving around in there, brother! Come on. We have to go," a voice yelled through the closed door.

Ella stifled a laugh when she heard Christian begin to grumble to himself as he sat up, swinging his legs over the side of the bed. Rolling his shoulders, Ella heard his back give a couple soft pops as he slowly stretched.

"Morning," she murmured, reaching out to run her hand over his arm. He turned his head to look at her and she immediately saw a warmth chase away the irritation from his face.

"Good morning, darling," he purred. Twisting slightly, he leaned down, giving her a quick kiss before getting up, the muscles on his back rippling as he moved.

Ella felt her mouth go dry as her eyes swept hungrily from his shoulders to the sexy smoothness of his lower back. He was perfection. Christian must have felt Ella watching him because he looked over again, giving her a devilish smile as he leaned down to grab his jeans off the floor. "You keep looking at me like that, I won't be going anywhere."

"Maybe that's what I'm going for," Ella smiled and propped the pillow behind her so she could sit up. "Will you guys be gone long?"

"We should be back sometime this afternoon, unless we find something right away and need to get back here sooner. Also, Manuel is going to be doing research all day. If he finds something, we could be heading back here to meet up." He pulled a t-shirt over his head and glanced over at her. "I won't be more than a phone call away, though."

"I know," Ella said quietly, pulling the sheets up around her chest. "I just... I don't know. I'm just worried."

"Well, don't be. Why don't you just relax today, sleep in a bit, enjoy the quiet...?" He wiggled his eyebrows as he ran his tongue over his lips. "Maybe enjoy a nice bubble bath while you think about what we did last night, and imagine what I plan to do to you tonight."

Ella felt her cheeks heat up as she laughed. "You're so bad!" she joked, throwing one of the pillows at him.

"I'm bad?" Catching the pillow easily, Christian laughed and sent her a quick wink. It seemed he was about to say something else when more yelling was heard through the door.

"Christian, I know you two are...enjoying your afterglow and all..." This statement was followed by the sound of several male chuckles, "but the hour is getting late, and–"

"I'll be right out!" Christian bit out as he grabbed a gun holster from a trunk against the wall. Ella shook her head as she watched him check his gun before walking towards her. "Don't pay attention to them. They just want to give me a hard time."

"It's okay, Christian." Ella smiled as she leaned up to receive another quick kiss from him. "I'll see you when you get back."

"Call me if you need anything...anything at all."

"I will. I promise," she said, watching him send another smile over his shoulder. He stood there for a moment, looking at her. His eyes were filled with an emotion so pure, no words were needed. He quickly disappeared through the door, quietly closing it behind him.

Rubbing a hand over her face, she glanced over at the clock next to the bed. "8:30," she said with a yawn, slowly sinking back down into the bed. It was way too early for her to get up and start getting ready to meet Father James. Part of her had wanted to tell Christian she was going to step out for a bit, let him know where she was going, but she knew he would just worry. Curling on her side, she felt the wonderful soreness in her muscles, the kind of soreness one gets only from a good night of lovemaking. She smiled as she thought back over the night. Everything had been perfect. At first, she had feared he would just leave, that he didn't want to be with her the way she had wanted to be with him.

So when he not only turned back toward her but pulled her into his arms, Ella had thought she was going to faint...again!

Glancing at the clock again, she sighed. *A little longer, then I'll get up and get ready to go*, she thought. Turning her face into the pillow, she breathed in deep, inhaling Christian's musky scent. Images of the night ran through her mind as she slowly fell back to sleep.

Manuel sat in their home library, carefully going through some of their oldest books. The boys had left just a bit ago to see if they could find Castigo, and morale had been high. Christian had even stated, several times, that he was sure they would find something.

Manuel hoped they would, too. Not just for Christian's sake, but also for Ella's.

He laughed as he remembered the look on Christian's face when he had emerged from his bedroom. Getting up to look through the shelves again, Manuel couldn't help but smile. Christian had been so closed-mouthed on the subject and, no matter how much they all had given him a hard time, he had just smiled, telling them to mind their own business.

Of course, there was no guessing about what had happened last night. Shit, Manuel had needed to turn his IPod up as loud as it would go to drown out their moans. Not to mention the sudden power surge that flew through the house, causing the lights to go crazy. Manuel laughed again as he picked out another book from the shelf. Those two were definitely perfect for each other. He had never seen his brother so happy. Before Ella, Christian had been distancing himself. Manuel had been worried about him. Really worried. Now, with Ella in his life, he was beginning to act like himself again. As much of a pain in the ass that was, Manuel was thankful for it.

That power surge that had flown through the house, though... Not exactly a subtle occurrence. Manuel, like everyone else, had been aware of it. Hell, you would have had to have been dead not to! He could see the questions in his brothers' eyes as they watched Christian emerge from his bedroom, but they all seemed to have silently decided to leave it alone...for now.

Manuel had a feeling he had an idea what that surge had been about, but figured he'd wait until later to really look into it.

First things first, he thought, walking over to the couch. Several books were out on coffee table, all of them open to pages filled with demon history, natural psychic history, and prophecies.

Sitting down, Manuel began to pour over the multiple books.

Chapter after chapter, he searched for any information that could help them with their current situation...or even shed light on what their current situation even was!

After almost two hours, Manuel could feel a headache forming behind his eyes. Setting the book he had been scanning back on the table, he leaned back, a feeling of irritation slowly building within him. So far, he had figured out nothing.

Sure, some of the books had *hinted* at a level of demon who was unable to leave hell. These demons would entice mortals, playing with their minds in order to get them to do what they wanted. This was usually done through dreams or, if the mortal had a weak mind, while they were awake. Nowhere did it say anything about who was in charge of this happy little group of nightmares, or if there was more to them than just influencing humans. Even when they were hinted at, there was no actual accounts of anyone dealing with them or what to do if you had to.

Manuel shook his head and scanned over the books littering the table and floor. *This is crazy*, he thought, running a hand through his short hair. How could a group of demons, especially ones at this level, not be mentioned in more detail throughout their books? They had the most extensive documentation on Earth and...

His train of thought stopped. They *didn't* have all the information. There was one book he had forgotten about.

It was an extremely old book, one that had been passed down for centuries, long before they landed on Earth. They had tracked it to a local library that specialized in old and unique books. Finding it at this library was one of the main reasons they had decided to stay in Fhallon.

He needed to see that book!

Getting up, Manuel went over and glanced out the window. It was overcast and, from what he could smell, it was probably going to rain.

"Perfect," he whispered. "I guess I won't need to travel by car today." With time running out, he would move the fastest way he knew how.

Stepping away from the window, Manuel cast his eyes to the floor. Taking in a couple deep breaths, he pictured the alley by the library. The cool brick walls. The damp asphalt. His body shuddered slightly as he felt his power spreading through him. The tingling always started in his fingers, but it wasn't an uncomfortable feeling. As quickly as the tingling started, it immediately spread up his arms, through the rest of his body. The air around him crackled as Manuel closed his eyes. With a last shudder, he felt his body get light as he vanished.

Moments later, Manuel emerged from the alley. Glancing around, he slowly made his way towards the library entrance. People slowed as they walked past him...some sneaking sly glances his way, others openly gazing at him curiously. By no means a towering presence, he supposed he did stand out a bit. With his short, spiky brown hair, his gothic cross tattoo on his back peeking out from the collar of his shirt, and his dark amethyst eyes... Well, people tended to take a second look.

Manuel's lips twitched as he caught a few passing remarks from the four females standing by the steps that led up to the library doors. He paused slightly, throwing them a smooth smile. They all turned towards him with wide eyes, small gasps escaping as they longingly gazed at him. Manuel could hear their heart rate increase, the heat beginning to radiate stronger off their bodies as their lust for him intensified. Licking his lips, he savored the warmth. Nothing like knowing you're wanted, craved. His smile grew a little more as he watched all four females turn a bright red.

"Ladies," he murmured with a slight tip of his head.

"Hi," they said in unison, their voices breathy, as he began to make his way up the steps. Giving them a last smile, he walked towards the door. Manuel had to let out a soft chuckle as their giggles followed him into the library.

Once inside, he took a deep breath. There was nothing like the smell of a library. All the old books, oiled wood shelves, and worn carpet... Looking around, he wondered at the amount of books lining the walls and cases, yet the only truly magnificent part of this library was beneath it. It was a treasure not many even knew existed.

Making his way to the back of the building he quietly pushed open a bare wooden door. Nobody stopped him or gave him a second glance. Another thing he loved about being in a library. Everyone was so involved with their books, no one gave a thought to him. Closing the door behind him, Manuel stood there for a moment.

Before him was an old staircase leading to the basement. Smells of mold and dust tickled his nose as he slowly descended down the softly lit stairway. It was rather narrow. So much so, one would think they were going to find themselves in a room no bigger than a closet at the end. However, once they reached the bottom, they would find that they were way off. Reaching the last step, Manuel glanced around.

The room opened wide, the stone walls lined with bookshelves, two rows of bookcases in a line down the center. There were no windows, so all the lighting in the room came from several dim drop lights hanging from the ceiling, as well as a few lamps around the room. The shelves were stacked full of books, some with the binding so worn, you could hardly make out the titles. Nothing was labeled. It wasn't unorganized, but if you didn't know what you were looking for, you could be walking the aisles for hours. Your only saving grace would be the lone person sitting at the desk placed between where you enter and the books.

Looking towards the desk, Manuel prepared himself to great Thomas, the man who had been posted at the desk since they moved to town. The *only* one who had always been at that desk. Manuel and his brothers liked to refer to Thomas as the "Gatekeeper". The nickname had been Nicholas' idea. Manuel had laughed and joked about him liking his *Ghostbuster* movies a little too much.

Manuel's grin gave way to a slight frown as he realized Thomas was not at the desk. *He must be putting some of the books away,* Manuel thought, walking further into the room.

He scanned the space around him. Something felt different. The scent of lavender caught his attention as he walked forward. Making his way towards the desk, his eyes narrowed. The lavender smell was getting stronger and, unless Thomas had a really well-kept secret, Manuel was pretty certain the smell was not coming from him.

"Hello," Manual called out, trying to keep his voice low. The last thing he needed was to get into a confrontation with someone because he scared the crap out of them. Taking in another deep breath, he could now smell the scent of lavender with an undercurrent of honey. It was so strong, he could practically taste it. Narrowing his eyes, he gazed past the bookshelves. Manuel could sense some movement coming from the back of the room. "Hello? Is anyone down here?"

His question was greeted with a sudden shriek from the back of the room, quickly followed by the sounds of several books hitting the ground. Quickly walking in the direction of the noise, he came around the bookcases and stopped short. The sight that met him was not only a surprise but rather comical.

A female, maybe in her late twenties, was kneeling amongst several books scattered at her feet, her auburn hair falling around her face. Manuel could clearly make out the cuss words leaving her mouth in a rush as she scooped up one book after another, forming a neat pile next to her. He watched as her fingers gracefully curled around each book and, although he could tell she was agitated, she took care with each book as she rested it atop the stack.

Suddenly realizing she still didn't know he was there, Manuel cleared his throat. "Hello... Do you need a hand with those?"

The female let out a startled gasp as she quickly stood up and spun around. Manuel felt his heart skip as he was suddenly met with the brightest green eyes he'd ever seen.

"W-what?" she asked, her voice shaking a bit. Manuel didn't need to hear that to know she was extremely startled by his presence, though. Taking a slight step back, he gave her his warmest smile. Her eyes briefly flicked over him before settling back on his face. Seeming to realize he was probably the one who had called out a minute ago, her cheeks turned to an even darker shade of red. "I mean, no, thanks. I... Can I help you with something?"

"Yes, actually. I'm looking for a very specific book. It's called *Dierum Immortalibus*. Last time I was here, Thomas said he had it." Manuel watched her eyes narrow slightly as she seemed to fall deep in thought.

"The *Chronicles of the Immortal...*," she said, more to herself than to him. "Yes, I know just where that is. Not many people come looking for that one." She gazed at him. "It's extremely old and hard to understand. Do you speak Latin? If not, you will definitely have a bit of trouble with it."

"Yes, um... I am able to read a bit of Latin. I'm doing a research paper, and that book has some information in it that I need." *Not quite a lie*, he thought. He noticed her tilting her head slightly as she considered what he had said.

"Must be a pretty compelling research paper," she commented.

"Yes, well... It's always been an area that has intrigued me."

"A little dark for my taste, but I can see where it could pique someone's interest," she replied, pushing her dark auburn hair behind her ears. Glancing at the aisles, she began to make her way down the one farthest to her right. "This way then," she murmured with a slight wave of her hand.

Manuel followed a few steps behind. Although a little more comfortable, he could tell she was still shaken from his sudden appearance. Not wanting to scare her more than she already was, he decided it was best to hang back a little.

Beautiful, he thought, watching her hips sway slightly as she walked. He could see her curves with every step she took, even though she was obviously trying to hide them beneath her modest outfit of grey slacks and dark purple blouse. Her outfit, along with her straight hair and simple white cross, made her almost the ideal librarian. *All she's missing are the black-rimmed glasses!* Manuel chuckled at the thought.

Seeming to hear him, the woman stopped suddenly and glanced back at him. A look of annoyance flashed through her pretty green eyes. Just as suddenly as the emotion was there, it was gone. If he had blinked, he would have missed it. *So there's some fire in there*, he thought. Giving her his most innocent look, Manuel smiled and she turned back with a soft huff. Her fingers brushed the shelves as she slowed her steps, glancing over the books until letting out a soft sound of triumph.

"Here it is." She removed the book from the shelf, her eyes lighting up with admiration as she ran her hand over the cover. "What is it specifically that you're looking for in this?" she asked, looking up at him, her stare steady as she waited for his response.

"It's a little hard to explain," Manuel answered, glancing from the book in her hands, then back to her face. "It's one of those I'll know when I see it types of things."

"Well, there really isn't very much room down here to spread out so you can do your research..."

"Actually, I was hoping to check it out."

"Oh, well, we don't check out–"

"I've done it before...with Thomas," Manuel stated softly. "You can check in your files. I'm sure he's made a note of it."

He watched as she glanced down at the book in her hands. "I'm really not supposed to and, if you haven't noticed, Thomas isn't here anymore. I am." Her voice got stronger with each word.

"Are you trying to say it's *my* fault he's not here anymore?" Manuel felt a wave of anger run through him. "Is that what you're saying?"

"Well, no, but I don't know why he isn't here. Maybe he's been checking out books he wasn't supposed to for too long."

Manuel sighed and ran his right hand through his hair. This woman was exasperating. Maybe he needed to be a little more forceful. Clearing his throat, he hardened his gaze. "Listen..."

"Hayley," she said quickly. His eyebrow raised a bit as he rolled her name over in his head.

"Listen, *Hayley*, I need that book. What if I promise to have it back by tomorrow?"

"This must be an important research paper."

"Oh, it is, and I have an approaching deadline. So if I bring it back tomorrow, can I take it?"

He watched as Hayley tapped her fingers on the cover, her eyes so steady, they seemed to be looking right into his soul.

Finally, she let out a soft sigh. "Okay...but just this once!"

"Deal!" he said with a smile. Manuel wanted to reach out for the book, but he could tell that, even though she said it was okay, she was still not too sure. "I'll go ahead and fill out a card for you so you have a record of it. But I *will* bring it back tomorrow. I promised." With that, he watched her give a slight nod, then began to make her way towards the front of the room.

At the desk, Hayley rummaged through a couple drawers. Manuel watched, grinning as she pulled folders and paperwork out, her eyes narrowing as she went through drawer after drawer. "Well, I don't have any of the cards for you to fill out..." She brushed her hair behind her head, her frustration causing her eyebrows to draw together.

"Here," Manuel said, leaning past her, his arm brushing hers as he reached for a notepad and pen. He couldn't help but smile as he heard her soft intake of breath. Quickly jotting down his information, he handed the pad back to her. "Now you have my information. I'll be back tomorrow to drop off the book."

He watched her eyes scan the pad. She nibbled on her lip as she seemed to memorize the information. Glancing back up at him, her eyes narrowed. "Okay, *Manuel*. You better bring this book back tomorrow. I can't even begin to go into the crap I'll get if they find out it's not here."

Nodding, he picked the book up off of the table and began to make his way towards the stairs. Pausing, he glanced over his shoulder to find Hayley still standing there, gazing down at the notepad in her hands. He felt a rush of heat run through him as he watched her.

Seeming to feel his eyes on her, she glanced up and gave him a small smile. "See you tomorrow, Manuel."

He smiled back, enjoying the warmth in her gaze. "See you tomorrow, Hayley," he said, surprised at how much he was already looking forward to it.

With that, he turned around, beginning to make his way up the stairs. *Now is not the time!* He needed to get his mind back into his search. Glancing down at the book in his hands, he frowned. Who knew what information could be within these pages? It could hold nothing, or it could hold information that would change everything. For now, any thoughts of Hayley would have to wait. He was surprised at the sudden sigh that rushed from him at the thought. Halfway up the stairway, he paused and glanced around to make sure he was alone, then vanished, heading home.

Chapter 25

Ella slowed as she pulled up in front of the church, already wishing she had stayed at the house, remained in the warmth and safety of Christian's bed.

She had told Father James she would come, though. The worry of disappointing someone who had always been so good to her was overwhelming, even more than the feeling of unease which had come over her as she had been rushing around, getting ready.

Glancing at the church through the passenger window, she felt a chill run down her spine.

Sighing, Ella looked down at her cell phone on the seat beside her. She had just finished a rather lengthy conversation with Cindy. She had always been like a sister to her, the closest thing to family Ella had since her grandma passed. The conversation had been a lot of questions on Cindy's part, with an equal amount of short answers on hers. She hadn't exactly lied to Cindy... She just hadn't told her the whole truth.

No matter how much she wanted to, she couldn't tell Cindy about everything that had been going on. It was hard enough for her to come to terms with it all. She couldn't put that on her best friend. *Maybe someday, when things calm down...* Even if she did tell her, what would she say? What would she think?

She'd probably think I deserve to be in a straitjacket, Ella thought with a laugh.

After some back and forth, Ella had finally promised to meet up with her later. Cindy had laid on a rather thick guilt trip about her being away for so many days. Something about never calling, writing, or sending flowers. Ella couldn't tell her no.

Getting out of the car, she pulled her coat tight around her. The wind had started to pick up. It hadn't been this windy when she left the house. *Strange*. Looking up, she noticed the clouds had really started to roll in. Thick, black clouds were taking over the once bright blue sky. A chill ran down her spine as she looked at them. Wrapping her arms protectively around herself, Ella attempted to shake off the sense of dread.

Come on, Ella. Get a grip on yourself. There's no reason to be freaking out. I'm at a church!

Walking quickly, she made her way around the side of the church, heading towards the garden in the back. Once through the gates, it didn't take her long to reach the bench where Father James was waiting for her. As she made her way across the gravel path, she studied his appearance. He seemed so tired with his head resting in his hands. Not wanting to startle him, Ella cleared her throat .

"Father James," Ella said, stopping in front of him.

He looked up at her with red-rimmed eyes. "Ella, I'm so glad to see you. I...I started to think you had changed your mind." Concern laced every word.

"It's good to see you, too, Father. I'm sorry I'm a little late. It took me a little longer than I thought to get here." Glancing around the garden, Ella noted how secluded they were. "It's getting kind of chilly out here, Father, and you look tired. Wouldn't you be more comfortable going inside?"

"No, no...," he said with a quick shake of his head. "This is fine. Why don't you come and sit with me?" He patted the spot next to him on the bench.

Sitting down, Ella couldn't help but notice that the gentle smile on Father James' face wasn't quite reaching his eyes. Those happy, caring eyes she was so used to seeing were now shrouded in fear. A need to leave washed over her. Her fingers twitched as she glanced over towards the path out of the garden. Looking up, Ella noticed the clouds were much darker than before and, as she watched, she saw the sun completely disappear from sight. Shivering, Ella looked back at Father James, finding him staring intently at her.

He licked his chapped lips as he placed one of his cold, shaking hands on hers. She glanced between his hand and his face as her unease began to grow. "Ella, I fear I have turned down the wrong path."

Confused, Ella shook her head. "What do you mean, Father?"

"I was weak," he said softly, a tear sliding down his wrinkled face. "I lost my faith and, in doing so, fell prey to the darkness."

"W-what are you saying?"

"I just want you to know that I'm so sorry. So, so sorry."

The wind began to blow harder, leaves and dirt flying into the air. Ella felt the debris rolling over her just as her hair whipped around her face. Running her hands along her head, she held her hair back from her face, blinking rapidly. Her mind was racing as she tried to figure out what he was saying. "Sorry? Sorry for what? I don't understand."

He squeezed her hand. Muttering, he leaned in towards her.

"What? I can't hear you?" she said, her voice starting to sound frantic. She leaned towards him, her eyes widening as she finally made out his words.

"He made me do it. He made me call you, get you to come here. I didn't want to, but my family... He threatened my family. He said he would do such horrible things to them. I-I can't fight him. I'm just too weak."

Ella sprang up from the bench. She watched as tears fell down his face, his eyes taking on a wildness. "Who? Who wanted you to call me?"

She saw his mouth move, but any words became drowned out by the growing wind. Backing away from him, Ella began to shake. She needed to get out of there. Reaching for her phone, Ella's hands shook as she tried to call Christian, only to find she had no signal.

"Shit," she whispered. Looking back towards Father James, she found him still staring at her, repeating something over and over. His face had gone completely white, entirely drained of color. He began to rock back and forth, his tear-filled eyes never leaving hers.

Taking another step back, Ella felt her foot catch on the border around the statue. She stumbled before regaining her balance, dropping her phone in the process. *No...no...no!* Ella looked around her, searching frantically, finally spotting it beneath a nearby rosebush. Quickly, Ella started to lean down to retrieve her phone when she froze as the sound of Father James' screams reached her.

Ella gasped, spinning towards him. He was now standing by the bench, his eyes wide, his mouth open in a silent scream, pointing wildly at her. His head shook back and forth as his mouth moved without a sound.

When Ella opened her mouth, she suddenly felt a large hand wrap tightly around her face. With a jerk, she was yanked backwards, her body pulled roughly against her assailant's. The smell of sulfur hit her. It came on so strong, it threatened to choke her as she sucked in air through her nose.

Oh, god! she thought as she began to buck and kick. *It's a demon!* Ella couldn't believe she had been so stupid. Why hadn't she just listened to her gut when she had felt something was wrong? Trying to think of something she could do, Ella grunted and raked her nails across the hand covering her mouth.

She could feel the skin beneath her nails give way, but there was no change. Attempting anything she could to get free, she threw her arms back and forth, screaming into the hand restraining her. Although her screams were muffled, they echoed loudly through her head.

She felt a thick arm wrap around her, pinning her arms to her sides. The hand on her mouth pulled her head so far back, she was arched against the demon's shoulder, her feet barely touching the ground. Feeling his hot breath against her ear, Ella shuddered, a tear sliding down her cheek.

"Shh," a deep voice growled. "Do not fight me, *femina*."

Ella wiggled as best she could, grunting against the demon's hand. She felt disgust rise in her as the demon sniffed along her neck.

"We have been looking for you, Ella." Her name rolled off his tongue in a whisper. "It is time for you to come home."

Ella's eyes widened as she sent out a silent scream, concentrating with all her might. She brought an image of Christian into her mind, repeating his name over and over, praying he would hear her. The tears ran down her cheeks, and she felt her stomach churn, the demon's hot breath crawling across her skin as he chuckled softly.

That sound, that evil sound, vibrated through her. It was the last thing Ella heard as the world dissolved into blackness.

Chapter 26

CHRISTIAN!

His name echoed through his head as he slowed and looked around. Ella's voice was laced with fear and anguish as it tore through him, shaking him to his core. Something was wrong, but before he could yell out to the others, a sudden spasm stopped him in his tracks.

Christian shuddered when he felt a coldness begin in his chest. His breathing became labored as he tried to suck in air. The cold quickly spread throughout his body, causing every one of his muscles to tense. His heart began to beat erratically, shuddering, feeling like it was about to burst right from his chest, and his lungs hurt as he desperately tried to pull in air. Panic gave way to fear as he fell to his knees. It was not *his* fear, though. It was Ella's, and he was drowning in it. It was a fear like nothing he had ever felt before. It rode through him, wave after wave, as the coldness took hold of his mind.

Then, just as suddenly as it had started, the feeling vanished. His lungs burned as the breath he had been gasping for was finally pulled in with a rush. Eyes widening further, Christian glanced around him. He could see Cyrus and Nicholas standing over him, their mouths moving, but all he could hear was his name still echoing through his head.

Gasping, he stumbled to his feet and, turning to the side, braced himself against the brick wall. There was a ringing in his ears that slowly became just a low hum and, after several minutes of concentrating on taking one breath after another, he could finally hear his brothers' concerned voices.

At some point, Darren had come up on the side of him. Christian felt their concern radiating through the air, but all he could think about was Ella.

"What was that?"

"What happened?"

"Are you okay?"

All their questions came at him at once, but Christian just kept shaking his head. How could he answer them when he, himself, wasn't sure what had just happened? All the feelings in him began to give way to anger, a silent rage that began to build. Reaching for his phone, he started dialing Manuel's number.

"Something happened to Ella," Christian growled, dragging in one shaky breath after another, attempting to calm his nerves.

"Hey. You guys find anything?" Manuel said after one ring.

"Are you home?" Christian blurted.

"Yeah. I stepped out for a bit, but I'm back at the house now. Why? What's going on?" Manuel's voice had taken on an edge of concern.

"Is Ella there?"

"I haven't seen her. I assume she's still in your room."

Christian leaned his head against the brick wall, a growl threatening to come out as he felt a familiar pressure in his back. "Go check... Please."

"Yeah. Hold up."

He could hear Manuel making his way through the house. His footsteps sounded rushed as he quickly walked towards Christian's room. Christian felt the rage in him begin to grow. *How could this have happened*? He should have stayed with her, made sure she was safe. His thoughts were interrupted when he heard Manuel quietly tap on the door. Then the taps became loud knocks when she didn't answer. Christian strained his hearing, praying he would hear the door open.

Maybe what just happened was some kind of a sick game! The demons just trying to mess with me, he thought. Hope that this was the case coursed through his veins, even though he knew it wasn't.

By now, Cyrus, Nicholas, and Darren were standing close by him, all their faces etched with worry as they waited to find out what was going on. Christian could hear

Manuel calling out her name, asking her if everything was okay. *She's not there*, he thought, a pain spreading in his chest. His anger must have begun to show in his eyes because he felt his brothers begin to tense.

Christian glanced around, looking to see if they had drawn any attention. He knew he needed to get out of there because every cell in his body was screaming. Still calling out for Ella, Manuel opened the door. Taking a step away from his brothers, Christian looked at them. He continued to put more distance between them as he listened to Manuel's voice become more and more frantic.

Suddenly, he was back on the line. "Christian, she's not here," Manuel breathed out. "I... I don't know where she went. She couldn't have gone–"

The rest of what he was saying was lost on Christian as a sudden growl erupted from him. After a roll of his shoulders, he vanished, reappearing in front of their house seconds later. With a few quick steps, he was inside, practically running towards his room. Christian burst through the bedroom door to find his brother still standing there, phone up to his ear and talking away. Manuel turned to him and, blinking a couple times, closed his phone.

"So... At what point during my crazed rambling did you decide you were done listening to me?" Manuel asked.

"When you told me Ella wasn't here," Christian stated quickly, looking around the room. Her phone wasn't on the charger, her jacket was no longer thrown over the back of the door, and her shoes were gone. *Had her Jeep still been outside?* he thought wildly. He had run inside so fast, he hadn't stopped to look. Shaking his head, Christian's mind went over and over their last couple of conversations. For the life of him, he couldn't remember Ella mentioning having to go anywhere. Actually, this morning, she looked like she was planning to lounge around until they got home. *Why hadn't she mentioned to me that she was planning to go out?* If she had, as much as he would have tried to convince her to say in, Christian would have stayed behind to go with her.

The sudden sound of heavy footfalls from down the hall told him the others were home. Christian moved close to the bed as they all came through the door, hovering close by him.

"So what the hell's going on?" Cyrus asked, his voice slightly strained as his black eyes scanned the room, landing on him.

"Ella's gone," Christian answered, meeting his brother's dark stare. "Even before I called and asked Manuel to check, I knew she wouldn't be here."

"How did you know?" Nicholas asked, his own eyes filled with confusion and worry.

"I... I heard her call to me. She screamed my name, then everything was cold. I don't know how, but I knew something had happened to her."

"But how–" Nicholas started.

"Their souls bonded last night," Manuel whispered.

"Bonded?" Christian asked, his head whipping around to look at Manuel.

"It's rare between angels and humans, but it can happen. All humans are born with a soul mate, somewhere, whom they may or may not ever meet. It's a tricky thing finding one's soul mate, but when you do, the souls bond forever! Ella is your soul mate, Christian, and the connection between you two strengthened when you found each other."

"How could I have a soul mate?" he asked, shaking his head. "That just doesn't make any sense. I mean, I was never supposed to even be down here on Earth."

"Weren't you?" Manuel asked simply.

They all glanced from one to the other, thinking about what Manuel had just said, each taking a turn shaking his head in disbelief.

"Can I use this bond to help me find her?" Christian asked, deciding to ignore the implication that all this was planned.

"I don't exactly know how it works," Manuel said, "but we'll find her, Christian."

"Of course we will!" Darren agreed. "When Ella reached out to you, what do you remember happening?'

"How is going on about what happened to me going to–"

"Trust me, Christian. We want to rush out there to find her, too, but we need to understand what's going on first." Darren took a step closer, his eyes filled with concern. "Tell us what happened."

Christian sighed as he looked back at Darren. Rolling his shoulders, he attempted to release the tension building in them. "I heard her calling my name. I remember thinking she sounded afraid and I needed to let you guys know. All of a sudden, I couldn't breathe. There was a cold feeling in my chest. So cold, it was painful." He rubbed a hand over his chest as he remembered the pain. He had never felt anything like it before. "My heart was beating wildly and I couldn't stop shaking. I thought the pain was never going to end. I tried to pull in air, but my lungs hurt and I started to panic. Then I felt a sudden stab of fear shoot through me, like no kind of fear I've ever felt. Suddenly, it just stopped.

All the pain, all the fear... It just went away and I could breathe again."

A silence fell over the group. Christian could hear his heartbeat in his ears. He needed to find Ella, and quickly. He knew who had her... Well, it was more like an educated guess, but it was a strong one. It was the only conclusion that made sense. All that was left was to say it out loud. Clearing his throat, he looked at each of his brothers, finally voicing what they were all thinking. "The demons have her. I just don't know where they took her."

"Well, she wasn't taken from here. If she was, we would have known as soon as we stepped into the room. So wherever she was taken from must be close. I mean, she wouldn't have gone far," Nicholas said.

"Why do you say that?" Christian asked.

"She would have planned on coming back, so it would make sense that she'd stay around town," Nicholas responded.

"I agree," Darren said with a nod. "She definitely would have stayed close."

Christian looked from one face to another. His heart was still racing as he furiously tried to think of where she would have gone. "Cindy!" he suddenly said, reaching in his pocket for his phone.

"Who's Cindy?" Cyrus asked.

"She's Ella's boss and best friend. When we first brought her here, Cindy was the one Ella called to take care of her house and her cat," Christian mumbled, searching through the recent calls. "She asked to use my phone to make the call."

"That's great and all," Cyrus said with exasperation, "but why is she important right now?"

"Because if Ella was going to see anyone, it would be her," Christian said, finding Cindy's number. Taping it, he listened as the phone began to ring. "If not, she may at least know where Ella would go."

With each ring, Christian felt his heart race. *What if she doesn't answer?* Anger was still rolling through him, threatening to take over. Running a hand through his hair, he felt himself shaking. He couldn't shake the feeling that he needed to move. Maybe he was wrong. Maybe Cindy wouldn't know where Ella was. What if he was just wasting time? He should be out there looking for her. He should be doing more to–

"Hello?" a soft voice said, interrupting his frantic thoughts.

"Cindy?"

"Yes. Who's this?"

"Cindy, is Ella with you? Do you know where she is?"

"Who is this?" Her voice came across a little more agitated.

Christian gripped the phone, trying to calm himself down. "This is Christian."

"Christian?"

"Yeah. Ella has been staying with me and–"

"Oh, Christian! Yes. Ella has told me about you. Why are you calling–"

"Listen, Cindy, Ella isn't here and I need to know... Do you know where she was going today?"

"Actually, she called me not too long ago. She was heading over to the church to see Father James, then we were going to meet up for a bit. Why? Is something wrong?"

"No, no. I just need to talk to her really quick and I wasn't sure where she had gone. Um... Do you know what church?"

"Why don't you try her cell? I'm sure she can just–"

"Just tell me what church!" He heard a sharp intake of air as she gasped at his tone. Taking a deep breath, Christian closed his eyes. "I'm sorry. Please, just tell me which church she was going to."

"Okay, but I still don't know why you don't just call her." She was quiet for a minute, and Christian could hear her shuffling through some papers. "Here it is... She's at St Anne's on Courtland Avenue."

"Thank you, Cindy," Christian said, hitting END. She had been starting to say something when he hung up, but he really didn't have time to chat. *Once I get Ella back and she finds out I hung up on her friend, I'm sure going to get some shit*, he thought as he began to make his way down the hall. Glancing over his shoulder, he saw his brothers following close behind him.

He knew they were aware of where they were headed, just as he knew they would all have his back. Christian had a strong feeling things were going to get a lot worse before they found Ella, but they *would* find her. They had to. Taking a deep breath, he stepped into the backyard and paused. He could feel the anger rolling through him. His gut told him that the priest was somehow involved in what happened to Ella. He wasn't sure how he knew this, but he learned a long time ago to trust his instincts.

Looking back towards his brothers, he nodded. "Time to go talk to a priest, boys," he snarled, watching each of them nod. Then, as the air shifted around them, they vanished.

Chapter 27

Andras looked down at where Ella lay. *She really is a beautiful creature*, he thought as he reached down, running his hands through her rich brown hair. Even in sleep, he could feel the power rolling off her. He could taste it in the air.

Andras' eyes traveled up and down her body, slowly taking in each curve, each pale flash of skin. Licking his lips, he leaned down, sniffing slightly. The smell of roses reached him and he shivered, a rush of lust running through him.

Qual had shown up with her just as he had planned. Ella had been over his shoulder, having passed out, so Andras had told him to lay her on his desk. It may not be the most comfortable place but, with its sturdy legs, it was an ideal place to chain her.

Andras looked at her hands securely chained above her head. Not that there was really anywhere for her to run, but this would help make things a little easier. *At least for me*, he thought with a sneer. Hearing a soft moan, his eyes traveled back to Ella's face.

Her head turned to the side as she began to slowly move around. Andras leaned back, watching her. Her breathing changed before she blinked her eyes open. Slowly looking around her, confusion laced her face as she seemed to attempt to make sense of where she was. He watched as they began to widen, landing on him. The haze that had been in them when she had first woken was now gone, replaced by panic. Andras saw her mouth begin to open as she took in a gulp of air. Before she could utter a sound, he placed his hand over her lips.

He leaned close to her ear and whispered, "Shh, Ella. Not that anyone would come if you screamed, but I just think things would be so much easier if we could bypass all that unnecessary nonsense." Andras felt Ella's body shudder violently, the chains around her wrists shaking as she pulled on them. She tugged on them so violently, he heard her whimper. He glanced up and noticed a thin line of blood coming from beneath the cuffs. Reaching his other hand up, he pushed down upon her hands, holding them tight so she could no longer pull against the cuffs.

He waited a heartbeat before pulling back to meet her wide-eyed gaze. "Now, why would you want to go and hurt yourself?" Andras tisked, tilting his head. "I am going to remove my hand and you are going to stay quiet...and still. I would hate to have to restrain you further."

Pulling his hands away, he watched Ella lick her dry lips, fear coming off her in waves. Like the predator he was, Andras moved a couple steps back, enjoying the way her eyes never left his. Smiling, he felt his heartbeat speed up. "Do you know how long I have been looking for you?"

Ella just stared back at him, tears beginning to run down her cheeks.

"There is no need for tears. You and I are going to get along just fine. You will see." He stepped towards her, running a hand just above her legs. He could feel the power just below the fear radiating off her. Andras knew that, soon, he would be able to control this power. Soon, Ella would no longer fear him. She would not just do what he asked her to, she would *want* to do it!

He could feel his own power licking just beneath his skin, wanting desperately to crawl over her, claim her as his own. She *would* be his, regardless of the remaining essence of that Guardian curling protectively within her. Andras could see it in the depths of her eyes, but he wasn't concerned. Sure, this would take a little more doing than he had originally thought, and would probably be a little more painful on her. It usually was when you had to sever a bond like that. It would be worth it, though. After all was said and done, he knew Ella would agree.

She gasped a bit as he placed his hand upon her. "Wh-who are you?" she whispered, her voice quivering slightly.

"Andras," he answered with a smirk. He felt his power start to slide down his arm, tingling his fingertips.

"What do you want with me?"

Andras didn't answer. He watched as her cheeks flushed, his power now gliding across the surface of her skin. She closed her eyes tightly, surely feeling the heat as his power began to swirl with hers. Pushing it farther into her, Andras watched with an arrogant smile as he saw her power, so innocent and pure, beginning to blend slightly with his own.

Suddenly, he felt her pushing back at him, her own power attempting to stop him from engulfing hers. She was strong. He felt her, like white hot lightning against his skin, as she lashed out at him. Grinding his teeth, Andras focused on her core, the very center of her power, willing it to bend to him. A sheen of sweat now covered both their bodies, each fighting to dominate the other. Her power suddenly stabbed into him, causing his concentration to break. Rage filled him. From deep within himself, Andras felt his darkest power unleash. He willed all of it to the surface. She *would* bend to him!

The air in the room changed as he leaned over her. "Look at me," he demanded. He watched as Ella squeezed her eyes shut, panting slightly. "I said, look at me!" he snarled, putting the full force of his power into each word, pushing it into her.

Ella's eyes snapped open. He could see the light within them waiver, a darker tint beginning to swirl through them.

"To answer your question," he began, his voice just above a whisper, his face right above hers. Andras could feel her warm breath as she gasped with each flex of his power. "I want you...all of you! *You will be mine*!"

"No!" she screamed. Andras felt her body bow, her power sending shivers down his spine, the air around her beginning to glow. "I will never be yours!"

With that, Andras let out a growl as their powers collided, crackling around them in flashes of light. So violent was their power that, at that very instant, the walls themselves bled.

Chapter 28

Appearing in the street next to the church, Christian felt a wave of dizziness come over him. Bending down, he placed his hands on his knees and, pulling in a couple deep breaths, he gave his head a shake.

Ella, he thought with a cringe. Something was happening to her. He could feel her power reaching out to him as he pulled in a hiss of air between his teeth. Focusing on her power, he reached for her. He could sense a coldness, a darkness trying to wrap around her. Closing his eyes, he felt himself shudder as he attempted to help her.

Feeling a hand against his back, Christian glanced over his shoulder, the sense of Ella's power fading. Whoever she was fighting was strong. He needed to get to her.

"What's happening?" Darren asked him, his eyes narrowing.

"I'm not sure," Christian said with a shudder. "We have to hurry, though."

Darren nodded. "Okay. Why don't you and I go inside? The rest of you, go around back and see if you can find any trace of Ella or this priest."

Nicholas, who had walked a couple steps away from them, turned. "There's Ella's Jeep."

Christian growled as he straightened himself, the need to find this priest overtaking him. "Let's go," he said gruffly, moving towards the church. He could hear Darren behind him as he swung the large wooden doors wide open. The air inside was thick. The smell of varnish and incense flooded his nose as he made his way past the first set of pews, spotting a priest kneeling in the front row. As he got closer, he could hear a soft mumbling coming from the man. Christian saw his shoulders shake slightly as he quietly cried.

Glancing around to make sure they were alone, Christian reached where the priest was seated. He heard Darren make a humming sound behind him, probably trying to tell him to calm down, but he was way past that. Reaching down, Christian grabbed the priest by the collar and yanked him up. The man let out a startled yelp when he found himself airborne.

Spinning the priest around in the air Christian reached for the front of the his robe. Pulling the scared little man towards him, he let out a soft growl. "Where is she?" he hissed into the priest's face.

He watched as the man's eyes grew wide, his mouth opening and closing like a fish out of water as he stared back at him.

"Where is she? Where's Ella?" he asked again, giving the priest a rough shake.

Tears began to fall down the priest's face. "I... I don't know. She was taken."

Christian was shaking, his anger threatening to take full control as he clenched his jaw. "*Who* took her?"

"A demon... He... He made me do it... He made me call her and have her come to the garden."

"What demon?"

"I... I don't know. Please! I don't know who he was, but he threatened my family." The last part of his sentence became muffled as he began to sob.

"Christian," Darren said from behind him. "He doesn't know anything."

Shaking his head, Christian gripped the priest's robe tighter, pulling him off of the ground until he was just balancing on his toes. "You have to know more. Tell me what else you know?"

The priest, gasping for air, held tightly to Christian's arms, his eyes bulging out of his head as he began to mumble.

"Christian, put him down!" Darren said a little more forcefully. "I'm telling you. He doesn't know anything."

Refusing to give up that easily, Christian's eyes narrowed. "Do you at least know where she was taken from?" His voice rumbled through the empty church.

The priest gasped a couple times, his throat working hard beneath Christian's grip as he tried to pull in air. "The... The garden...by the statue!"

In a fit of disgust, he tossed the priest to the floor. Turning from the quivering heap. Christian found Darren staring at him. Rolling his shoulders, he just shook his head.

The look on Darren's face told him his brother understood that he was barely holding on. With a nod towards the door, they both made their way out, leaving Father James to silently cry at the foot of the alter.

Walking through the garden, they quickly found the others making their way towards them.

"The priest called Ella to come here. He said a demon made him do it, and that he took her from the garden," Darren informed the others, because Christian was in no mood to chat. His eyes were already scanning the area for the statue.

"Weak little piece of...," Cyrus muttered. "Where in the garden?"

"By the statue," Darren responded, looking around.

Out of the corner of his eye, Christian saw each of them glancing his way. He knew they wanted to know exactly what had happened in the church, but he didn't have time. Walking past them, he continued down the path, finally spotting the statue.

Circling it, he looked for any sign she had been there. Seeing some drag marks on the ground, he had to swallow the scream threatening to burst from him. His brothers had spread out around the area. He glanced over towards Manuel, hoping he would be able to catch a scent, something that would help. He was one of the best when it came to his sense of smell and, as he watched Manuel take in one deep breath after another, he held his breath.

"I got her phone," Nicholas yelled. Christian quickly made his way over to him, taking it from his outstretched hand. "It was under this rosebush. Looks like she either dropped it or it was tossed there," he continued as he stood up.

Christian looked down at the phone. Its case was cracked. The more he looked at the damage, the more he felt his stomach drop.

Manuel came to stand next to him. "Can I see it?" he asked, holding out his hand. Christian looked over and, after a pause, dropped the phone in his hand. He watched as Manuel lifted it to his nose and took in a deep breath, closing his eyes. Christian watched him take a step back, the air around his body shivering as he pushed his power out around him. Manuel turned his head to the side as he closed his eyes.

Christian held his breath again as he waited. *Please... Please, find something*, he thought.

Suddenly, Manuel's eyes snapped open, startling them all, as a low growl burst from him.

"Shit...," Christian breathed.

Manuel's purple eyes lit up as he meet Christian's gaze. "I know where she is," he whispered, his power spreading from him, causing the hairs on Christian's arms to stand up. It felt like a cold breeze against him as his eyes slowly began to turn black.

"Where?" Christian asked.

He felt the others step in closer, each adding their own power to Manuel's. Christian hissed when he felt Darren's power against his back. Its warmth mixed with the chill of Manuel's, causing the air to spin around him. Nicholas and Cyrus added their power, each sending his own unique feel across Christian, his own power growing within him.

Rolling his shoulders, he felt his power intensify, the pressure in his back beginning to build. With a sharp intake of air, his back bowed and, in a flash of light, his large black wings exploded out of his flesh, reaching high above him. His flash of power was answered by each of his brothers until they all stood there, wings flexing high into the sky, a wind of their own making surrounding them.

Christian shivered as their combined powers completely engulfed him. He could feel Manuel's power leading the rest, gathering their strengths to his as he prepared to lead them in the direction they needed to go.

Christian's eyes narrowed as a low growl vibrated through him. "Show me..."

Chapter 29

It was dark when Christian and his brothers found themselves deep within a cave. With only the tiniest bit of light to guide them, he could just make out the jagged rock edges surrounding them. Blinking, Christian reached out to touch the cavern walls, expecting them to be cold. He let out a hiss when he had to quickly pull his fingers back. The rocks felt like they were on fire.

Giving his hand a shake, he looked over at Manuel. His brother's eyes, now black, where glowing softly. "Where are we?" Christian whispered.

"On the edge of Hell," Manuel answered.

"On the edge of...," Nicholas sputtered. Shaking his head, he glared at Manuel. "Haven't we spent all these years trying *not* to come here?"

"This is where Ella is," Manuel stated calmly, looking around them. "Come on. We need to get moving."

The rest of them grunted in acknowledgment as they began to move farther into the cavern. Christian watched as Darren gave Nicholas a friendly little shove. Nicholas shook his head, but began walking. With each step, they all seemed to stand a little straighter.

The air around them was thick and humid, and Christian could feel a thin sheen of sweat beginning to build on his skin. Some ran down the side of his face as he took shallow breaths of the stale, warm air. Making their way around one corner after another, Christian began to worry that they were lost.

He trusted Manuel's ability to track anything, but even Manuel surely had his limits. This wasn't exactly a place they had been to before. Suddenly, he started to notice the cavern was getting brighter. Just as he was about to comment on the fact, he saw Manuel raise his hand. Much to Christian's relief, they seemed to have reached the mouth of the cavern.

Coming to a stop beside Manuel, Christian glanced in front of them. He wasn't sure what he was expecting to see. He had always wondered what it looked like down here. Were there really fire pits? Maybe a dry wind eating away at the surface? He had lists of things he thought may be down here, but a city skyline definitely wasn't on that list.

There were buildings of all sizes. Some so tall, they would put the greatest human skyscrapers to shame. All looked old and worn. Some had holes in the sides, like a huge demolition ball had taken a chunk out of them. Narrowing his eyes, he could see broken windows and what seemed like a light dust occasionally lifting off the ground.

Between them and the edge of the city, he could make out just a few small, stringy, cactus-like plants. However, they were brown instead of the normal green. Other than those, the ground was covered in sand and rocks.

His eyes were drawn to the sky when he felt a shadow pass. Gasping, he couldn't believe the colors swirling above them. It seemed like the sky was on fire, flames and smoke swirling around each other.

"It's like those pictures of Mars," Nicholas whispered. Christian turned to find Nicholas right behind him, staring up at the sky.

"It is," Darren murmured, coming up next to them.

Christian looked back towards the buildings. Ella had to been in there somewhere. His eyes scanned one building after another. *Which one, though?* He could feel his chest clench as he took in a gulp of the warm air.

"Christian."

He turned to find Manuel looking at him, his brother's eyes back to their original amethyst color. *How long have we been standing here?* Realizing he had probably been repeating his name,

Christian gave himself a mental shake. "What?" he whispered.

"You know how you asked if your bond with Ella would be able to help you find her?"

Christian narrowed his eyes. "Yeah."

"Well, it can. You can follow that bond to her."

"How do you know that?" Darren asked, glancing between the two of them. Christian noted the look of uncertainty in his eyes.

"I read it in the book I got from the library today."

"What book?" Darren asked.

"*Dierum Immortalibus,*" Manuel responded, glancing around at the wide-eyed look they were all giving him. "I was trying to find more information on the demons we're up against and that seemed like the right place to look. While going through it, I came across some information on what it could mean for an angel's and human's soul to bond." He shrugged, looking back at the landscape.

"And did you learn anything about the demons?" Cyrus spoke up. He had been leaning against the rock wall the whole time, glancing around him suspiciously.

"Not much. I did learn they are good at getting into and manipulating the minds of humans. Also that the leader is a real piece of work. Powerful, too. Other than that, there really isn't any information on him or those who follow him."

"Is that because nobody has ever come across them?" Nicholas asked.

"Or they didn't live to talk about it," Cyrus grunted.

They all turned to give him a look. Cyrus raised an eyebrow at their glares but, instead of explaining his comment, he merely smirked.

"Nice," Darren muttered. Cyrus shrugged in response.

"Enough of this," Christian growled out. Looking over towards Manuel, he took in a deep breath. "How do I use the bond to find her?"

Nodding, Manuel gestured ahead of them. "Use your power, like you do when you're searching for a demon or evil spirit. Send it out. When you find Ella, you'll know it. The book says it should feel like a warm and safe glow, drawing you in."

Standing there for a moment, Christian thought over what Manuel had just told him. He had to admit that he had his concerns about opening himself up down here because he didn't know what to expect once he did. It was sometimes hard for him to deal with the feelings he got when he came across *one* dark soul or demon, let alone a *group* of them.

Shuddering, he ran a hand through his hair, remembering the cold feeling he would get when he would come across a demon. Christian always spent so much time keeping his power under control, he never really had to think about sending his power out. For as long as he could remember, it was something he had been able to do.

Images of Ella came to his mind. Her beautiful brown eyes, so full of life. The way she had looked at him with trust, and maybe the beginning of something else just this morning. Just thinking about it had caused his heart to swell within his chest. He should have been there for her. *But I'm here now!* His teeth ground together when he thought of what he would do to whomever was holding her. And Heaven help them if they hurt her.

Looking towards the buildings, he felt himself begin to open. As his power flew towards the building, he allowed his power to run free. He felt the intensity of the heat in the air, the dryness of the ground. The closer he got, he started to feel a coldness run through him. Christian hissed as his body shuddered. He felt a hand against his back. He knew it was one of his brothers, but didn't know which one. Christian was about to turn and see, but with the sudden rush of power he felt pour from that hand into his back, he didn't care. He was just thankful for the extra boost.

Using this extra power, he concentrated on adding it to his to help push his power farther. Weeding through the cold spots, he concentrated on finding Ella. With each cold wave he came up against, he became more and more worried.

Christian tried not to linger too long in hopes that he would be able to flow his power through this little city of Hell without notice, although the likelihood of that happening was getting smaller by the second.

Then, just as his patience was coming to an end, he felt her. It was faint, so he willed his power to hover for a second to make sure. When a warmth came over him, his mind reached out to her, willing her to answer him. *Ella? Ella? I'm here.*

Christian paused, allowing his power to pulse like a beacon. He knew it was risky. He didn't know who would be able to see his power, but his only concern right now was Ella.

Christian...?

Christian gasped when he heard his name. *Ella*! Her voice sounded weak, but it was her. He felt a rush of relief soar through him. She was alive.

Hearing her voice, his mind was suddenly filled with the image of a wood room. It was a dark image and hazy around the edges, like looking through a foggy window. He must be seeing what Ella was. *Hold on, darling... We're coming!* He sent the message to her before pulling back.

Taking a couple deep breaths, he pulled himself together, looking back at his brothers. They all looked at him expectantly. "I know where she is. She's weak, but she's alive." This was met with some sighs of relief and grunts of approval. "We need to get moving, though."

"Okay, here's the deal," Darren said, stepping in front of the others. "We don't know what exactly is out there, so we're going to stick to the shadows. Get to the building that Ella's in, take care of whoever's may be in there, and get the fuck out of here." He stopped and looked around. His gaze was steady as he looked at Christian. They stared at each other for a bit and, although Christian knew what was coming next, he let Darren say it anyway. "And Christian? Try to keep it together, okay?"

Giving a quick nod, Christian moved past Darren, his need to get to Ella taking control. Crouching low, he quickly moved over the flat terrain towards the first building. He was going so fast, he didn't even know if he was touching the ground. When he finally got to the edge of the building, he flattened his back against it. The bricks were hot, even more so than the cavern walls. He gritted his teeth as he felt the heat sear through his shirt. Resisting the urge to pull away from the wall, he glanced to his right and saw all of his brothers beside him.

Looking away from them, Christian leaned over, peering around the corner. Letting himself open a little, he could sense some demons close by. It didn't take long for him to spot them.

There were four, maybe five demons standing across the way. Their skin, what he could see of it, was a milky white, which contrasted greatly with their glowing red eyes. Their appearance was extremely human-like. Then again, they all had long trench coats on so their looks could be deceiving. For all he knew, they could have tentacles instead of hands, and extra heads hidden in there somewhere.

Shaking his head, Christian's eyes narrowed, watching them as they talked. He couldn't make out what they were saying, but one of them seemed agitated. The irate demon shook his head, pacing in front of the others. One of the demons motioned towards the entrance of the building where they were standing. The others looked that way, but the agitated one only shook his head again. *Go on... Go inside, you vile idiots!* Christian thought, waiting for them to move.

Next to him, Cyrus let out a low growl. He couldn't really blame him. He was just as frustrated, if not more. They were so close to Ella, but had to sit here and wait. This was ridiculous! There had to be another way.

Christian looked around and, pulling away from the wall, glanced up. The building they were up against had to be about nine or ten stories high. If they got onto the roof, they could just move from rooftop to rooftop. They'd be able to get to Ella even faster that way, but there was always a chance they'd be seen. Then again, if there were demons on the roof, they would be seen regardless.

Taking another slight step away from the wall, Christian placed his palm against it. He gave the briefest glance to his brothers before closing his eyes. The flair of tension quickly rolled through his back as he willed his wings to appear, making sure to keep them close behind him. Christian figured a pair of black wings, even in Hell, may draw a bit of attention.

Looking up, Christian bent down. With only a soft whisper from his wings, he launched himself into the air, landing effortlessly on the roof. He remained in a crouched position once he landed. Flattening his wings behind him, he looked around. It didn't take long for his brothers to join him, each landing with little sound.

Looking out, Christian was both surprised and relieved to see all the rooftops empty. He had been expecting an attack as soon as they landed. *Nice to be wrong every once in a while.*

"Now what?" Cyrus hissed between his teeth, his black eyes glowing.

"Just a couple buildings over," Christian answered, keeping his voice to just above a whisper. Staying low, they traveled across the roof towards the next building. The roof was covered with small, black rocks, the heat from the sky turning them into hot coal. Gritting his teeth, Christian crawled to the edge of the roof. Peeking over, he could see the demons down on the street.

"We have to get over to the next roof without them seeing us," Darren whispered next to him.

Christian looked across and noticed that the distance to the next roof was quite a gap. With no cover, they would definitely be noticed. Glancing back towards the demons, he knew they would have a clear view of them. Out of the four of them standing there, one was sure to notice a group of angels with huge wings flying through the air. Tapping his finger against the short wall, Christian groaned. There had to be a way!

"I got this," Cyrus said from behind him.

Christian, along with the others, turned to face their brother. "What do you mean, *you got this*?" Christian hissed, his eyes narrowing.

"Just what I said," Cyrus responded with a twitch to his lips. "You guys need those demons to get distracted so you can go save your girl, and I'm bored. I'll go do my thing and meet you guys back at the cave."

Before any of them could comment, Cyrus was already back to the other side of the roof and over the edge.

"Fucking, Cyrus," Manuel muttered as he leaned back over the wall.

They all watched as the demons below continued their conversation, the agitated one waving his arms around. He seemed truly upset about something, shoving one of the demons closest to him. Christian could tell that the angry demon was the tallest and, although none of them were bulky, he seemed to be the most muscular, his trench coat fitting more snuggly on him than the others. *Probably the equivalent of hired muscle*, Christian thought, shaking his head. There are thugs on all levels.

"There's Cyrus," Darren whispered. Christian glanced in the direction he was pointing and spotted Cyrus looking around the corner of a building across the street from them. "Crap, he moves fast. Didn't even notice him crossing the street."

Nodding his head, Christian watched as Cyrus peeked around the corner. He quickly glanced up at the rest of them and smiled. Most of his body was hidden in the shadow of the building, but his face was in the light, causing his scar to be a stark white against his naturally tan skin. It stood out like a beacon, seeming to even further emphasize his coal black eyes as they began to glow. Cyrus looked away from them and back towards the demons.

Christian held his breath as he watched his brother step around the corner of the building. Glancing over, he realized the demons still hadn't noticed any movement. Looking back, he noticed Cyrus' wings were now uncurling, large and black behind him. The silver tint his feathers always held shimmered like diamonds against the blackness.

As Cyrus moved out of the shadows, he seemed to pull the darkness with him. Christian had seen him manipulate the darkness more times than he could count, but it never ceased to amaze him. The darkness furled out behind him and curved around, spreading high above Cyrus' head, seeming to come to life. He watched as his brother crouched down and spread his wings.

Taking a breath, Cyrus flapped them, lifting himself into the air. With a thrust, he was moving quickly towards the demons, the darkness following close behind. Everything behind Cyrus was now covered in a dark, black fog.

Right before he was on them, one of the demons turned, his eyes growing wide when he spotted Cyrus. The demon only got a chance to yell out a brief warning to the others before Cyrus was on them, the darkness swirling, hiding them from view. Christian watched for any sign of his brother, but all he heard was a lot of cussing and yelling. Taking a shaky breath, he looked over at the others. "Let's go while he has them busy." Without waiting for a response, he got up and quickly leapt towards the other roof.

Moving fast, he flew from one rooftop to the other. With each jump, he not only prayed Cyrus would be okay, but that he would find Ella in time.

Ella.

Her name began running through his head. He felt a pull on his soul as he moved forward. Opening himself up, he sensed the warmth of their bond wash over him. As he landed on the building she was being held in, he felt his whole body shudder.

Stopping, he looked around. There had to be some sort of a hatch or doorway on the roof. He felt his brothers land by him, each looking around as they crouched down.

"Is she in here?" Manuel asked.

"Yes. We need to find a way to get in."

"Okay. Well, there must be a way in from up here," Nicholas said as he began to make his way around, his hands skimming over the hot rooftop.

Grunting in agreement, Christian began to search, as well. Finding nothing, he felt his frustration grow. How could there be no way in? No hatch. Not even a freaking ventilation shaft. Running his hands through his hair, he felt a pain begin in his chest.

"Deep breath, Christian," Manuel murmured. "Let me see if I can do something here."

Christian turned towards him. Manuel's amethyst eyes began to glow darkly as he held his hands over the rooftop. The rocks below him began to shake as his power poured out. It flicked over Christian, curling through the air as it flew over the roof. He could almost see the roof below them buckle from the force of Manuel's power. Just as he thought his brother was going to give in, he heard it. The noise was faint, but Christian heard the sound of a wall cracking.

He watched in awe as the rocks began to roll away from Manuel, the air around him beginning to glow. "Step back," he hissed, throwing his arms out to his sides. Moving back as quickly as possible, they all had to catch themselves as the ground beneath them shuddered. A large crack flared out from in front of Manuel, running out a couple feet before collapsing in on itself. As a rush of dust lifted up, Christian flapped his wings a couple times to clear the air.

Blinking, he couldn't help the grin that spread across his face as he saw Manuel kneeling by a hole in the roof. "Ladies first," he said, glancing up at him. Christian, in turn, flipped him off as he made his way over and looked into the hole. Manuel chuckled as he pulled out his sica.

The debris from the ceiling was scattered all across the floor, completely covering, a rose-colored carpet. Taking a closer look, Christian realized the rose color on the floor was not the carpet, but was from a liquid dripping down from the ceiling. Reaching down, he ran his hands along the jagged edge of the hole. His fingers dripped with the sticky substance as he pulled away, holding his hand up to his face. Inhaling deeply, he was surprised by the sudden metallic smell that hit his senses. Blood?! *The building is bleeding*? "What in the...?" Shaking his head, he forced himself to look away.

Looking back into the hole, he realized they were standing above a hallway. Taking in another deep breath, he found there were no other smells reaching up to meet him. To be sure they were alone, though, he opened up all his senses and allowed his power to flow. Nothing!

Listening for a couple minutes, he smiled at the welcoming silence. No yelling about the sudden hole in the ceiling or the loud noise of the roof cracking. Christian nodded in satisfaction.

Motioning the others to follow, he stepped over the edge, landing effortlessly upon the carpet. When he gave a quick flick of his wings, the debris moved away from him. Moving off to the side, the others jumped into the hallway one by one.

"Why is the ceiling leaking on me? Is that blood?" Nicholas whispered, giving his wings a shake. Christian spared him a quick glance before looking over towards the others.

"Hmm... I've never made a building bleed before," Manuel stated, looking around. He gave Christian a quick wink before he backed up to leave room for Darren.

"Which way?" Darren asked, landing behind him, not even sparing a glance at the blood now splattering the walls.

Christian sent his powers down the hallway as he searched for Ella. He knew she was on the top floor...her power was so strong, it was suffocating him...but which way? Looking to his left, he stared down the hall. Several feet from them were two doors, one on either side of the hall. He found the same as he looked to the right.

His power flowed over the doors, slipping beneath them as he felt for her. *Ella where are you?* There was so much power within the walls that, although he could feel the pull of their bond, it was almost overpowered by the scorching heat in the walls. Finding nothing in the rooms closest to them, he pushed his power further out. Just as he felt he was nearing his limit, a sudden rush made him pause.

Whipping his head to the right, he noticed a door at the end of the hall. It was a bit darker than the rest...a richer wood with a cold knob. The power radiating out of the room was stifling. Through the coldness, though, he felt the warmth... He felt Ella. Without saying a word, and before he was even aware of doing it, he moved towards the door.

By the time he reached it, his hands were shaking from the effort to remain in control. The others were close on his heels as he slammed into the door, ripping it right off of its hinges and sending it crashing to the floor. Within seconds, Christian's eyes locked on Ella's.

She was lying across a large wooded desk, her arms chained above her head. His eyes followed the chains to where they were wrapped around the legs of the desk.

Scratches lined the legs from the chains rubbing against them. From the blood running down Ella's arms, it was clear she had been fighting her restraints for a long time.

Rushing over to her, Christian saw the tears of relief slipping from the corners of her eyes.

"Christian," she gasped out, her voice raw from emotion.

"Shh, it's okay. I'm here now," he whispered, wiping away some of her tears. Her face turned into his hand and she let out a soft whimper. "You're going to be okay."

"No, I won't," Ella murmured softly.

"Of course you will, honey," Christian said, gently running his fingers down her cheek.

"But I'm bad, Christian." Her voice hitched. "I'm evil and dark and–"

"Shh... You are not evil, Ella. You are sweet and kind–"

"No... No...," Ella whispered, tears running down her face as she shook her head. "I was made for darkness."

Christian watched as her eyes filled with sadness. A black cloud of her growing sorrow was swirling around her. It gathered around him, seeping into his very being. Her raw emotion rolled within him, causing him to want to wrap himself around her, protect her from all the evil surrounding them. "No, Ella," he forcefully said. Placing his fingers gently under her chin, he tilted her face up so he could meet her eyes. He put all the emotions he felt for her, all his love and trust into his eyes. Breathing slowly, he willed his warmth to wrap around her, to chase those fears from her eyes. "No, my love. You were not made for evil. You were made for *me,* and I will get you out of here."

Christian glanced up and saw Manuel at the head of the table. He had placed his sica beside Ella and his fingers were working quickly to release her from the chains.

A sigh of relief slipped from her as Manuel released one of her hands. Christian brought her free hand down, rubbing his fingers over the gashes and kissing her palm gently. "Just one more. Then I'm taking you home."

"He's coming," she mumbled.

"What?" Christian leaned in closer. He had heard something but she was almost too weak to get a sound out. "What did you say, darling?"

She looked at him, her eyes getting wider by the second as her body began to shudder uncontrollably. "He's coming."

"Who's coming, Ella? Who?" Christian watched as her bottom lip began to tremble. "Ella... "

A sudden wave of power rushed through the room. All of them jerked their heads towards the door just as a gust of air rushed through it. The force knocked Nicholas and Darren off to the side, both of them slamming against the dark wood walls. Christian leaned over Ella to protect her, as Manuel ducked behind the table.

"What the fuck?" Nicholas coughed.

Christian looked over towards Manuel. "What was that?"

"I think asking *who* would be a much better question! Would you not agree?"

Swiveling around, Christian found a demon standing smugly in the doorway. He was dressed in a black suit, his white shirt open at the top. Christian noticed gold cufflinks on his sleeves as he reached up and straightened his jacket.

However, it was the demon's eyes that caught his attention. They were mismatched. One was a deep chocolate brown, while the other was a dark forest green. Both were holding so much darkness within them, Christian could see it from across the room.

Christian felt a tightness in his chest as he stared at him. The demon's mouth began to twist into a sick smile as they stared at each other. "Who are you?" Christian asked, his mind registering the movement of his brothers around the room. "I asked you a question."

"Yes, you did," the demon responded. His voice was rich. Each word rolled from his lips with a smooth flow. Tilting his head, Christian watched as his eyes left his, scanning over his brothers before looking back at him. "I must insist you answer one of mine first."

Christian stood up straighter. Keeping himself firmly between the demon and Ella, he narrowed his eyes. "And what question would that be?"

The demon's eyebrow raised slightly. "What are you doing hovering over *my* female?"

"*Your* female?" Christian choked out as he felt rage begin to build within him.

"Yes...*mine*! She has always been for me. Sweet little innocent Ella. Oh, the plans I have for us."

"*She. Will. Never. Be. Yours*!" Christian ground out as he began to build his power within him. He would not let this demon get her. He saw Darren slowly get to his feet, then lean against the wall, his eyes never leaving the demon. Nicholas was watching him, as well.

"Even if you take her now, take her home and watch her every day for the rest of your miserable existence, she will always be mine, Guardian. Always!" the demon sneered, glaring at him.

"Christian, he's just trying to get you to lose it," Manuel whispered from behind him. "He's lying to you, saying anything to get you angry."

"Yes, Christian," the demon said with a laugh. "We would not want you to lose control, would we?"

Christian's vision waivered as he stared at the demon. He could feel a coldness begin to curl within him. His breathing was ragged as he shook his head. Taking a step towards the demon, he felt his hands clenching at his side. "Who the *fuck* are you?"

The demon's eyes flared as his power forcefully flowed out. Christian's breath caught in his chest as it slammed against him. Out of the corner of his eye, he saw his other brothers stumble beneath the weight of that power. The demon, seeming to notice his distress, pushed more of his energy onto him. He reached his hand towards Christian, letting out a growl as his eyes burned into his. "I do *not* appreciate being talked to like that. You will learn some respect."

Christian's knees felt weak as his body shuddered from the assault. Sweat now covered him as he fought off the evil swirling around his body. His chest was tight, and he was fighting to take a breath. Just as he thought he was going to faint, the demon pulled his power back. Gasping,

Christian leaned over, pulling air into his burning lungs, blinking to clear his vision.

"That is better. Now, where were we?"

Christian tilted his head up, rolling his shoulders as he glared at the demon. He could hear the rest of his brothers hissing lightly as they all tried to recover. "I asked you for your name, demon?"

"Ah, yes. That is right." The demon took a step into the room, opening his arms wide. "My name is Andras and this," he said, gesturing to the room, "is my office."

"Well, Andras," Darren spoke up, drawing the demon's attention away from Christian. "Are you the one responsible for the demons we have been running into lately?"

"Yes, they are mine, just like Ella."

"How do you figure?"

"That is simple. Ella was made for me. One of mine was sent up top, found the perfect female and, after a little persuasion, lay with her to create Ella."

"You mean he rapped an innocent woman," Darren stated, only his eyes showing the anger that filled him.

"You say raped. I say persuaded. Is there really a difference?" Andras said with a shrug.

A feeling of disgust and rage ran through Christian as he got to his feet. He could feel Ella behind him and, in that instance, knew the feeling was one they both shared.

Manuel let out a grunt. Christian looked over at his brother and noticed him slowly moving towards the head of the table. Their eyes met briefly before Christian turned back towards Andras.

He watched as Andras glanced over his shoulder. Seconds before two more demons appeared behind him, Christian heard a low drumming. His eyes narrowed at the new arrivals.

The one to Andras' right was a little shorter than his boss, but bulky. He wore a black leather jacket that was tight around his shoulders, hanging loose enough that Christian could make out the butt of a gun hanging from a side holster. The demon had silver hair and piercing blue eyes. They glinted as he glanced first at Andras, then towards Darren, who was standing close by.

Darren, on the other hand, hadn't taken his eyes off Andras since the demon showed up.

The other demon was taller than Andras, but less bulky than the other. His short black hair was ruffled, almost giving him a boyish look...if he wasn't surrounded by an aura darker than a moonless sky. The demon had a sneer on his face as his icy silver eyes scanned the room, suddenly coming to a stop as he let out a deep chuckle.

"Why, Nicholas, it is so nice to see you again," he murmured.

"Castigo," Nicholas hissed back, flexing his wings. "I can't say I feel the same."

"Oh, you hurt my feelings," Castigo said with a small pout. "And here I thought, after our last encounter, we had really made a connection."

"We made a connection all right."

The two seemed to square off, each wordlessly daring the other to make a move. The low drumming was growing louder in Christian's ears as he glanced back and forth between them. *So that's Castigo*, he thought.

Looking at the three demons, he could feel his anger building, his heart beating in time to the drumming in his ears. The longer Christian stared at them, the louder the drums seemed to get.

Shaking his head, he concentrated on pushing the noise away, but it was starting to get harder to ignore. Rolling his shoulders, he glared at the trio. The demon with the blue eyes turned and met his glare. His silver hair was pulled back and his presence, not unlike Andras', seemed to demand their attention. Christian glanced over at Ella. They locked gazes and she mouthed, *Drums*. She looked over at the demons in the doorway.

Concentrating on the conversation, Christian soon realized Andras and Darren were still bantering back and forth.

"You can't possibly think you're going to win this." Darren hissed, taking a step away from the wall. Christian could feel the power rolling off him as he moved closer to the demon.

Andras laughed as he took a step into the room. "Why, of course I am going to win. I think, deep down, you know this."

"Deep down, I know you are, at best, a mid-level demon filled with delusions of grandeur. That's what I know, Andras."

"Delusions of grandeur? Hardly. I *know* how important I am, Guardian...just as I know how powerful I am. And mid-level? Really? Your ignorance is astounding."

"Oh, and how powerful are you?" Darren responded, ignoring Andras' last comment.

Andras tilted his head, looking devilishly at Darren, a thin smile slowly forming on his lips. Christian could feel the power within the room growing by the minute. He glanced over at Darren, wondering what his brother was up to. Surely goading Andras into a fight wasn't the best idea right now, was it?

The drums grew even louder as the other two demons stepped further into the room. Each moved off to either side of Andras, flanking him.

Nicholas was now directly in front of Castigo. Both of them were shifting from one foot to the other, attempting to anticipate what the other was planning. Christian watched as Nicholas' red eyes flashed dangerously.

The demon with the blue eyes was staring at Darren, seeming to be debating on moving towards him. The demon's jaw clenched as he looked over towards Andras, then back at Darren.

Christian was about to speak when he felt the pressure in the room release, then everything seemed to happen at once.

Manuel snapped open Ella's last cuff and flung it to the ground. She sat up quickly, swinging her legs to the side of the desk and, upon standing, seemed to shudder under the weight of the power flooding the room.

Andras lifted his hands up and released such a powerful wave, a crack formed along the wall. It split open, blood oozing out. The drumming in Christian's ears seemed to grow to a deafening level as he sensed his own power swirling dangerously within him. He concentrated on keeping it in check as he felt himself stumble back. Ella jumped back on the desk and placed one of her hands on his back, her warmth surrounding them both.

The second they connected, he felt a moment of clarity.

Looking up, he saw Castigo pinned against the wall by Nicholas, his white wings flapping furiously as he lifted the demon by the throat. Castigo's silver eyes glared down at him as he released a loud growl. His hands reached for Nicholas' face, fighting to get him to let go. Lifting his arm, the demon slammed his hand down into the bend of Nicholas' elbow. He howled in pain as the demon followed this action with a kick to his stomach. Christian watched as Nicholas doubled over, knocked to his knees. Christian began to take a step towards him to help when a sudden grunt from the other side of the room drew his attention.

Darren was locked in a battle with Andras. Crack after crack appeared in the walls behind Darren, Andras sending waves of power straight into him. He saw Darren's deep sapphire eyes slowly turn black, his own power rolling around him as he battled off each of the demon's attacks.

"Christian!" Manuel yelled.

Christian turned just as he saw the third demon moving toward him. His power slammed into Christian, threatening to send him flying over the desk. If it hadn't been for the sudden flare of power from Ella, he was sure that was exactly what would have happened. The demon stumbled a bit as Christian pushed Ella's and his combined power into him. He could feel their warmth colliding with the demon's coldness.

Concentrating on that feeling, he shoved out his power, willing him to back up. Christian needed to keep the demon away from Ella. Although she was sharing her power with him, Christian could still sense how weak her time down here had made her.

He was concentrating so much on the feel of their power fighting against the demon, it took him a moment to register the glint of light off of the gun now pointed at him. The demon seemed to have given up on the power battle.

He grinned at Christian as he steadily pointed the gun at his chest. When Christian stepped towards him, he shot, the sound echoing through the room, along with Ella's scream.

Clenching his jaw, Christian braced for the bullet, but all he felt was the rush of power coming from behind him.

In surprise, he watched as the bullet stopped in mid-air. It spun for a second before being sent back the way it had come. Glancing over his shoulder, he saw Ella had risen to her knees upon the desk. Her hands were spread out in front of her and the power around her was swirling with such strength, her hair was floating off her shoulders.

"*No*!" she yelled.

That one word had such force behind it, he saw the power rush from her, seemingly having a life of its own as it roared through the room. Christian felt his vision clear, the drumming in his head ceasing.

Spinning around, he watched as Andras and the other two demons were thrown backwards. They were forced into the wall so hard, Castigo was pushed right through it. She sent out wave after wave. Christian could see Andras trying to get up, but her power was pinning him to the ground.

"*Ella*!" Andras yelled above the roar of her power, his mismatched eyes glowing dangerously as he clawed at the floor.

Christian heard a loud crack from behind him and, with a quick glance, saw a hole forming in the wall. It was wide and showed a clear view of the outside. Manuel ran to it in a flash.

"Okay, ladies and gentleman. It’s time for us to take our leave," he shouted.

Nicholas and Darren ran towards the hole, their wings tight to their bodies as they jumped through it, then opening wide as they soared into the air.

Christian gave Manuel a quick nod as he twisted towards Ella. Manuel let out a growl as he leapt through the hole, flying out of sight.

Christian wrapped himself around Ella and he felt his wings stretch out, lifting them off of the ground. He could hear the demon's yells and snarls behind him as he carried her through the hole, swiftly moving after the others.

Within moments, he landed at the mouth of the cave, the others waiting for them before turning to head inside.

"It's about time." They turned to find Cyrus leaning against the edge of the cave. "You guys look like shit."

"Later, Cyrus," Darren mumbled as he motioned for the rest of them to follow him.

They followed the same route they had taken upon their arrival. It seemed hotter than Christian remembered, but he figured a lot of it was because of his tingling nerves.

Christian held Ella close to his chest as he moved. She was shivering, tucking her head into his chest.

Coming to a stop, Christian glanced over at Manuel, who was already building up his power. His eyes glowed darkly as he looked around, meeting his brothers eyes. Each of them nodded as they willed their own power to join with his, causing the air around them to move wildly.

It was a rush that Christian felt deep in his very core. Ella shuddered against him, but the warmth of their power seemed to stop her shivering as she glanced towards the others. Christian felt her power as it mingled with his, causing his skin to tingle.

Manuel let out a sigh as he pulled the power into him. In a sudden flash of light, a rush of power shot out, engulfing them and sending them home.

Chapter 30

Andras stood in his office, staring at the city through the new hole in his wall, a slow drip of blood still coming from the gaping wound. His poor building just couldn't seem to catch a break today.

He knew he should feel anger right now but, as a whole, things had gone rather well. His time spent with Ella had been...productive. She had fought him like the lioness she was, and his power had the battle wounds to prove it. Andras rubbed a hand across his chest as he smiled.

Oh yes. It had been a battle.

Even the encounter with the Guardians had turned out to be rather insightful. Their power had been impressive. His body shivered as the memory of the rush of power swirling in the room swept over him. There were kinks in their armor, ones he planned to explore more.

He chuckled as anticipation ran through him.

Just as the Guardians had shown up, Andras had gotten word that the last of the souls had been taken. It was only a matter of time before the veil would come crashing down. He remembered the feeling of empowerment he had felt as he had made his way towards his office. It had been so strong, even the sudden knowledge of his guests hadn't caused it to waiver. If anything, it had made him feel even stronger as he had faced off with them.

Andras gazed at the sky. The sky he had looked at for as long as he could remember, and one he was soon going to be leaving. He was sure the sky he was going to be seeing would be much different from this one.

Having never been up top before, Andras felt almost giddy, not that he would let his feelings show to the others. He needed to command control over them, making sure they not only respected his leadership, but understood the consequences of any insubordination. Now, more than ever, he needed to make his presence, his position of being in charge, known – at any cost!

Looking down, he saw several of his demons standing in the street. They were agitated and Andras could feel their anger. The fact that not one, not two, but *five* Guardians had slipped past them was mind-boggling. Andras was disappointed but, as he had discovered, there was a silver lining to even this unwanted event.

As soon as word had gotten out about their "guest", there had been a rush of demons to his building, even though it had been too late for any help. Soon enough, they had all felt the need to start stating the obvious. The most annoying was the question of whether or not *he* had noticed the angels leaping from the hole in his office.

With a growl, Andras looked away from the group and back towards the sky. *Idiots... I'm surrounded by idiots!*

He heard a throat clear behind him. Looking over his shoulder, he spotted Aragon standing in the doorway, the door itself now propped up against the wall.

"Yes, Agalon?" Andras said with a sigh.

"Um, sir, do you want us to go after the Guardians? Their power trail is still fresh in the cave we had tracked them to. We could easily follow it and find out where they went."

Andras turned, taking a good look at his second-in-command. Agalon was a mess. There was a tear in his shirt where the bullet had entered his shoulder, dried blood causing the shirt to stick to him. That bullet had been meant for the pesky Guardian, Christian. Something about that angel made his teeth grind. The bullet should have put an end to him. It, along with many others, had been specifically made to take out an angel. He had overseen the melting of one of his cursed blades to make these bullets. They were not to be used lightly! Not to be wasted! Yet there it was...embedded in Agalon's shoulder. The wound looked angry and, if Andras was being honest, pretty painful, although you wouldn't know he was in any kind of pain by looking at him. As ever, Agalon was focused and unmoved.

Damn his little feisty lioness. She *would* have to rush to the rescue at the last moment. With her sudden burst of power, everything had changed.

Shaking his head, Andras sighed. "You should get that bullet out."

"Yes, sir. I plan on it. I just thought, while the trail was still fresh, we should–"

"No! I got what I needed. We have other plans to concern ourselves with right now."

"But Andras–"

"Are you questioning me, Agalon?" Andras growled.

"Of course not."

"Then forget about the Guardians for now. They will be dealt with, just not right away. They would expect us to go after them now."

Agalon nodded as he tilted his head. "We will wait until they are no longer looking for us to attack."

"Yes. As I said, we have other plans to work on right now. But once enough time has passed, and they are no longer looking over their shoulders, we will attack." Andras growled out the last couple of words. "For now, go and take care of that wound, Agalon. Then get the others in here. We have a lot to go over."

Agalon bowed slightly as he backed out of the room.

Looking back out the hole in the wall, Andras couldn't help the smile that began to slowly creep across his face. All things considered, this was turning into a good day. A good day indeed!

Chapter 31

Several weeks had passed since they had rescued Ella. It seemed like just yesterday that Christian was running around, threatening a priest, and getting into a fights in an office building in Hell. Laughing, he leaned back in his chair. He looked around their kitchen, enjoying the rays of sunlight streaming through the windows. Sitting at the table, he took another sip of his coffee as he looked over the listings he had for a new house.

Shortly after they had gotten back, he had made it clear to everyone that Ella was going to be stay with them. Besides a couple of raised eyebrows, everyone had just smiled. To his relief, Ella hadn't complained one bit, either. She had looked at him with a knowing look in her eyes, as if she had been expecting this outcome all along.

He couldn't be happier. Getting to curl up with her each night and wake up to her body nestled into his each morning, seemed like the greatest gift. At no point in his time here on Earth had Christian ever thought he could be this happy. It was like a prayer he had never known he was saying, or even thinking, had been answered.

Manuel was right. Maybe they *were* meant to be here all along.

Thinking about Ella made him smile. Their lives had been fated to meet from the beginning. Ever since that moment in the alley, their futures had been intertwined.

He wouldn't have it any other way.

His chest still tightened when he thought about how he had almost lost her. He wasn't sure what Andras had wanted with her, but he thanked Heaven every day that they were able to get there in time to bring her back.

After getting her away from Andras and getting her home, Ella had been exhausted. She had slept for almost two days before finally coming around. Christian knew the whole experience had taken a lot out of her, but he had still been worried. He had paced back and forth in his room so much, there was now a permanent wear spot in his carpet.

Darren had spent a lot of time sitting with him, keeping an eye on both of them. Christian had stated repeatedly that he was okay, but the others had just smiled and nodded. They hadn't believed him, but none of them had said anything.

When Ella had finally come around, she had seemed...different. Christian sensed a bit of darkness in her that hadn't been there before. Then again, you couldn't spend time down in Hell without coming out a little tainted. At least that was his opinion. Darren had assured them all that she was fine, though. He had come to this conclusion after spending several hours talking to her alone.

Christian hadn't been too keen on the idea, but Darren had assured him it was going to be okay. He said he just needed to talk to Ella without him there. Something about him being a distraction. Christian had finally given in and anxiously waited in the kitchen with the rest of them. After what felt like forever, Darren had emerged from the room. He had smiled and told them that, although Ella's aura was slightly tainted from the ordeal, she would ultimately be fine.

"She's going to be okay, Christian," Darren had told him later that night.

"Are you sure?" Christian had asked. He had studied his brother, in the hopes that his face would give away some knowledge. "I'm just so worried... "

"Trust me, Christian. She's good." With that, Darren had patted him on the back and changed the subject. As frustrating as it was, he knew Darren would tell him if there was something going on he should worry about. At least, he hoped.

Christian still didn't know exactly what Ella and Darren had talked about, nor did he know what took place between her and Andras, but he figured that when the time was right, she would tell him. The last thing he wanted to do was push her for details. He trusted her and, when she lay next to him each night, whispering about how much she loved him, Christian knew all he needed to.

To further help her feel better, he had called Cindy and invited her over...much to the dismay of the others.

He laughed as he recalled her reaction once she was in the house. Cindy was a feisty woman, her hand on her hips as she eyed them all. After she had finally gotten over the shock, she had flown right into a rather sisterly role, demanding to know their names and what their intentions were with Ella. It hadn't taken long to appease her. A couple smiles here and there, plus the promise she could come see Ella whenever she wanted, had done the trick. However, Christian was sure it was the promise from Ella to have her stay over, plus the long eye contact between Cindy and Darren, that had ultimately helped. Shaking his head, he looked back down at the papers in his hands. All of those events had led him to what he was doing now.

After Cindy had helped them get all of Ella's things into the house, Darren had decided it was time for them to move. More people meant there was a need for more space. Plus, they each enjoyed their privacy.

In a small house with thin walls, privacy was hard to come by.

Feeling a pressure against his leg, Christian glanced down. Holly, Ella's cat, purred loudly as she looked up at him. Smiling, he reached down and lifted her onto his lap. Right away, the little black cat had claimed all the males in the house, letting them know she was here and, when the time suited her, her needs would not be denied. She especially seemed to like Nicholas, but when he wasn't available, any of them would do.

He scratched lazily behind her ears as she settled into his lap. His mind again drifted back to the events that had taken place when they had gone for Ella.

The demons they had come across had been powerful. Darren had refused to talk about his personal battle with Andras, but they all knew it had taken a toll on him. He had pulled back from the others a bit, refusing to talk about it and just commenting sporadically on what had happened.

Christian felt that he was just trying to hide how worried he was, but he hoped Darren would open up about it sooner rather than later. After all, they were all worried. Nothing had been solved while they were down there. Yes, they had gotten Ella out of there, but they ended up leaving with more questions than they had going in.

On the other hand, Cyrus had been more than happy to talk about what he had done. It seemed he had more fun fighting with the group of demons than he had in a long time. He had left them broken and bloody...a couple of them not even getting a chance to fight back. "They didn't even know what hit 'em!" he had commented with a laugh, his black eyes twinkling more and more each time he got to tell the story. It was nice seeing Cyrus excited about something. Ever since...

Christian blinked a couple times as unwanted memories threatened to emerge. It was safe to say they had all been through more than their fair share of darkness. Cyrus more than the rest. It was good to see him smile, even if it was only temporary.

Once back home, Christian had assumed they would be attacked. He had feared something would happen before Ella was fully recuperated but, thankfully, everything had remained quiet. Manuel had commented that they were probably waiting before coming after them.

That hadn't been very comforting, but at least they may have some time to figure out what exactly they were up against. Manuel had assured them he would find the answers they needed. Seeing that he was the best in researching things, everyone had relaxed instantly. If Manuel said he would find something, he would.

There was something about Manuel lately, though. Not only was he a bit moodier than usual, but he was hiding something. Three days after they had returned, he had taken off like a bat out of hell, yelling something about being late to return a book. They had all just glanced at each other. Darren had shrugged it off and shook his head. A couple hours later, Manuel had shown back up...an odd look on his face and a lot more quiet. He hadn't seemed upset, but something had definitely gotten his mind working.

Just another mystery to add to the list, Christian thought as he looked down at Holly. She was purring loudly, her green eyes gazing up at him. "At least there's no mystery where you're concerned, is there?"

"She likes you, you know?"

Turning, he found Ella standing in the kitchen, leaning against the counter. He smiled at her as he set Holly on the floor. Standing up, he began to make his way over to her. "Well, with Nicholas out, she seems to think I'll do."

Ella smiled at him. "Nicholas is really good with her."

"He does what he can. I think he's always wanted a pet and, after seeing Holly, he's decided to adopt yours."

She reached up to wrap her arms around his neck. "As long as he doesn't take off with her...," Ella laughed as she kissed him on the cheek. "I've grown quite fond of the little furball after all this time. I mean, she's been my only companion, outside of Cindy, for the last couple years. They were the only thing keeping me from feeling alone."

Leaning back, Christian stared into her eyes. Ella was looking at him with such trust and love, he felt his heart skip a beat. He knew he would do anything to keep her safe and in his arms. Christian never wanted her to feel alone again. It hurt his heart to think she ever felt like that, but he knew he would be the one to change that. "And now?" he asked, watching her eyes light up.

"Now... I don't feel alone anymore," she whispered. Smiling, Christian bent down and kissed her. He felt her body lean into his as he deepened the kiss, enjoying the rush he got every time she was near. Ella pulled back and sighed. "I feel safe..." She leaned in and placed a kiss on his right cheek. "I feel wanted..." She placed a kiss on his left cheek, lingering a little longer.

Christian shivered as he felt her breath against his face. Her hands slid down from his neck to grip his arms. Leaning back, Ella blinked several times as she smiled. "I feel loved..."

"Good," he whispered as he kissed her again. Christian knew he felt the same for her. No matter what may happen, what trials their future held for them, what fate had planned, he would always have Ella, always have this moment. Christian tightened his grip on her, pulling her close to him as he kissed the top of her head. "I always want you to feel like you're feeling right now. I love you, Ella, and I promise to keep you safe. Always."

"I love you, too, Christian," Ella whispered, sighing against him as she held him tight. "Always and forever."

Did you love spending time with Ella,
Christian, and the rest of the
Guardians?
Want to know what happens next?
Then be sure to keep on the lookout
for...

Bound in Fate

The Fallen Guardians Series,
Book 2

Coming 2016

Acknowledgments

There are so many people that I would like to thank, and I know that I won't be able to name them all, but I'm definitely going to try. This book has truly been a joy to write. With this being my first novel, I had no idea what to except but I made the choice to jump right into it and couldn't have done it on my own.

First I would like to thank my family, both by blood and by choice, for being my support team. You guys have stood by me throughout it all, my joys and fears, panic attacks and happy dances! Mom, dad, Katie, and Lacey (and the rest of my family and friends) - I love you guys and look forward to continuing on this journey with you all by my side.

I want to send a huge thank you to the love of my life, John. You heard, and had to deal with, it all. Without you here to ground me, to remind me why I needed to push on when all I wanted to do was stop, I don't know what I would have done. I love you.

Thank you to my cover designer and one of my best friends, Diana, for all of your help. I absolutely love this cover and can't wait to see what other wonderful ideas you come up with as we go. Luv ya girl!

Thank you to my editor, Kim. You are absolutely amazing! I don't think I can truly put into words just how much I appreciate all that you've done for me.

I would also like to send a huge thank you out to some of my favorite authors. Specifically to Michelle Rabe, Rissa Blakeley, Franca Storm, Ashley Wheels, Aden Lowe, Kris Norris, Sapphire Knight, Tess Oliver, and Alana Sapphire (to name a few...lol)! Whether you have inspired me with your work, with a kind word here and there, or with your friendship, I will always be grateful for you.

And, last but most definitely not least, I want to thank all of you, the readers - from the bottom of my heart. The fact that you chose my book, my very first novel, to read means more to me than you'll ever know!

I hope you all have enjoyed reading Divinely Entwined as much as I've enjoyed writing it.

"You are my drive, my inspiration, and the life behind my words!" ~ E.F. Rose xx

About the Author

E.F. Rose lives in the Central Valley of California, surrounded by her family, friends and boyfriend. She has always enjoyed writing and considers herself to be a multi genre author, with urban fantasy and dark romance being her main focus. If she isn't writing up a storm, than Emily can probably be found either online chatting with friends, reading a good book, or out enjoying life.

My Work

Echoes (A Book of Poetry)

Divinely Entwined (The Fallen Guardians Series, Book 1)

And look for the release of Bound in Fate, Book 2 in the Fallen Guardians Series - coming 2016

Contact Information

You can email me at

emilyfrose13@gmail.com

or follow me on....

Facebook @ www.facebook.com/DarkestRose13

Twitter @ www.twitter.com/Emily_F_Rose

www.ingramcontent.com/pod-product-compliance
Lightning Source LLC
Chambersburg PA
CBHW052034260626
47163CB00007B/331